WORMHOLE
TO WAR

OTHER BOOKS BY JAMES C. GLASS

NOVELS

Shanji
Empress of Light
The Creators
The Viper of Portello
Toth
Visions
Branegate
Sedona Conspiracy
Eagle Squad
Synths

COLLECTIONS

Matrix Dreams and Other Stories
Imaginings of a Dark Mind
Touches of Wonder and Terror/Voyages in Mind and Space
Strange Worlds, Near and Far

WORMHOLE
TO WAR

JAMES C. GLASS

WILDSIDE PRESS

FOREWORD

Discovered by accident, it was first thought to be a Branegate, a hole in a Brane connecting two universes, but it was not. Formed from a primordial string, a strange folding in spacetime connected three points separated by over seventy thousand light years, two bridges connected weakly. Over millennia the midpoint was stabilized using vacuum state energy, allowing a stopping and transfer point for safe and repeatable travel from the home world of Kratola to its colonies on Gan and Galena seventy thousand light years distant.

The colonies flourished, paid heavy tribute to their mother world for hundreds of years, received benefits in terms of special building materials, agricultural chemicals and free labor. Despite this, desires for independence grew among the colonists, chiefly advocated by a mysterious organization of high technologists known popularly as "The Immortals" for their advances in medicine and biological sciences.

The situation worsened when a religious coup by zealots on Kratola established rule by a council of bishops and forced a puppet Emperor on Gan to enforce their control over the colonies. This led to two revolutions on Gan: one against the Emperor, and one against a usurper secretly connected politically to the bishops, both happening within one generation. Both revolutions succeeded. During the second overthrow Kratola tried to intervene by sending military forces to close the transfer point connecting the two spacetime bridges between their worlds, but were repelled by new technology from The Immortals, who then took charge of the port there and dismissed administrative personnel who had been loyal to Kratola.

The port had become a community with a cluster of large stations including an entertainment center called Pleasure City which attracted tourists from three worlds with more conservative cultures.

It was renamed Port Nexus, a new governor appointed, and new security chief and police chief were hired to restore order and safety to the port. But the bishops, twice frustrated by their failed attempts to control Gan and Galena, had not given up. Disgraced by their setbacks, they cruelly tightened their rule on Kratola and plotted to take back power over what they perceived as their rightful colony worlds.

But first, they had to seize and control Port Nexus.

From *A Brief History of Gan*
Chapter XIX, "The Troubled Years"
by Trae Nowak, Peoples; Press, 1024 AC

CHAPTER ONE

Stefan Fechter had just finished another synthetic meal and changed clothes to spend an evening at Pleasure City with Pavel when the call came in from the Governor's office. The lady herself was on the line, so the matter was urgent and his evening plans probably canceled. He stifled a stab of resentment. For the first time in his military career, his boss was a woman.

"I hope you don't have any plans for tonight," said Governor Madelia, "but it's an emergency situation. We have an uninvited guest arriving in half a cycle, and security will have to be tight. He's not a popular person here, especially with people who grew up in the colonies."

Stefan's heart sank. "A Bishop," he said.

"Bishop Halmai. He's not as despised as Caleb or Zuhair, but it's bad enough. The bastard claims he's just passing through the Gate on business, and he wants to discuss travel restrictions through the Gate. He's miffed about the approvals he had to get to come through here."

"That's krack," said Stefan. "He's miffed about the ban on military vessels. It's only four years since the Bishops tried an invasion of the old colonies. Why is a Bishop even allowed to come through here?"

"Part of the peace deal," said Madelia, "and part of the deal that eventually brought you here. I'm sorry, Stefan, but he's arriving in half a cycle, and I want you and Pavel to be at my meeting with him."

"Halmai won't stand for it. He'll want to meet you all alone. You know the Bishops' attitudes about women in responsible positions. They were vocal enough about their opposition to your appointment."

"Tough krack," said Madelia. "My loyalty is to Gan and Galena, and they know it. It's another reason I picked you, Stefan. You said your loyalty was to the people of Gan before you came here."

"That was my Academy oath, and it includes Galena. Too bad there had to be a revolution, and my oath screwed up my career."

Bitterness dripped from his voice.

"But you were reinstated when the revolution was over. You did the right thing. It was your chance to leave, and I feel fortunate to have you as my Security Chief. Port Nexus has new leadership, and we're on a new path. Pavel is on his way here, and I'll have a room arranged for you to lay out the security protocol for the meeting. Can you be here before red light?"

"I can leave right now," said Stefan. "Be there in a few minutes."

His office was only a few minutes by belt from the Governor's suite. A moving belt walkway went around the entire circumference of the great spoked wheel that was Station Alpha, the administrative center of Port Nexus. On either side were offices, cafeterias, meeting rooms, entertainment and recreation areas, even two little parks with artificial grass, plants and benches with tables for a relaxing hour or two. A curved ceiling was painted with frescoes of scenes from Gan and Galena, rolling hills and fields of grain and grasses under a yellow sun. Bright lights went through a cycle from yellow to red to dim violet and back to red and yellow to complete a daily cycle of one Gan day, to which all clocks and watches were set.

It was easy to forget that on the other side of the lovely ceiling frescoes was vacuum, and the blackness of deep space.

Stefan hopped on the belt and only a few minutes later hopped off when he reached the large double doors of the Governor's suite.

The Governor was there to greet him.

Kira Madelia was a striking woman at sixty, large boned and six feet tall, with silver-gray hair pulled back in a bun. Her tight, black suit with purple shirt gave her an elegant, military look. She smiled, and held out her hand and her grip was firm when Stefan took it. The smile reached her eyes, so dark brown they were nearly black. She was wealthy beyond imagination, having retired after selling her agricultural machine business on Gan in order to do something new. And she had helped fund revolutions that had first overthrown a Bishop-controlled Emperor and then a usurper who was a closet supporter of a home world thirty thousand light years from Gan.

She was quite capable of leadership and commanded the respect of somewhat chauvinistic military professionals such as Stefan Fechter.

And he liked her.

"So sorry again," she said. "Pavel told me you guys had some entertainment planned for tonight."

"It can wait. I don't get paid for entertainment," said Stefan, and smiled.

"Pavel is at the dock, and he'll be here shortly. I've set up the big room for you, and breakfast will be brought in."

"I recommend protocol for complete secrecy. I wouldn't want to give this guy any publicity he can use."

"Agreed," said Kira. She led him into her suite to a long room with a table for twenty, and sixteen computer stations, all bathed in low, red light. A huge coffee urn was at one end of the table. "I'll need everything to be ready by next red light," she said.

"Should be ready before breakfast," said Stefan.

"Knock, knock," said a voice from the doorway.

Pavel had arrived.

Pavel Fiala, in his thirties, was a decade younger than Stefan, dark hair and eyes, a thin, high-cheeked face with a prominent nose, a man whose relaxed manner made him easy to work with. But beneath the calm exterior, Stefan had quickly discovered a man with the strength, tenacity and attitude of a third generation cop. Pavel was officially in charge of the police units at Port Nexus and Pleasure City, a force of over four hundred men, and he was second in command to Stefan for overall port security. There had been an instant bond between them even at Stefan's first interview for the job. And a personal friendship had developed noticeably over the two weeks Stefan had been on the job.

"Sorry I'm late," said Pavel. "I had to call Carra and cancel out plans."

"Tell her I'm sorry when you get a chance," said Kira.

"She's fine, just disappointed. She wanted to meet Stefan, and so does her boss and some other important people. There's a big buzz about the new guy in the city."

"You have a girlfriend?" asked Stefan.

"Carra Cozza, a dancer at the Red Palace Casino." Pavel smiled. "She's mine, so don't get any funny ideas when you meet her."

"We'll arrange a city tour for Stefan after our uninvited guest leaves," said Kira. "What I need now is the security plan for his visit. I agree it should be private and without publicity. I don't want word getting out that a Bishop has even been allowed here. It'll only stir up supporters of Kratola."

"Even after the war?" said Stefan. "They got their asses kicked when they invaded Port Nexus, and that was only four years ago, and now they're sniffing around again and we're allowing a visitation. I don't understand that, Ma'am."

"I don't either," said Pavel softly.

"I have to know what they're after, what they're probing for, to figure out their new strategies. They haven't given up, guys. They know a direct invasion won't work; the Guppies from Gan will just show up again and blow them away. But they do have supporters here, and on Gan. They will work to destabilize our governance of the Gate and any political system on Gan that they can't influence."

"Sounds like a good reason to bring down the Bishops' rule on Kratola."

"That's not our mission, Stefan," said Kira, "but I'm sure the idea has been entertained by the freedom fighters on Gan and Galena."

"And they have the Guppies to do it with," said Stefan. "Nothing can stand against those monsters." He wiggled an eyebrow at Pavel, who smiled back, then, "Okay, so let's entertain our visitor, and show him how tight our security is. No favors."

"Agreed," said Kira, "but be respectful. You can do that and still be firm."

Stefan nodded. "Done," he said. "Give us three hours. We'll have to make some calls and change docks for some incoming merchant vessels."

"Breakfast in three hours, and coffee's on the table. I'll see you then." Kira left them in the room and closed the door behind her.

Stefan looked at Pavel. "I would be very happy to watch a flight of Guppies show up with their big energy weapons and level the palace on Kratola with all the Bishops still inside it."

"Dream on," said Pavel.

They got down to work and massaged a standard security protocol to fit the unannounced visit by a representative of a hostile state, deploying special police and military squads to entry and exit points at Port Nexus and on Station Alpha.

Kira returned, and they had breakfast together, and then they retired to private rooms for a three hour nap before rising to greet their guest.

CHAPTER TWO

There was no sunrise or sunset at Port Nexus. The entire complex of space-port and constructed stations floated at a distance of two light years from a K-type star known as Lyrae 53. There was only the blackness of space and the twinkling of distant stars and colorful lights from the stations, especially those flickering from the great globe of Pleasure City. Four massive moon-sized orbs framed space filled with a flickering green glow that showed the great wormhole connections to two civilizations that had once been one. Hidden from view was the remnant of a primordial string pinching spacetime to a long line connecting regions over seventy thousand light years apart in normal space. The orbs, filled with closely spaced sheets of superconducting foil extracted vacuum state energy to stabilize a troubling weakness in the local wormhole structure, enabling a stable break providing two exits or entrances for travel in two directions.

The wormhole itself had been discovered dramatically by accident nine hundred years in the past near a fledgling colony on Kratola, and over the centuries the new colonies on Gan and Galena, now heavily populated and highly successful, had developed gradually some seventy thousand light years distant.

But problems had developed in the relations between the worlds.

In recent decades, Kratola had been ruled by religious zealots known as the Council of Bishops who demanded worship of a primal being manifested by the vacuum state, and they had founded the Church of First Light. Tithing was demanded from all citizens. At first the ideas and philosophy were accepted: all power comes from the Field, past, present, future defined there, death leading to reincarnation in the Field and a return to new existence. The church grew rapidly on Kratola and the colony worlds, but decades of living with tithing and dictatorship by a religion-controlled government eroded the faith of many people. Kratola remained under the iron fists of the Bishops, but on Gan and Galena, first against a fumbling Emperor and then against a church supporting billionaire who had replace him, there was revolution.

The Bishops tried to intervene, and there was a short war that included an attack on Port Nexus, then called Grand Portal.

The Kratolan ships were repelled and destroyed by forces from Gan, monstrous ships called Guppies because of their peculiar shape, heavily armed and armored and projecting a field that could make enemy ships simply disappear.

The war was four years in the past. A peace treaty had been agreed upon, staff of Port Nexus now replaced with senior personnel loyal to Gan and Galena, and the military force of the Bishops had been officially outlawed and disbanded.

Maybe.

There were rumors that there was again a military buildup on Kratola, and now a Bishop was arriving to attempt a change in the new rules governing Port Nexus.

Here we go again, thought Stefan, as he and Pavel boarded a military shuttle for the trip to the port.

The flight from Station Alpha took an hour. There were several observation ports in the craft, and it was the first time Stefan had relaxed time to observe the environment of his new home.

He was quietly staring out a port when Pavel said, "Must be a big change for you."

"What?"

"Well, you've spent your whole life under a bright sun on Gan. This must be a visual come down."

"Pretty bleak. I can see Pleasure City out there, though. Pretty lights."

"That's what most people come here for," said Pavel. "Lots of tourism, people come to gamble, drink, and have affairs, and then they want to see the Nexus. Not much tourist travel all the way through in either directions because of the restrictions on Kratola."

"How long have you been here?" said Stefan.

"Just over two years. I signed on for ten, and possible renewal."

"Me, too. Time will tell if I have reason for renewal. I just got here, and now I'm entertaining a Bishop."

"Yeah," said Pavel. "When I take you to Pleasure City it'll perk you up some."

"You just want to see your girlfriend."

"I hope she's more than that. Since I met her, the past year has gone by very fast."

"Ohhh," said Stefan and smiled.

"Do you want to do the talking when we're with Bishop Halmai?"

"I think so. Give me a nudge if you think I'm saying something out of line. I'll be respectful and polite, but I won't take any krack from this guy. And I probably won't believe anything he says."

"Sounds personal," said Pavel.

"It is. I'll tell you about it sometime."

"I can guess. I read your file."

"Oh, oh," said Stefan.

"First thing I said when I read it was that finally we'll have a professional man in charge. And Governor Madelia said the same thing."

"Thanks, Pavel. That's encouraging, and I think we're going to do a good job for her."

Pavel stuck out a hand, and Stefan shook it warmly.

As they neared port, the faint green of turbulent gases within the space between entrance and exit stabilization rings suddenly brightened, a brief flash, and then dimming again. A vessel had arrived, probably the one bearing their visitor. The port station was a line of seven cylinders, connected by tubes, and open rectangular structures on one side that were docking bays for shuttles and smaller commercial vessels.

They docked at Bay 4 and took a vacuum tube train to Bay 2 where the Bishop's vessel would be docking. Stefan had arranged for the pickup to be made by two military shuttles, one intended for the Bishop, the other for any additional entourage that arrived with him. The Bishop had been informed that no welcoming ceremony was planned, and security would be extraordinarily tight for his own safety, Stefan had been relieved when there were no immediate objections before the Bishop's arrival, but knew that could change in minutes.

The cylindrical vessel from Kratola was approaching Bay 2 when Stefan stepped off the tube train and into a van with two officers armed with rifles and sidearms. Four guards remained on the train. The lobby had been cleared of all except technical personnel. A small crowd had gathered there, and protested loudly when forced to move elsewhere. It was likely the Bishop had informed local supporters about his visit in the hope of some positive publicity.

The medium-sized commercial vessel came in through the wide opening to vacuum, descended slowly and docked without a bounce. The door closed, air pressure restored in minutes, and the transparent plasteel door to the lobby swung open. The van was driven into the bay and stopped as a ramp descended from the vessel. As it touched down, two troopers in full armor came down the ramp and stood at port arms on either side of it.

Bishop Tibor Halmai was the first to appear in the doorway. He was a short, portly man dressed conservatively in a gray suit and a silver collar. His face was round, his nose small and sharp, and he smiled faintly as he descended the ramp. Behind him trailed four people, one a woman, all of them there to look after his creature comforts after an arduous three hour trip.

Stefan and the driver of the other van stepped forward as Halmai and his entourage approached. Up close, Halmai's eyes were small and closely spaced, their color nearly as dark as his black hair. He started to extend his hand but hesitated.

Stefan thought of snake eyes. He did not extend his hand, but bowed stiffly and said, "Welcome to Port Nexus, Excellency. We will take you directly to your meeting. I'm Stefan Fechter, the head of security here. We have a separate van for your staff, and we'll look after them during the meeting. A lunch will be served."

"How nice," said Halmai, but for just an instant his eyes narrowed. "I'm honored by this meeting with your Governor. Will it be private?"

"I will also be attending," said Stefan, "and our police chief. It is a matter of security, Excellency."

"I see," said Halmai, but his smile faded away.

Stefan gestured, and Halmai got into the back seat of the van as his entourage was led to the other van. "I will be leaving my guards by the vessel," he said, and paused, then, "It is a matter of security," he said, and smiled again.

Stefan got into the front seat by the driver and the van sped away down a tunnel to the awaiting shuttle back to Alpha Station. He had not planned for a conversation, but Bishop Halmai wanted to talk, and had questions.

"This was my first time through the Gate," said Halmai, "and I'm surprised by the emptiness here, with no sun for light and warmth, just the blackness of space between stations I wonder that people would want to live here."

"It takes some getting used to," said Stefan, "but our needs are satisfied."

"I take it you weren't born here," said Halmai.

"I was born on Gan and grew up there."

"Ah, a colony man," said Halmai, "and a Zylak supporter."

"Gan has a four-hundred-year history, Excellency. The people there don't consider themselves colonists. They are an independent world. And I have no political party affiliations."

"Interesting," said Halmai, and Stefan's heart thumped hard just once. *I shouldn't have said that,* he thought. *Watch your tongue.*

"A world with sunlight and fresh air," said Halmai, "and yet here you are. What brought you to Port Nexus? Are you a military man?"

Ah, now he's probing. "I had a twenty-year career in Gan special forces, and retired as a battalion commander, Excellency. I was not happy about it. I was ready to work when the job here was offered to me, and that was a Gan year ago."

"It must be a simple job for you after being a battalion commander. The force you lead here must be much smaller than that."

"We have substantial security and police forces here," Stefan lied, "but I'm not at liberty to give you any numbers. Ah, we've arrived."

The van came to a stop by the ramp leading up to the shuttle, and the two guards there came to attention.

Stefan led Halmai and his entourage up the ramp and Pavel followed behind them. He'd not spoken one word to Halmai, playing subservient. Everyone had assigned seats, with Halmai in a luxurious cubicle for special guests. Stefan and Pavel sat just aft of the pilot's compartment and watched him. The man had a communicator in his left ear, and was already talking to someone when the hatch closed and the shuttle made its slow, stately exit from port.

Halmai was engaged in conversation much of the way, with long pauses during which he only listened during the flight back to the administrative center on Alpha.

"Who do you suppose he's talking to?" asked Pavel.

"Probably someone on board the freighter that brought him through the Gate. For all we know, there are other officers and troops on board that ship. My bet is he's reporting first impressions and getting new advice."

As they approached their destination, an image came up on the viewscreen, a slowly spinning spoked wheel of clear, double-layered plasteel some twelve kilometers in diameter with a three layered solid equatorial band that was the base of the living area there. The giant door of the airlock in the outer shell of plasteel was already opening to receive them.

They entered the lock, the outer door closed and then there was the sound of rushing gas as they were pressurized. The inner door opened, and they floated inside majestically, turning towards a long, narrow city sprawled beneath them in two directions. Halmai watched all this on the view-screen with a grin on his face, and even for Stefan and Pavel the sight would never become old.

The shuttle landed vertically at a small flight port two kilometers from the administrative center and the offices of the Governor. Halmai's entourage was spirited away in two vans for a short tour of the city. Stefan and Pavel accompanied the Bishop in an air-taxi to the roof of the capital building and took the elevator one flight down to the Governor's suite of offices. Two soft knocks on the large double doors, and Governor Kira Madelia was there, hand outstretched, a welcoming smile on her face.

"Bishop Halmai, how nice it is to meet you. Welcome to Port Nexus," she said.

"It is my pleasure, Madam," said Halmai, who took her hand gently, bent forward and kissed it grandly, his other hand placed over his heart.

Pavel smirked at Stefan and received a frown in return.

There was a circle of four plush chairs in the office and they sat there, Halmai placed with a direct view of the video screen.

"What a lovely view," said Halmai, smiling. "This place is beyond my imagination with an unusual beauty all its own. All those colorful lights against the blackness of space, and no bright sun to spoil the contrast. Oh, I think I just saw a green flash in the distance."

"The Gate brightens when a ship comes through," said Kira. "Another freighter has arrived."

"I'm sorry to say that my profession requires I lead a rather cloistered life," said Halmai. "This is the first time I've left Kratola. My trip here was amazing for me, all the strange glows streaming by us, and the explosion of light when we arrived here. My knowledge of the technology is poor, and I really must read more about it. My studies in seminary were focused on theology, politics and history, and many other subjects were neglected. I am a Keeper of the Faith, you see, but I have serious interests in history and interplanetary politics. These are also of interest to the government on Kratola, and there are some issues my fellow Bishops have sent me here to explore with you."

"Issues about the Gate?" asked Kira.

"Yes, but others as well. We are so distant, yet communications between the colonists and their home-world were open and cordial until recently, and that has led to some unfortunate incidents. I'd hoped to discuss this with you privately, Madam. Will this be possible?"

"You said you wanted to discuss military use of the Gate, Excellency, and that is a security issue. These gentlemen oversee military and security forces for Port Nexus, and I respect their opinions on other issues as well. They also have many contacts with Gan and Galena and keep me informed of events taking place there. I do see why the Bishops might have some concerns. Can we get down to specifics?"

Halmai looked sharply at Stefan and Pavel, and then smiled faintly. There was a pause, and then, "Very well, Madam, I will trust your judgment. Our concerns are primarily about the colony worlds, and Port Nexus is a secondary concern if military action should become necessary."

"Military action against Gan and Galena?" said Kira. "I thought that was settled four years ago. Those worlds are completely independent of Kratola. What right do you have to interfere in their affairs? Stefan, are you aware of any problems there?" She turned and raised an eyebrow at him.

"Yes, Ma'am. There was serious unrest on Gan while I was there. The man who replaced their Emperor has been forced out. The claim is he was an agent of Kratola. There were more demonstrations, then open revolution. The man was killed, and now a democratic form of government is being formed there. I haven't heard of any problems on Galena, or effects on commerce. The problems are totally internal."

:We are particularly concerned about a group claiming to be immortals," said Halmai. "They are a religious cult backing all the continuing unrest and are oppressors of the Church."

"The Church of First Light, you mean. Your Church," said Stefan.

"There is only one Church," said Halmai.

"No human can live forever," said Kira. "Why do you say they're a cult?"

"They fit every definition of a cult: secretive, isolated, opposition to normal society," said Halmai.

"Maybe," said Stefan. "They were around over a hundred years preaching democracy and religious freedom when Gan still had it. But things changed. The Emperor backed officials of your church in going after those people, and they went underground. The Church persecuted the Immortals, not the other way around. Sorry to say I was a part of it for a while."

"They are endangering both the Church and the governmental body of Gan," said Halmai. "Interplanetary commerce of the planet will soon be in danger, and steps must be taken to prevent it."

"A military intervention?" said Kira.

"That is possible, Madam."

"But you tried this before when the Emperor was overthrown, many lives were lost here against your forces, and Gan's advanced weapons nearly destroyed your military. Another war will not be a solution. You might try diplomacy."

"Negotiations are not possible as long as the Zylak cult of so-called immortals is allowed to exist," said Halmai.

"Look," said Kira, "the new treaty between Kratola, Gan and Galena promised complete independence and no possibility of military interference between them. This includes a ban on any military vessels, personnel or supplies being transported through the Gate in either direction. So, what are you suggesting?"

"The treaty should be changed to protect civilians on Gan from the revolutionary activities of a cult."

"The treaty was approved by a vote of the people on all the involved worlds," said Stefan. "They would have to approve any changes, Excellency."

Bishop Halmai scowled at him. "That is your opinion, sir. There are times when true leaders must take charge and do things without waiting for the approval of an ill-informed public. I came here to discuss this with Governor Madelia, not her associates."

Stefan felt the slap but saw Kira's face immediately redden. Her shoulders stiffened, and she spoke slowly and softly.

"Excuse me, Bishop Halmai, but I feel it is you who is ill informed. I concur with what my associate, as you call him, just said. The treaty is clear on the movement of military vessels, personnel or supplies through the Gate. It is not allowed, and I will honor that as long as I am Governor of Port Nexus. We work for the people on both sides of the Gate who approved the terms of the treaty, not just a few who would change things for their own convenience without a vote."

Halmai grinned nastily. "Madam, you were placed in your position by the leaders of three worlds, not by a vote of the people. You do owe us some consideration."

"And I am giving you that," said Kira. "I will be generous and not take what you just said as a threat to my position, but my associates here might feel differently. We will continue to honor the terms of the treaty, and ban any military use of the Gate. The Council of Bishops was mistaken in thinking I would feel otherwise. They're certainly free to present their arguments to the people for a vote of change, and I would accept their wishes. That is the solution to your problem."

Halmai scowled again and sighed. "I had hoped for more. Problems are solved simply when there is cooperation among leaders. My colleagues will be quite disappointed by your response, Madam."

Stefan put a finger on his ear communicator as if he was listening to something, and then, "Excuse me, Ma'am, but I have an urgent call. May I take it outside your office?"

"Certainly," said Kira.

"Hold on a minute," said Stefan to a silent communicator, and left the room. He went across the hall to a conference room, closed and locked the door behind him, and called the security office at Gate Port. "Give me Del," he said. "This is Stefan Fechter, and it's urgent."

Seconds later the man was there. "What's up, sir?"

"A Bishop came in on a freighter two hours ago. Has it been checked?"

There was a pause, then, "Manifest checks out. They unloaded plasteel, liquid helium and some fabric bales, less than half a hold's worth. Pretty big ship for such a small load."

"I want the ship density scanned, stem to stern, high sonic frequency. Focus on the bow and stern areas, Keep a low profile on the scanning operation."

"You suspect smuggling, sir?"

"Maybe, but do it quick. They'll be out of here in a couple of hours."

"You've got it, sir."

"Thanks, Del. Report to me. Don't tell anyone else about it."

Stefan went back to Kira's office and the trio of glum looking people there. Kira was reading something, and Halmai pointed to it as she read. "The second suggestion might be more appealing to you. An exception to military passage could be allowed in case of declared war or reckless endangerment of citizens on any of the treaty signers."

"It still has to be voted on," said Kira.

"I've sent copies to the state acting heads of Gan and Galena," said Halmai, "but the powers of deciding when to allow the exceptions would rest in your hands, Madam."

"Then we'll await the decision of the people," said Kira, and then looked at Stefan as he sat down again. "Any problems, Stefan?"

"A minor thing. It's taken care of. Sorry about my brief absence."

"Duty calls," said Halmai, smiling, but the smile did not reach his eyes. Stefan could sense from the man's rigid posture and clench of hands in his lap that the meeting had not gone well for the man, and he was anxious to leave.

Kira tried to make small talk with questions about the challenges of the government on Kratola, but Halmai's answers were short and uninformative. Finally, the man stood, rather rudely Stefan thought, and said, "Well, I think I've done everything I can do here. Thank you for your comments, Madam. I will convey them to the council, and hopefully our problems will be solved on another day."

"I'll see if your ship is ready," said Stefan, and he left the room again.

He called Del at Port Security. The man answered immediately, and gave him some alarming news. Stefan's first reaction was anger, his second caution. He had to consult with Kira before Halmai got on the freighter.

He had only a few minutes to do it, while Pavel was escorting their guest down the elevator to an awaiting air-taxi. Kira was horrified, and then angry. Stefan told her what he wanted to do, and she told him to do it, her eyes blazing.

Stefan caught up with them at the taxi, and the ride back to the shuttle was silent. Pavel sensed something and kept looking at him until Stefan looked back and shook his head.

There was more silence on the shuttle. Halmai looked displeased and was not in a talkative mood.

Stefan waited until they had reached port and were on the tube train only minutes from Halmai's departure. The Bishop was sitting by himself as part of the protocol until Stefan walked up and sat down opposite him.

Halmai looked surprised. "Sir?" he said.

"There is something that needs to be said before you leave. Please convey this to the Council of Bishops if we are to have any further contact with them."

"Such drama," said Halmai, and smirked at him.

"It's about the ship that brought you through the Gate. If that ship, or any ship like it, ever comes through the Gate again it will be boarded and seized, and the captain and his crew will be arrested and imprisoned."

"What?" said Halmai, appearing astonished.

"I don't have to explain to you why this is being said, and I speak for Governor Madelia. Please be sure the Council understands that."

Halmai opened his mouth to speak, but Stefan stood up and walked away from him.

Another minute and they were off the train and Halmai was angrily stalking up the ramp to the shuttle without looking back, and then the hatch was closing, and the shuttle was gone.

Pavel turned to Stefan and said, "Man, you got to him about something. What is going on?:

"Something sneaky," said Stefan. "But I'm hoping that I didn't just start a war."

CHAPTER THREE

Five hundred miles from Port Nexus the nearest of four fuel refineries and storage stations floated in the blackness of space. Five miles across, a giant metal sphere bristled with tubes connecting smaller spheres, re-mindful of a model of some enormous molecule. Freighters came and went daily, docking at random locations on the smaller spheres to transfer their loads of condensed hydrogen and helium taken from two gas giants orbiting Lyra 53 nearly two light years distant. The crews, some with families, were born, grew up, gave birth and died on those ships, only a few of them ever visiting Port Nexus even once in a lifetime. The fluids they brought were condensed and refined into tanks and pellets used in the several fusion reactors that serviced Port Nexus, and they were delivered on a regular schedule to each customer.

On radar, from Port Nexus, a fuel station was just a blob on a screen. Only within a hundred miles could any detail be seen. Only within that distance could one see that one of the smaller spheres was not a sphere at all, but a strange looking ship, smooth surfaced, small vanes protruding aft, a long, sharp bow forward and a huge bulge amidships, looking vaguely like a huge, pregnant fish.

A Guppy was permanently docked at the fuel station. It came from Gan, had been manufactured there. Four years ago, three of them had suddenly appeared when Kratola forces attacked Port Nexus. They had decimated those forces with a bewildering array of weapons: lasers, smart missiles, rail guns and a strange, glowing energy ball ejected by a sharp proboscis that could strike a target and cause it to simply disappear without any explosion or debris. It was said to be a weapon provided by the Immortals, a group of freedom fighters who were masters of technology, and powers approaching that of a God.

It was said they had left Port Nexus after the war to focus on restoring democratic rule to the citizens of Gan.

The Immortals had not left. Their influence had determined the new staffing of the port, and they maintained a nearby military presence with the knowledge of only a Governor and a few Gan agents in the port.

A Guppy came and went on a regular basis. It did not depend on the great wormhole at Port Nexus for travel. The same force that allowed it to make enemy ships disappear could fold space rapidly for repeated jumps over distances of thousands of light years, a power that was still known to only a few. The Guppy now docked had recently arrived, and the crew prepared for a five cycle stay. One man left the ship, took a moving beltway to the central ball of the refinery and found an office there overlooking the towers of cyromachinery.

Dane Taasaar, a senior officer of the Gan Intelligence Agency, was there to greet him. "Hi, John," he said, and extended a hand.

John, the second reincarnation of Leonid Zylak, shook the man's hand, and they sat down at a table with plates and utensils and a big platter heaped with meat sandwiches made onboard the Guppy. Dane bit into one and chewed. "Always a treat," he said, "but the artificial stuff is getting better year by year."

"We're working on it," said John. "There's more coming over from the ship. I'd like to unwind and review some strategies before I head to Kratola again. We're making progress, but I need to speed up the unrest. Decades of dictatorial rule should make people angry, but instead it has turned a lot of them into sheep."

"The Bishops have had over thirty years to do it this time," said Dane.

"Yes, but for the last four years there's been a bad economic downturn on Kratola. A lot of businesses on Gan and even Galena have canceled contracts with them in fear of more war. The money people are getting nervous, and I'm concentrating on them now."

"It's going to be a slow process," said Dane.

"I know. It would be a lot easier to just go in there with half a dozen Guppies and blow that palace away to another part of the universe. My fear is that the entire population of Kratola would hate us for the invasion, and I don't want that. It should be their job to bring down a bad government and replace it with one of their own choosing."

"Well, you have the time," said Dane, smiling as he picked up another sandwich.

"I can think of a lot of things I'd rather be doing with it. Now I'm hearing a Bishop made a surprise visit to Port Nexus. I need to know what he's sniffing around again for. What have you heard?"

"I think you'll like it," said Dane. "It was Halmai who made the visit."

"The little greasy one?"

"Supposed to be subtle at diplomacy, but the way he was treated he wasn't so subtle this time. There was no ceremony, no publicity, and Halmai found himself meeting with three people, not one. Both security guys were there. Halmai insisted that military ships should be allowed through the Gate. Some phony excuse about preventing religious persecution. They didn't buy it, but that's not the fun part. During the meeting, he was trying to sneak a disguised military ship into Port Nexus. But our new security chief had the ship scanned, something I've never heard of happening before, and he caught it."

"Oh, oh," said John.

"No, there were no arrests or charges, the chief issued a warning, and in the process gave Halmai a new bung-hole. Governor Madelia was actually giggling when she told me about it. She is very happy about that new guy.

John shook his head. "Maybe. Depends on the reaction of the Bishops. We'll see. Do you have a file on the Security Chief? I remember he came from Gan and had some problems there."

"Got it," said Dane. "Give me a call when you're settled, and I'll have it sent to your room."

"And a beer," said John.

"That we have in plentiful supply," said Dane.

CHAPTER FOUR

The marble towers and turrets of the palace and tabernacle of the Church of First Light gleamed in morning sunlight. A wide staircase led up to the complex from a square courtyard with lawns and beds of red flowers and a great golden sphere from which water from many orifices flowed into a large pool. The complex was bordered on all sides by a twenty-foot steel frame fence with gates front and back for entrance and exit

The previous evening there had been a mass, and sixty or so of the faithful had attended after enduring document checks and searches at guard stations by the gates. During all of the day and night armed guards continually patrolled the perimeter of the property with orders to shoot anyone who dared to enter without permission. Now, in morning, there were no visitors, but by dusk a crowd would begin to gather by the front gate with their signs and megaphones and burning torches, and protests that changed from day to day. Two years ago, there had been no protests. The unrest was something new, undoubtedly orchestrated by outside influences.

The Council of Bishops had had enough of it. A quiet purge of dissent leaders had already begun. Several people had simply disappeared, and two awaited public execution for the unrest they had inflicted on Kratola's citizenry. But so far there had been no effect on the size of the crowd in front of the gate each evening. Public executions might have an effect. Anything more would have to wait for the buildup of military forces after the disaster at Port Nexus, and that was proceeding rapidly.

Caleb Aluna, Prime Minister of Kratola and First Speaker for the Council of Bishops, stood on a palace balcony and watched a VTOL shuttle coming in from the west. Halmai had called in from the shuttle terminal, a brief call that was nothing but bad news. Caleb went inside as the shuttle passed overhead for a landing on a pad towards the rear of the palace.

Two hundred steps later he reached the assembly chamber for the Council of Bishops, a small room with four thrones facing each other from four walls. There was no room for observers or visitors, only the four men who ruled Kratola under the laws of the Church of First Light, men descended from priests who had led a successful coup to obtain power over a hundred years in the past.

Zuhair Pasela and Galen Dietzen were already there, seated opposite each other, and they nodded to Caleb as he entered the room. "Tibor has arrived. He should be here in a few minutes." Caleb sat down on a throne and sighed.

"Have you talked to him?" asked Zuhair, who was the oldest among them, and had served two terms as Prime Minister.

"Briefly," said Caleb. "The news isn't good."

"I'm not surprised," said Galen, always the cynic. At forty-five, he was still young, only a few years older than Tibor, and had much to learn about dealing with recalcitrant but powerful colonists.

Zuhair rubbed his graying beard with a rough hand. "We certainly don't need more problems to deal with. Maybe I should have made the visit."

"Now, now, we're not going to blame Tibor for this. It was a risky visit, and he was willing to do it. No blame from either of you," said Caleb firmly.

No sooner than he'd said it and the door opened, and Tibor Halmai was there, looking tired and a bit disheveled. He shuffled into the room and sat down heavily on the remaining throne.

"Welcome back," said Caleb.

Tibor glared at him. "I'm glad to *be* back. I accomplished nothing, and by some miracle I wasn't arrested and shot!"

Caleb chuckled. "Come, now, it couldn't have been that dramatic. I've heard it, but tell Zuhair and Galen exactly what happened."

Tibor did so, in a five-minute tirade, voice increasing in pitch, face flushing deep red until he was shouting, "He scanned a diplomatic vessel! When in the history of the Gate has that *ever* been done?"

"Please," said Caleb. "A scan is routine for ships suspected of smuggling. It happens rarely, but it happens."

"A diplomatic vessel with a Bishop on board is treated as a smuggler," said Tibor, calming some. "Do they *want* to start a war?"

"Oh, that would be great news," said Galen.

"Doesn't sound to me like they fear one, though," said Zuhair.

"I went in there calmly with the spirit of negotiation, and I couldn't even get started. They slammed the door in my face politely, and then scanned my vessel."

"But no arrest, no seizure, nothing," said Caleb. "We tried something illegal and got caught. This is informative. We won't try it again. And it's clear we'll have no influence with Port Nexus administration. They are owned and controlled by Gan and protected by Anton Zylak's merry little band of so-called immortals. They are the real enemy. We have many friends in Port Nexus. We need to organize and empower them to change control of the Gate. The change must be done from within. Even with a military buildup we cannot win a war against Gan. The appearance of a Guppy in our skies will signal the end of us. It must not happen. We have talked about this before now, as I hope you all recall. We even made a tentative plan.

"Infiltration," said Zuhair. "We have moved fifty agents into Port Nexus during the past few months, and I've heard no news of their activities. What are they doing?"

"Nothing for now," said Caleb.

"All having a good time in Pleasure City?" said Galen. "That's where the cell was being organized."

"And organizing is what they're doing. I want fifty more agents there before the cell becomes operational. If any disruption were to begin now, I'm sure it would be less than a week before the new Security Chief figured things out and closed the Gate to all non-commercial traffic from Kratola. Security is still lax there. They require no visas, no background checks for visitors. It won't be long before they have it."

"People walk freely in and out of the terminal," said Tibor.

"As did five of our agents who left the ship after you did," said Caleb. "They were not stopped or questioned, even when they bought shuttle tickets for the city. Everything was wide open."

"That is really rather stupid," said Zuhair.

"But they are not stupid people, and they will learn quickly. We had friends who determined the old rules. Now we do not. I've ordered ten agents transferred to Port Nexus each week at least for the next month, and more if we can get away with it. We'll develop other smaller units among our friends. Two or three months maximum, and they will be ready for mischief."

"Let the chaos begin," said Galen, "including sabotage and murder, I suppose."

"Proceeding carefully," said Caleb. "We don't want to provoke a Gate takeover by Gan. That would be the end of commerce for us."

"I'm surprised they haven't done it by now," said Tibor. "We couldn't stop it. They've done half the job by hiring administration who are overtly loyal to the colony worlds."

"Bad for their image. Zylak's band is pro-democracy, remember? It's better to manipulate freedom of choice," said Caleb.

"Ah, something we might like to try ourselves," said Zuhair.

Caleb bristled. "Excuse me, but that sounded like a criticism."

"I would call it a suggestion. We've been talking about disruption, and suddenly we have it at our own gates. It's a recent thing, and I have my suspicions about it because it has been growing since the Port Nexus war we lost so badly. It was, in fact, humiliating. Our citizens seem to have lost respect for their government, and I've heard no discussions about it in this room. Please lead us in dealing with it, Caleb, before it gets out of hand."

"Arrests have been made, Zuhair. Executions will be public. Our power has been absolute for generations, and the people know it. They do not dictate policy to their leaders. They are not qualified to do it," said Caleb grimly. "Pure democracy is the worst form of government. The best is a benevolent dictatorship. That knowledge is ancient."

"Perhaps the key word there is 'benevolent'," said Zuhair. "We can at least appear to be listening to complaints by our citizens. They only need to think they're being heard. Trying to satisfy everyone only leads to chaos, we all know that. But who knows, an occasional suggestion might be useful, especially from our business and industrial community. It's not just common folk demonstrating at our gates. I would designate some prominent citizens to advise us about existing problems, and to publicize those interactions so people feel recognized. I think it would quickly cool many demonstrations based on a frustration they have. Having said that, there is another cause that bothers me more deeply. I don't mean to lecture, Caleb. I admire and respect what you've done through these difficult times."

"Well, I thank you for that," said Caleb, his face coloring. Tibor and Galen sat motionless, eyes wide, lips pressed tightly together during the conversation.

"We have talked about disruption today, and I fear the same thing is happening to us," said Zuhair. "The colony planets have become our mortal enemy. Of this, I have no doubt. A total war with considerable loss of life would be wasteful and would not be tolerated by their people. But they will destroy us from within, spreading dissatisfaction, dissension, emotional chaos and rioting until we are toppled from power. It has begun, I am certain of it, and we must counter it any way we can. Let our intelligence service earn its keep, our assassins do their jobs, our propaganda agency smother the people with kindness and understanding, even if it means some policy changes we're not happy with."

There was a long silence in the room, and then Caleb spoke.

"Thank you, Zuhair. You have given us much to think about. There is one thing we can do now. Our first public execution is set for tomorrow morning at first light in the courtyard. Please, all of you be there for it."

CHAPTER FIVE

"If the Bishops think we'll ever trust them again, even for a visit, they are badly mistaken." said Kira. "Bringing a warship through the Gate qualifies as an act of war against Gan and Galena, and it was definitely a threat to us."

"Not exactly a warship," said Stefan. Rolls and Gan tea had been served to them, and they were sitting across from each other at a small table in the Governor's office.

"What do you mean? It certainly had the armament for one."

"Well disguised, though, modeled after a pirate ship. I'd call it a raider, with the appearance of a light freighter, but bays with laser-canon fore and aft and a small rail gun turret hidden beneath the bridge. That's enough firepower to take out our terminal quick, and three of them could overpower the small number of Novas and C-class fighters that survived the war here. Only six left, and I need at least twenty more. We need to talk about that, Ma'am."

"I know, I know," said Kira. "So why didn't they attack even with one ship?"

"I think they were probing our security. The cargo was small, the manifest in order, and then they were suddenly scanned. Halmai was obviously surprised by that. He was scared. I don't think he expected us to detect a fraud."

"And now they know better," said Kira.

"Ma'am, we have no control over what comes out of that wormhole. If there's a threat, we have to stop it on entrance with flying firepower we don't have. I consider what just happened as a good warning."

"I've made our needs known to Gan and Galena months ago, and I've had no response. They're busy setting up a new government for the second time in only a few years. They need to be reminded."

"I'm familiar with the chaos," said Stefan. "I dealt with it for two decades."

"We have local Gan contacts in Pleasure City, and I have a private channel to them. I've been holding recent requests until the new government is settled in. They're electing a legislature and a Prime Minister soon. Any decision about aid will have to come from them. Pavel can help. He's close to Gan contacts in the city. We can start now. Call him, tell him what you need and when. He can get you in touch with someone. I'll use my own channel and do the same."

They finished their tea. Stefan returned to his office and called Pavel, whose main office was near him, but the man wasn't there. A secretary said he'd gone to the second level precinct office in Pleasure City for an information briefing and would be there for three cycles. She gave him a number to call.

Stefan called, and Pavel answered. "We have to meet right away with any contacts you have on Gan," said Stefan, and he told Pavel how they needed to proceed in rebuilding their forces quickly.

"There's someone in town, now," said Pavel. "Can you be here at red light? We can meet and have dinner afterwards. Hey, do a cycle here. With luck, you can meet my girlfriend."

"Should work. I'll take the 1500 shuttle. Where do we meet?"

"Red Palace Casino, front entrance. I'll be there We'll eat in the casino. Any cab will take you there. It's in sector 2, second level. Okay?"

"See you then," said Stefan, and broke the connection. He called Del, told her to arrange the shuttle that first stopped at Pleasure City before going on to the terminal. Four hours to departure. His desk was heaped with files of every senior officer at Port Nexus, and records of the brief battle that had destroyed a sizable fraction of port forces. It disturbed him to see that the performance of port fighting ships seemed to have done more harm than good in defending the terminal, and in some cases had even inflicted damage to the Guppies that had come to their rescue.

Whose side had the port forces been on?

Del had to call him twice to remind him of his trip, and in the end, he had to sprint on moving walkways past astonished people to catch his shuttle. Belted into a soft couch and sipping a hot tea through a straw he was finally able to unwind after an hour. The flight took nearly two. Pleasure City was a bright gem in the surrounding blackness of space, a double-walled rotating sphere of clear plasteel surrounding a curved plate four miles across on which rested a city that was the true life center of Port Nexus. Hanging beneath the city plate were featureless blocks of buildings housing two fusion reactors and all the equipment necessary to power a city of two to four thousand souls and provide a temperature-controlled atmosphere of constant composition. Narrow streets meandered between buildings up to four stories high, complexes of shopping centers, casinos, eateries and loud entertainment centers in the middle of the city, banks, a few factories and commerce buildings around the periphery, all of it lit up in a rainbow of colors that could be seen thousands of miles away.

The shuttle went through a double lock of plasteel and descended to a terminal with ten gates near the edge of the city plate. Before Stefan had even found a taxi, the shuttle had taken off again for Nexus terminal.

The taxi had no driver. Stefan climbed into the car and punched in his destination and bank card I.D. The door closed automatically. "Welcome to Pleasure City," said voice from a speaker. "We'll do all we can to make your visit a pleasurable experience. Please fasten your seat belt."

With the click of a seat belt locking, the car began to move. The ride to Red Palace Casino took only a few minutes, even at low speed. There was increasing traffic near city center, but only a few private cars. It was dinnertime, and the cafes were packed, only a few people walking the streets. He passed Black Diamond Casino on his right and his destination was coming up on his left, perhaps a hundred yards away. The facade lights of two casinos so close together were so bright they lit up the street like a sun.

Pavel was waiting outside the sliding glass doors and waved as he saw Stefan approaching.

Stefan sniffed the air as he got out of the cab, and his stomach grumbled. "What is that wonderful smell?"

"That's real meat grilling, real deal, straight from Gan. They actually pipe the scent our here from the kitchen. Nothing synthetic in this town, unless you have to have it. For a nominal fee, of course," said Pavel.

They went inside the Red Palace Casino, and it was fairly quiet. Casinos hadn't changed much in hundreds of years: machines and wheels and tables for cards. Many dealers stood waiting patiently at their stations, a few tourists working the machines. At the other side of the big room an alarm went off. Someone had gotten lucky. There was scattered applause, the sound of more tokens being eaten by the machines. Fifty years before, a gamblers' revolution had returned machine play from auto to tokens, and people strolled the room carrying buckets of them.

Most of the buckets would be empty within hours.

They had to walk through the entire gaming area to get to the restaurant.

"My friend is holding a table for us. This is the busy time for food," said Pavel. "I need to give you a heads up about this guy. He came to me two weeks ago and introduced himself, says he's a liaison rep for the new government on Gan and he's opening an office here. I think he's Gan intelligence. He might be an immortal."

"Do you believe that stuff?" said Stefan.

"No matter. He's part of a new government. When I mentioned you, he jumped at the chance to meet. But I really know little about him."

"Okay, so let's meet the man," said Stefan.

They entered a crowded restaurant. Odors of meat cooking assailed Stefan's senses, and he swallowed hard. From a corner of the room a man was waving to them. He stood up as they approached the table.

"Hi, Zeke," said Pavel, "I want to introduce you to my boss Stefan Fechter, the new Security Chief for Port Nexus."

The man shook hands with a hard grip. "Nice to meet you, sir. I am Zeke Azel, and I'm a new representative for Gan. I've just arrived to set up an office in the city, and I'm glad we're able to meet so soon."

They sat down. Zeke looked like a factory worker: heavy shirt, canvas pants and work boots. He had a square face and chin, dark hair and stubble. Dark eyes inspected Stefan closely. He seemed intelligent, with just a hint of something dangerous behind those eyes. He looked to be around forty.

If he was an immortal, there was nothing unusual to see.

"Are you with Gan intelligence?" asked Stefan.

Pavel's eyes widened, but Zeke just smiled. "Very direct, sir. A good start, I think. A part of my job will be to broker good working relations with yourself and Pavel here, and so I'll be open and honest with you from the beginning. Yes, I'm connected to Gan intelligence, but I also answer to our new Prime Minister when he's elected a month from now. As I'm sure you know, Gan is in a state of flux these days. But we're coming together again. Ah, time to order something."

A waiter had come to their table with menus. His name was Mark. He took their order for drinks, and went away.

They studied their menus in silence. The waiter returned with their drinks, and they placed their food orders, steaks all around. "Nice to see I can get some real meat here," said Zeke.

"The synthetics are pretty good, once you get used to them. Cheaper, too," said Pavel. "I'll pick up the tab tonight," he added, and smiled at Stefan.

"It's your budget," said Stefan.

"I hope for the chance to reciprocate," said Zeke. "There are a lot of things we need to talk about that relate to our mutual security. Port Nexus is our only link to the old world commercially, and we want to keep it open if possible. But we also want to eliminate any threat of future war with Kratola, and as long as the Bishops remain in power that threat will be there."

"We're aware of that," said Stefan.

"I'm sure you are. Your recent visit by a Bishop has demonstrated the threat again."

Stefan's eyes narrowed. "What?" he said softly.

"You governor keeps us informed, sir. She trusts us absolutely, and I hope to earn your trust as well. We have many friends and supporters here in Port Nexus. They see things, sir, things that are important to your security, things that can be improved.

"For example, you did handle bishop Halmai's visit nicely, caught him in a deliberate sneaky probe of your security, but did you know that just after you picked up Halmai at the terminal, four men left his vessel and took a shuttle to here and checked in at the Black Diamond Casino across the street. They did not return to their ship and are still here. Why? Tourists? I don't think so. You keep no records of people arriving and leaving the terminal. You are wide open for infiltration by unwanted guests. In these times this is not good. We can help you with this. You provide the system, we'll provide the observers, at our expense."

Stefan blinked his eyes, feeling a terrible embarrassment, and Zeke saw it.

"We want to help in any way we can. We are not questioning your abilities or intentions."

"I should have seen that problem," said Pavel.

"Historically the terminal has always been open without restrictions. I saw it was a potential problem, but I was more concerned by rebuilding our defense capabilities after heavy losses in the war," said Stefan. "This is my error, Pavel, not yours."

"I hear no excuses, just acknowledge of a problem," said Zeke. "That is very encouraging, sir. Egos can be deadly in times of war, even a cold one, and that time will be with us until the Bishops are gone."

Stefan felt his face flush. "You plan to overthrow the government of Kratola?"

"That will be up to our legislature and Prime Minister in the months to come. Right now, it's talk, conjecture. Please do not repeat this to anyone except your Governor," said Zeke.

"Agreed," said Stefan, and Pavel nodded.

Thankfully, their steaks arrived, and they could just eat for a while and enjoy the meal while their subconscious minds dealt with sinister possibilities.

"You mentioned building up your defense forces," said Zeke suddenly.

"I was hired with the understanding that our C-class and Nova squadrons would be built up again after the beating they took in the war, short as it was. Governor Madelia has been holding up new requests for new ships because of the governmental changes on Gan.

"What do you need?" asked Zeke.

"Nine or ten ships for each class would bring us up to fair strength. I'll be adding a ground force, but we can handle that ourselves."

"A ground force on Port Nexus?"

"We have this city to defend, and Station Alpha, and several vital stations with small crews necessary to the operations of the Gate. They could be occupied in an attack, and there has never been a plan for defending them. Pavel's police are not equipped or trained for that kind of action."

Zeke nodded. "Okay, I'll pass on the request when our new government is seated if you have Governor Madelia send it formally to 'Office of Prime Minister' on Gan right away. I can't promise anything, but the Gate is vital to our commerce and there is support for it everywhere in our business community."

"Thank you," said Stefan, "and I appreciate your advice about terminal security. I'll get on that, but regulation may not be popular with the tourists. They have never had exit and entrance rules before, but we'll try to make simple for them. Without the tourists, Pleasure City would go dark."

Zeke smiled. "I'm sure that is not likely to happen, Mister Fechter. It has been a pleasure to meet you. I'm very encouraged by our talk. My office here is being set up as we speak, and here is my private number." He slid a small card across the table to Stefan. On it was only his name and a number. "If there's anything you need, or any help in contacting Gan officials, just call that number. If I have news I think you need to hear, I will contact both of you directly. I already have your contact information."

He turned to Pavel and held out his hand. "And I want to thank you, sir, for a fine meal. You've been silent during this conversation, but I've watched the glances between the two of you and it tells me you work very closely together."

"We do," said Pavel, and shook his hand.

"Well, I must leave now," said Zeke, and he stood up. "My office is just down the street, almost next door to the Black Diamond Casino. You can't miss it. The sign on our front window says 'Gan Tourism Bureau'. Pay us a visit sometime."

Zeke walked away, leaving Stefan and Pavel grinning at each other.

They ordered sweet, doughy desserts, and Pavel was on his phone, talking to his girlfriend briefly. He hung up, said, "She'll be here in a few minutes. She just finished a show, has another coming up, so she can't stay long. She works here, dances in 'Red Lights' and 'Dark Fantasies'. She's a line captain," he said proudly.

"Well, well," said Stefan. They sipped coffee and watched people for only a few minutes before a tall brunette dressed in a red, silk robe approached their table. Her hair sparkled with a dusting of colorful chips of something plastic. Her face was round, with full lips, a small nose and dark eyes lined in purple. Pavel stood up, held out his arms and enveloped her in a hug when she reached the table.

"Wow," said Stefan, smiling. The girl was lovely and gave Pavel a wonderful look.

"This is Carra Cozza," said Pavel, squeezing her tightly, "and this is my new boss, Stefan Fechter."

She held out a slim hand, and Stefan shook it gently. "Ah, you're the new guy who will protect us all," she said, but not with a disrespectful tone.

"That's the plan," said Stefan.

"Welcome, and good luck," said Carra. "I'm afraid your predecessor wasn't worth much."

"And that's why he's gone, "Pavel said. He pulled out a chair, and seated Carra. "Want some coffee?"

"Not before a show. It'll just make me want to pee. My, but you guys look good in your dress uniforms. People are looking at us."

"I think they're looking at you," said Stefan.

"Why thank you, sir," said Carra.

"Watch out for him," said Pavel.

"And you watch out for my honey," said Carra. "I love this guy."

"He's my right hand," said Stefan.

"I hate to be brief, but I have to change for another show," said Carra. "We'll get together again, and I'll bring along a girlfriend for your handsome boss. My big reason for meeting you now is to bring him a message."

"A message for me?" said Stefan.

"Yes, a message from my boss, Corinne Ariska. She owns this casino. She wants to meet you, now."

"Well, I..." Stefan paused, surprised.

"While you're doing that, I'll watch Carra dance. 'Dark Fantasies. Second floor theater. We'll meet there. I'll' show you how to get to her office."

"She's expecting you, and she always gets her way," said Carra. "Let's get him to the elevator, sweetie. I'll see you at the show."

She kissed Pavel firmly on the lips and walked away.

"Better go," said Pavel. "Boss is waiting."

"He felt like an automaton, but was curious, and followed Pavel and Carra across the gaming area to a small elevator by the cashier cages. Carra used a key to open the door. Inside was a panel with buttons for four levels, the top button labeled 'penthouse'. Stefan stepped inside. Carra leaned in and pressed the button for level three.

"Have fun," said Carra, and the door closed.

And the new security chief of Port Nexus rode the elevator to the office of Corinne Ariska, owner and operator of the Red Palace Casino.

CHAPTER SIX

The elevator rose slowly to level three and stopped, but the door did not open. Stefan felt a hint of apprehension and looked up and around him. In the upper corner of the elevator light reflected from a small camera lens, and suddenly there was a female voice from a speaker on the button panel.

"Your name, please."

"Stefan Fechter, Chief of Security, Port Nexus. I was told to see Corinne Ariska, and that she's expecting me."

"Thank you," was the reply, and the door slid open. A slim, young blond in a form fitting, black business suit was standing there with a data pad in her hand, and she smiled. "Follow me, sir," she said, turned, and walked across a large room with couches and chairs to a desk fronting large double doors, and he followed her. She knocked softly on the doors, and there was a muffled reply from within, and she opened the door for him.

"Mister Fechter is here," she said, and gestured for him to step inside.

Stefan had imagined meeting an older, severe looking woman who could own a business such as a major casino in a place so far removed from a planet-based city.

He was pleasantly surprised.

The office was vast, walls lined with rich, blond woods, a thick, orange carpet, a couch and plush chairs circling the room. There was a long table with ten chairs along one wall, and in the middle of the room was a massive, curved desk with computer consoles at each end and a video screen placed flat in the middle. A woman sitting behind the desk rose to greet him. She was a brunette, tall and slim looking in a red business suit, and definitely not an old woman.

"Welcome to the Red Palace Casino, Mister Fechter. I hope you enjoyed your dinner with us."

"It was excellent," said Stefan. "Nice to taste real meat again. You have quite a place here."

"I've done quite well, but hope to do better, Mister Fechter. Please sit." She gestured to a chair in front of her desk and sat down again. Stefan was waiting for her to introduce herself, but she did not.

"So, you are the new security chief for out little community here."

"Overall, yes, but my focus is on the military wing. My number one handles police forces in the city and port terminal."

"Pavel Fiala I know. Nice kid, keeps things peaceful in our sometimes rowdy streets. I like him. His girlfriend is one of our dancers, and I think the relationship is getting serious."

Nice kid? "Seemed that way at dinner tonight." *How old is this woman?* he wondered. Chiseled, sharp features, deep set brown eyes, she wasn't just striking, she was frigging beautiful. *Pushing forty*, he concluded.

"So, Mister Fechter, you are a professional military man, and you came to us from Gan. I'm also from Gan, but I've lived here now for twelve years. My father is still there. General Fabrik and Brokery. Maybe you've heard of it?"

"I don't think so."

"Specialized manufacturing and metals brokerage, important enough to keep the business safe through all the political changes. I fled the chaos, and father set me up here, but I've done the rest. There was an opportunity here, and I took it."

She paused, looked at him closely, then asked, "So why are you here, Mister Fechter?"

He'd had enough. "That's Stefan," he said. "And you are...?"

For the first time, a slight smile on that lovely face. "Corinne," she said. "Corinne Ariska, but you did know that."

"I just wanted to hear you say it. I was a brigade commander on Gan, served under an emperor and a wannabe emperor for seventeen years, had some political problems and retired early."

"My father knows your history. All of it," said Corinne.

Stefan swallowed hard. "Then you know I was court-marshaled for insubordination."

"And later exonerated," said Corinne.

"When the Emperor's palace was under siege, he ordered my brigade to attack the crowds, and I refused. My academy oath was to defend the people, not an emperor. He disagreed. After the revolution I was reinstated, but there were still bad feelings about me, and then the new government was also a mess, and then the war at Port Nexus. I had supporters who helped me get this job and leave Gan. It's still in chaos, but I think they'll get it right this time. They'd better. The Bishops are still up to no good." *Shut up! You're babbling!* He thought.

"You're not a fan of the Bishops?"

"Let's just say I'm not a religious person."

Neither am I. I just believe in good people," said Corinne.

"Like the Immortals?" said Stefan, and Corinne smiled again.

"Just people, but special, highly educated in science and technology, and a community of geniuses, I think. Father knows them, had them in our home when I was growing up. Just people."

"They're probably going to be the new government on Gan, and my hope is they'll help us to rebuild our defenses. If you have any contacts I might need for this, I'd appreciate your help."

"Let's see what comes up," said Corinne, without commitment.

"Okay for now," said Stefan. "It's been nice to meet you, Corinne. Thanks for the invitation."

"Nice meeting you, too. I do have a warning for you, based on my own experience."

"Oh? She still hasn't used my first name.

"Everyone who believes in freedom knows that the power and influence of the Bishops has to end," said Corinne. "Despite that, there is a division among our people that is mostly religion. We have many followers of the Church of First Light here, especially among people who originally came from Kratola, and though they don't support dictatorial behavior they see the Bishops as heads of the Church. To threaten the Bishops is to threaten the Church. The Bishops are aware of that fear, and they play to it. Whatever they do, the excuse is always action to counter endangerment of the Church.

"We are an isolated community here, and religion is important. Zealots are common among our citizens, and you can be certain they exist among your military personnel. You need to know their loyalties. The problem became real during the attack by Kratola four years ago. Your predecessor did nothing to stop it, and many of our ships actually attacked Gan forces that arrived to help us."

"I'm aware of it, and suspected divided loyalties were a factor. My desk is piled high with files of ranking officers. I started a review a few cycles ago. A third of them are originally from Kratola. I'll be interviewing all of them soon."

"Really," said Corinne.

"Three men are already suspect, from their performances during the war. Even split loyalties will not be tolerated."

Corinne looked at him closely. "I must say I'm impressed, Mister Fechter."

"That's Stefan, please."

She smiled, then, a real smile that reached her dark eyes. "Your military experience and bearing is showing—Stefan. Perhaps some things will be changing for the better around here after all."

"That is the plan," said Stefan, and smiled back at her. Very briefly, he had forgotten to breathe.

Corinne opened a drawer in her desk and took out a colorful bag with the Red Palace logo printed on it, and cloth handles for carrying. She pushed it across the desk to him.

"A little gift for you, something for the high rollers who bless our enterprise for their amusement. There are snacks and wine, and complimentary coupons for our restaurants and show rooms. Perhaps you'll find the time to return and enjoy yourself."

The bag was crammed full. Stefan took it without inspection. "Thanks so much. I have to warn you, though. I'm not a gambler."

"Oh, I think you are, just not in the casino sense, but do be aware of the odds in your game. It has brought me good fortune. Perhaps we'll have a chance to meet again sometime," said Corinne. She was not so serious, now, her expression softer. She touched something on her desk, the door opened instantly, and the pretty blond was there. "Please show Mister Fechter to the elevator."

She stood up, nearly eye to eye with him, extended a hand. Her grip was firm, and warm, and lingered for a few heartbeats.

"Thanks again," said Stefan, and then followed his escort to the elevator without looking back and took it down to second level where the showrooms were located. "Dark Fantasy' was well underway. He sat down by a confection kiosk and waited for nearly an hour for it to end. Pavel came out and saw him, giddy after watching Carra's performance, and they waited another half hour for her to appear. They had a sweet desert at a cafe, Stefan amused by watching Pavel and his lovely lady, the two of them unable to keep their hands off each other, and then it was time to leave. Carra promised to find a pretty companion for him for dinner the next time they met. She kissed Pavel long and deep, then went away to her apartment in the staff building behind the casino, leaving Pavel grinning.

"My life would be pretty dull without her," said Pavel. "She lights it up for me. We've got to find a woman for you."

"Right," said Stefan. "That would really complicate my life."

But then he thought about it again when they were on the shuttle. He thought about Corinne and had a sudden realization.

He wanted to see that woman again.

CHAPTER SEVEN

It was twenty-four cycles later before Stefan saw Corinne Ariska again.

Up early, a quick workout, meals at his desk, brief sessions at the shooting range, bed late, this was the routine for twenty-four straight cycles of work for a former brigade commander totally focused on his new job. With a list of immediate tasks in mind he was obsessed with finishing everything simply and quickly, but the mountain of files on his desk contained details and necessary cross checking that made it slow going.

The data disturbed his dreams several cycles before he was finished. In a few cases it was suspicious. There were sixty-five remaining senior officers and flight commanders registered in the defensive force of Port Nexus. Several officers had died in the war and had not been replaced. Five were simply missing, had not been seen or heard from for the past four years, and no search had been made for them. But overall, the statistics were encouraging and would simplify the interviews he had to make.

Nearly seventy percent of the senior people had come from Gan or Galena, though none were academy graduates. They had come out of Gan flight schools with academy associations, taught by active, senior pilots in Gan's merchant space force. And not one of them claimed any affiliation with the Church of First Light.

Alas, the other thirty percent contained potential challenges. All were from Kratola, had been raised there at one time or another, had been members of the military during the reign of the Bishops. To make it worse, half of those people, including two very senior officers professed affiliation with the Church. There were fifteen men who had been recruited the same year when Kratola had been paying especially heavy taxes for commercial shipments through the Gate, and Stefan's predecessor was first at the helm nearly six years before the war. For several of them, Stefan could find no details of their performance during the war, something that had been in every other file on his desk.

This he found highly suspect.

Over a period of four cycles he interviewed fifteen men, asking pointed questions about their politics, any ties to Kratola, and especially their version of their own performance during the war. The responses of four men were at first guarded, then hostile when he asked for witnesses to corroborate their stories. Most vocal was Alex Rotando, a wing commander based on Alpha Station.

"Why are you asking all this?" Rotondo demanded, red-faced with anger. "I'm telling the truth. I don't give a krack about your records."

"Everyone was debriefed after the war, and there are records of it. I found nothing for you. Why is that? Has something been removed from your records? That's my question."

"I told you what happened. Put it down, record it or shove it. I don't care."

"That's insubordination, Mister."

"Fugg it. I'll go to the Governor."

"Or maybe the Bishops?"

"At least they know how to rule a planet."

"Okay, you have an opportunity now to join their military again. You're fired, Commander Rotondo. Pack it up. I'll have the papers cut by red light, and passage for you on the next freighter to Kratola. A trooper will accompany you until you're onboard."

"You're going to pay for this," said Rotando menacingly.

"I already have, and so has Port Nexus. Now get out of my office." Stefan stood, one hand on his holster. "Now."

Rotondo didn't salute, turned and left the office, slamming the door behind him.

Stefan called Del. "Get a guard to go with Commander Rotondo and stay with him until departure. I'll bring out a draft of the orders to be cut. I've fired him. I want him out of port by the end of red light."

"Yes, sir," said Del.

That seemed to be the end of it. Stefan returned to his files, now including interview results for Rotondo. Four remaining files contained suspicious stories, but he'd been given names of people who could confirm or deny them. He decided to hold off final actions until the witnesses had been heard.

Suddenly there was a disturbance outside his office door, a crash, a shout, and then a feminine scream from his desk console. "They're fighting!" screamed Del, and there were sounds of a scuffle.

His reactions were automatic, without thought, the results of twenty years of military training. As he stood up, his right hand unsnapped his holster, and the big gun there had cleared the top of it when his office door burst open and Alex Rotondo was standing there with a rifle in his hands and wild, crazy eyes while behind him a guard was struggling to get up off the floor.

"I'm doing a favor for Kratola and the Church!" screamed Rotondo, and he was swinging the rifle arround to bear on his target when Stefan raised his fifty-caliber gun and shot the man twice in the heart at a ten foot range, slamming him into the door jam and spraying blood into the outer office.

The guard struggled to his feet. "Sorry, sir. He jumped me at the door and grabbed my rifle. You okay?"

"I'm fine," Stefan said coldly. Inside himself, he felt a terrible calm, and Del was looking at him with wide eyes and obvious fear that was somehow disturbing.

Stefan pointed at the bloody corpse crumpled by the door. "Get someone here to clean up that garbage. Send the body to Kratola. If they won't take it, eject it into space, but get it out of here. And trooper, get yourself to the infirmary for a checkup. I need you here."

"Thank you, sir," said the trooper, relieved.

Stefan looked at Del, who was still shaking. He went to her, put an arm around her slim shoulders. "Sorry you had to see that. No orders to cut now. Go home, and rest. I'll see you next cycle."

"I will, thank you," said Del softly, and then she looked up at him. "It wasn't just the violence or the shooting, sir. It was the look on your face when you shot him that really scared me."

"Yeah, well, I don't like that face much either. You don't forget these things, you move past them. It's over. Now go home and take it easy for a while."

Del found her purse and left quickly without looking back.

"Hope I didn't just lose a good secretary," said Stefan to an empty room.

The following cycle he found her at her desk again, working hard and giving him a little smile when he arrived. It was as if nothing had happened.

But it had. It was nearly ten years since he had killed someone in the line of duty. And that had been on Gan.

Stories got around quickly on Alpha Station. The cycle after the shooting, just before violet light, Stefan went to the shooting range for what he called his trigger tuneup, a regular but brief shooting session only several minutes in length. Someone was always there, usually a few troopers, occasionally a pilot. They saluted and greeted him, and made small talk, generally relaxed and friendly. But this time was different. Three men were there, drinking coffee after a shoot. They nodded to him when he arrived, and didn't say a word. There were eight shooting positions. Stefan got a silhouette target, hung it and cranked it ten yards down the line. He pulled out his auto -fifty and put it on the bench with two spare magazines. And then, in three rapid fire bursts, he emptied three double stacked magazines of ten rounds each at the target. When he cranked it back again, the head region of the target sported a three inch hole, and there were no fliers. He holstered the gun and magazines and left the room.

The three men watched him silently, and didn't say a word when he left.

* * * *

There was no staff outcry about the death of Alex Rotondo, and no public announcement about it. But two of the officers Stefan had suspicions about resigned their commissions and fled to Kratola before witness reports had come in about them. Two others were exonerated by their reports, and Stefan was left with the feeling that the loyalty status of his senior staff was now clean.

Kira had submitted a proposal to Gan to provide more C-class fighters and Novas in return for Gate tax credit over a ten-year period. Gan elections had been held, a new government coming into place, and Kira was expecting a visit by the new Prime Minister elect.

His name was John Haig, and he was said to be an Immortal.

Things had changed in a big way on Gan. It looked like the followers of Leonid Zylak, now long dead, and his Freedom Party were now in charge of everything. And it was not long ago that Stefan had led troopers to search out followers of Zylak for arrest and imprisonment under Emperor Osmond's rule.

The next task was the strengthening of terminal security, and initiating record keeping for entrance and exit at the port. Guard posts were added, and manned kiosks where people leaving or entering had to present a picture I.D. and thumb print card showing their home address. No other information was required, at least at first, to avoid complaints about privacy invasion. As it was, people would complain about lines and delays and intrusion.

And they did, but mildly, and strangely most of the complaining came from the tourists from Gan, and not from Kratola. For Stefan, this was a surprise.

His desk was clear for the first time in a dozen cycles, and he was thinking about calling Pavel and planning another visit to the city when Kira called him just before red light and said, "The new Prime Minister of Gan is here, and he wants to meet with both of us in extreme privacy. Have you eaten yet?"

"I was thinking about it."

"I'll have kitchen set up a buffet in the big room. Dinner at nineteen hundred, and then we meet. Don't mention the meeting to anyone."

"Got it. I'll be there." Stefan broke the connection.

No notice again. He called the terminal, got Control, identified himself. "Has any ship just come in from Gan? Any tourists? Any dignitaries check through the gates?"

He waited while the records were searched. Only merchant ships had arrived from both Gan and Kratola this cycle. No tourist vessels this time of week. And any arrival by a dignitary would have been noted in caps. There was nothing.

Stefan fumed How did he get here without checking in?

Del had gone home by the time he left the office and made the fifteen minute walkway ride to the Governor's suite. Kira was waiting in the meeting room and there were two men with her, going over the room with palm sized instruments. They looked up sharply when he entered the room, hands moving towards holsters on their hips.

"Stefan Fechter is my Security Chief," said Kira quickly. "they're sweeping the room for audio devices," she said to him.

"Well, I guess you never know for sure," said Stefan. The men scowled at him, recognizing the sarcasm. They finished their job and left the room. The buffet had been set up along a wall. Stefan opened closed food bins and sniffed. "Hmm, potatoes, veggies and faux stew. Not bad. Hope he's not a real meat lover."

"He's not," said a voice behind him, and Stefan was startled.

A man had opened the door and stepped quietly inside. "I got used to vegetables when I was hiding," he said, and extended a hand. "I'm John Haig, the new Prime Minister of Gan, and we have some important things to talk about. I remember you from commerce meetings years ago, Governor. Congratulations on your new position."

Kira smiled. "My congratulations to you as well, Prime Minister. This is Stefan Fechter, my Security Chief."

Stefan shook the man's hand. It was hard and calloused. The man was his height, dark eyes and stubble, and a square jaw. His presence was powerful.

"A former brigade commander, sir. I've read your record. At one time we were not friends, but now that appears to have changed."

"I worked under two rulers, sir, and things didn't work out well for either one of them." said Stefan.

"Indeed, they did not, and the people suffered from it. We plan to make life much better for everyone. And what happens here at Port Nexus is part of it."

Kira gestured at the buffet set up for them. "Please serve yourself, Prime Minister, and let's talk about our plans."

"That's John, Governor. First names, please, when we talk in private. Titles are fine for the public."

They served themselves, sat down at the table and ate leisurely. Kira talked about governing structures, new regulations and remodeling at Port Nexus. Stefan summarized defense spacecraft and personnel needs, including a modest boots-on-the-ground force, and then I.D. requirements for port visitation and expanded record keeping.

John Haig listened patiently until they were finished. He put down his utensils, wiped his mouth with a napkin and said, "This port was rudderless for so many years, and eventually it cost us a war. I'm really pleased by what I'm hearing. Kira, you've sent us a proposal for the buildup of defense capabilities, and I've circulated it among our industrialists, and it has been unanimously supported. We can begin shipments of vessels and parts within a month of Gan time. A contract will arrive soon."

Kira smiled. "That is good news," said Stefan.

"Won't we be violating Gate rules regarding military hardware?" he added.

"No. I'll tell you how we do that later," said John.

"The timing is good, since we've begun an accelerated production mode to build up our own forces, including Guppies, and this is the other thing I must talk to you about in absolute secrecy."

"Oh?" said Stefan.

"What can be secret about a military buildup by a new government that had losses in a brief war?" said Kira.

The main secret goes back to Azar Kahlil, who replaced Emperor Osman after the first uprising. He was a longtime resident of Gan, and a respected industrialist, and a talented and persuasive speaker."

"He was a con man," said Stefan. "I'd just been reinstated when the trouble began. Fortunately, I was behind a desk, with no combat role. Otherwise, I'd been court marshaled again and probably shot by the bastard. I'm sure you know my history."

"I have," said John, "and you're likely correct. Everything happened so fast. When the real man surfaced, and his true relation to Kratola was apparent, we were suddenly ruled by a closet Bishop planted there as a sleeping agent decades before. It was not a democratic change of government, but a deliberate, orchestrated coup by the Bishops of Kratola and our intervention was the only thing that stopped it."

"Intervention by you Immortals, and your Guppies," said Stefan. "The people themselves did little until the very end. They'd actually elected the man."

"They were fooled," said John. "Elections have always been a popularity contest. They're not perfect."

"We lost some good people during that second uprising," said Kira. "It must not happen again."

"And that is the problem. The risk will always be there as long as Kratola is governed by the Council of Bishops. They've not given up on controlling their former colony worlds, only retreated for a moment to rebuild their forces and plan new strategies. It won't be long before they come at us again with something new, and it will have to come through the Gate."

John paused for several seconds, considering something as Kira and Stefan frowned at him in the silence.

Finally, he said, "I tell you this in complete confidence, and what I say must not leave this room. It is not to be told even to your closest associates yet. Agreed?"

Now Stefan saw why the room had been swept for recording devices. He looked at Kira.

"I will agree to that," she said, "if it relates to the safety of Port Nexus."

"I'll agree to it, too," said Stefan. "The port must be our primary concern. If I listen carefully, I hear you suggesting an overthrow of the government of Kratola. I applaud that, but we can't provide any resources for it without risking our own defenses."

John actually smiled. "You are a good listener, but we aren't talking about resources. What I'm saying is the menace of the Bishops isn't going away, and a war with them is coming, and Port Nexus will be affected by it. We will not wait for Kratola to strike first again, if possible. Our legislature is in place, and the public awareness of Kratolan hostility towards us is at a maximum. Our forces are building. Guppy production is up threefold. In several months we will be up to full strength. When we are ready, we will attack the Bishop's palace and temple on Kratola and destroy both buildings and occupants."

"Without provocation," said Stefan softly, "and you'll have to bring military vessels through the Gate to do it."

"But you can't do that," said Kira. "The law doesn't allow it, and that was approved by everyone, including Gan."

John paused again, then, "Kira, the Guppies don't have to use the Gate. They can fold space as well as any wormhole."

Kira gasped in surprise. "I didn't know," she said softly.

"That's how you arrived here without checking in at the terminal. I looked for your arrival there before our meeting," said Stefan.

"The Guppy is docked behind a fuel depot, and I took a staff shuttle directly to this station," said John, and looked pleased at his little deception. "I expect this capability of a Guppy to also be treated as top secret."

"Of course," said Kira. "In a way I'm relieved. I was having visions of armies coming through the Gate in both directions at the same time."

"There will still be one direction to worry about," said Stefan. "We can only control the stability of the Gate. We can't really close it completely. How much war warning can we expect to have?"

"One year, not more than two, unless the Bishops initiate another strike. We want to go in with a sizable guppy force to take out Kratolan defenses. Our ships are not immune to missile or rail-gun attack. You'll have the fighting vessels you need in three months time, Stefan. I will personally see to it. If our attack goes as planned, Port Nexus will not be involved. That is my hope."

"Knowing your plans, of course, we are now officially collaborators," said Kira. "I don't know how our citizen population will react. There are more than a few supporters of Kratola here."

"I had to eliminate some on my staff," said Stefan.

"One with extreme prejudice, I hear," said John.

"The man drew first," said Stefan, "and you seem to have a lot of informants here."

"We are concerned about your safety. We will not interfere unless you ask for our help, ever."

Kira frowned at him. Stefan frowned back, aware of the sudden hostility in the sound of his voice. He paused, then said," Okay, I can live with that," extended his hand and John shook it warmly.

"We know how to contact you quickly by relay in normal space. We don't want to surprise you, and you already know we have agents here. They are good watchers. Please trust them as an extension of your own intelligence service."

"My number one is already taking advantage of that," said Stefan. "Thank you."

"Good," said John. "I think we're finished here. I have a new government to run, and I'm gone three days from Gan." He shook Kira's hand with both of his. "Best wishes for the job you're doing here. I'm afraid we still have some tough times ahead of us, but we will prevail."

"Good luck to you and your colleagues," said Kira. "I think the right people are finally in charge of things."

"The Immortals," said Stefan. "Mystical or not, they seem to support freedom and democracy, and that will be a big change for Gan. Your people have my complete support, even if I don't understand the immortality part."

John laughed, and clapped Stefan's shoulder softly with a hand. "We don't live forever, Stefan, but we do have advanced science and technology that is not revealed publicly. The Guppies are an example, but we also have medicine that is unheard of, and our people who take advantage of it can live very long and healthy lives. It is their choice to make. I hope the day will come soon when we can share our knowledge openly with everyone. Perhaps you'd like to be twenty years old again?"

Stefan chuckled, "Nah, I'll stick with forty-two."

"A good age," said John. I hope we'll meet again. In the meantime, good luck to all of us. A pleasure meeting both of you. My escort is at the door. Goodbye for now."

Kira stepped forward and gave him a hug, and John blushed. "Oh, my," he said, turned, opened the door. Two large men were waiting for him, the door closed and he was gone.

"I wonder if he's ever been hugged," said Kira.

"I think he'll need lots of them," said Stefan. I'm afraid he's right about the Bishops, and now we'll have to get ready for another war."

CHAPTER EIGHT

The small freighter from Kratola came out of the glowing, green cloud of the Gate vortex at 1900 and docked at the end of the terminal. Cranes began unloading a modest cargo of polymer panels for ongoing construction at Station Alpha, and a smaller load of carbon composite for transfer to Gan, since Kratolan vessels were no longer allowed to dock on that planet. A small group of tourists had come along for a fun weekend of pleasures in the city, and came off the vessel before the cranes began their work. There were twenty passengers in all, and sixteen of them presented their terminal I.D. cards at the exit kiosk and went out happily to catch shuttles, already in a holiday mood.

Four young men were new visitors and had to stop at the check in kiosk to fill out simple data cards, have a photo and thumb print taken, and then a five minute wait for the printing of a visitor I.D. in colorful plastic and decorated as a souvenir.

They waited patiently, without talking, and exited together, taking one shuttle to the city. Once there, one man made a phone call, asking for directions to their destination. They were large, muscular men, clean-shaven, square faces, and when taxis arrived, they rode in two of them to the Black Diamond Casino in the center of the city, and entered the large revolving doors there.

Down the street, above the office of the Gan Tourism Bureau, a security camera turned and focused on the men as they entered the casino. There was a soft click.

Inside, the men went to an information counter and identified themselves as job applicants. They were directed to an office on a balcony above the main gaming area. A secretary there asked to see their visitor cards and made a phone call. A moment later, a man entered the office, dark complexion, expensive suit, a noticeable bulge under his coat and a badge labeled 'security'.

"Come with me," he said.

They followed him to another office, unlabeled but with a large door, and entered it. Their escort pointed to a couch, and they sat. A young secretary behind her desk smiled and spoke, but not to them. "They're here," she said.

The door to an inner office opened, and a very large man filled the doorway. He grinned from a round, puffy face, a fat, unlit cigar protruding from his mouth, and the body of a true patron of good food.

"Come in, come in, and we'll get you settled," he said with a raspy voice, and the men got up and followed him inside. They sat in four chairs in front of his enormous desk as he settled himself behind it. The small room was littered with files and ledgers and reeked from cigar smoke. A brass tinted plate on his desk identified him as 'Guillermo Corrella', and he was the sole owner of Black Diamond Casino.

"I don't suppose you can share some names with me?" he said.

One of his guests leaned forward and placed a red, heart-shaped piece of plastic on his desk. "That's all you need to see," he said.

Corrella bit down on his cigar, and growled, "Okay for now, but when the time comes, you people had better remember who your friends are. I have my own guns, you know. You don't want to be messing with them, too."

"We do appreciate what you're doing for us, sir. It won't be forgotten," said the man speaking for the group. The rest of them just sat there sullenly, and never smiled.

"I know military when I see it," said Corrella. "It's good that they're finally sending us the right people for the job. A guy will be here in a few minutes to take you downstairs for assignment. We're just a way station; our cells are at several places in the city. I don't know any details, and neither will you, except for the cell you're assigned to. Any comments?"

"Just happy to be here, sir," said the spokesman, and then there was silence.

A knock on the door, and another man was there to take them away. They left without a word, and closed the door behind them.

"Assholes," muttered Guillermo Corrella, and then he lit his cigar again, and sucked on the chewed up end of it.

* * * *

Five blocks down the street, Stefan Fechter had arrived to give a presentation at Central Precinct with Pavel present. His purpose was to recruit a special team of officers for training in special operations and tactics in the city. To impress his audience, he wore his dress blues for the occasion.

The casino district precinct was known for its handling of public disturbances and petty crimes. For the tourists and hardworking people who lived on Alpha Station, the city itself, or the several small outlying stations of Port Nexus rowdy entertainment was in short supply. When they came to Pleasure City they wanted to play, and they often played hard.

The precinct office was a busy place when Stefan arrived. Several officers were there. A woman was screaming in one corner of the big room, took a swing at a man in dress blues and was stunned for her trouble. Two men were asleep on a bench, several others being interviewed for whatever reason, and there was a heavy, alcoholic odor in the air. On the way to Pavel's office, Stefan stepped over a suspicious yellow and greenish puddle that a workman was just beginning to mop up.

Pavel was on his phone, and hung up as Stefan entered his office. "Hey, look at you," he said, "all in dress blues. Your audience is waiting in the gym. We've set up chairs and a podium."

"Nice," said Stefan. They exited by a back door, walked a long, bare concrete hallway towards the rear of the station and could hear loud conversations from an open door at the end.

There were twenty occupied chairs in a wood-floored room bordered by mats, exercise machines and racks of bars and heavy plates, and a mirror covered one wall. Twenty men rose and stood at attention without command when they entered the room.

"At ease," said Pavel, and the men sat down in unison. They were all young men, early twenties, a year or two out of a level two class in Gan's academy. Stefan had been trained there what seemed like a century ago but had gone on to level four and a military career.

Pavel stepped up to the podium, but all eyes were on Stefan, who stood at parade rest behind him.

"Gentlemen," said Pavel, "this is a special day in your lives. You have been selected by examination and recommendations to form the first of four units to be called Shock Platoon. Together known as Shock Company, these units will be the equivalent of a ranger company on Gan, with high mobility and training in special weapons and tactics tailored to the defense of Port Nexus. You will be trained by former members of Third Mobile Infantry Battalion on Gan, and the originator of our program is a former commander of that Battalion. You know this man. His signature will be on your paychips. He has come out of retirement to be our Chief of Security at Port Nexus, and he is building our defensive forces to a level never seen before, and you will be a part of it. Please welcome Commander Stefan Fechter."

There was polite applause, Pavel leading it as he stepped aside and Stefan came to the microphone.

It was basically a pep talk, lasting only minutes, but designed to stimulate the interest and enthusiasm of the audience. They were hand picked, and special. They were mobile infantry, boots on the ground or ship to ship, dropping or flying out of spacecraft for ground, air or space attacks, and advanced training with harnessed flight propulsion units. There were weapons unknown to the public, smart weapons, stealth and exoskeleton technology, and composite armor. All of these things they would learn to use in ground simulations and field exercises at many locations within Port Nexus. There was also a mention of the public prestige in belonging to such a special unit.

Eyes were glittering in the audience when Stefan finished his short talk, and the applause this time was more enthusiastic than before. Pavel announced an orientation meeting at 0600 four days hence when two of the instructors would arrive. Both men had been trained by Stefan late in his career, were bored by retirement and had jumped at an opportunity to renew a military activity at his invitation, even though it was temporary.

Someone called "tain-hut!" softly, and the audience stood rigidly at attention as Pavel and Stefan left the room. In the hallway they could hear excited babbling coming from the gym. "Guess it went well," said Stefan, and Pavel smiled and patted his shoulder with one hand.

They sat down in Pavel's office. "I heard from Zeke again. They're all settled in. He wants me to be his first contact, since I'm here so much. Is that okay with you?"

"Sure. I'll be here more often when the new training begins. Any news?"

"He said they've seen some interesting things but wasn't specific."

"Well, specific is what we need. You know, it's 1600 now. I could take the shuttle back to Alpha soon or leave later and maybe have dinner at the casino."

"Want me to call Carra? She might be able to get a nice table companion for you." Pavel wiggled an eyebrow at him.

"Okay. I don't know if it's possible, but maybe her boss would have the time to join us? Should be relaxed at dinner, and I still have some questions she might answer."

Pavel had a slight grin on his face, a mischievous look. "Questions, right. Sure. I'll ask Carra about it. She sees Madam Ariska quite a bit about show scheduling and stuff. I'll call her right now."

He tapped on his phone, and waited a few seconds, then, "Hi sweetie. Stefan is here with me, and he's talking about dinner at the casino tonight. Hey, he wondered if your boss could join us. Yeah, that is interesting. Could you talk to her? Oh krack, I forgot. Well, he could eat there, but I don't think he'd want to do it alone. Okay. Okay. Call me back when you find out. Otherwise, I'll be there at 1900 sharp. Love you."

Pavel looked disappointed. "Rats, I forgot again. This is Carra's dark night. No shows. We usually get takeout at the cafe and go to her apartment, and—well, I usually spend the night there."

"How do you forget something like that?" asked Stefan.

"Yeah, bad me," said Pavel, "but Carra forgives."

"Well, I don't want to spoil that. I'll just take the next shuttle out."

"No, no, wait until Carra calls back. The lady is very creative about social things. Relax. Cuppa coffee? I'll get it."

"Sure. After the talk, I feel caught up on things."

Pavel got his coffee and poured one for himself.

They managed a couple of shot sips before Pavel's phone rang again.

"Hi. What?" Pavel turned to Stefan. "Is your phone on?"

Stefan checked and nodded.

"Yes, it's on," said Pavel. "Thanks, hon. See you later." He punched his phone off and smiled. "You are expecting a call," he said to Stefan. "Be nice."

"A showgirl?" said Stefan, and his telephone buzzed.

"Hello?"

"Commander Fechter?" the voice was female.

"Yes, it is."

"This is Ms. Ariska's office at Red Palace Casino. Could you be available for dinner at her residence tonight at 1900? It's just for the two of you, steaks medium rare, she says."

Stefan took a deep breath to control his voice. "That would be very nice. I'll be there at 1900. Thank you."

"Good. I'll tell her. Oh, she says please don't change your uniform. Dinner is formal this evening. Come to the third-floor penthouse at 1900. Someone will be there to bring you up in the elevator. Good-bye, sir."

Stefan hung up, shook his head, told Pavel what had been said. Pavel laughed and said, "You are one lucky man, and you probably owe Carra a dinner."

"Tell her she's got it," said Stefan.

CHAPTER NINE

Stefan and Pavel walked from the precinct station to the casino. Foot traffic was light until they neared the entrance, and a crowd was gathering further down the street on the other side. Stefan pointed and asked," What's going on down there?"

"Black Diamond Casino. They never have dark nights, but their shows are on the raunchy side. Lots of shiny boobs."

"Big competition for Red Palace?"

"Not really. Diamond caters to a different clientele. If you want class, Red Palace is the place to visit. I keep four officers inside Diamond on tourist nights, just to break up the fights. I won't say the owner is a low life, but I'd like to. He's from Kratola originally, and he is a card-carrying Bishop lover. His name is Guillermo Corrella."

"Sounds like a person of interest to us," said Stefan as they neared the entrance to Red Palace.

"Could be, but I doubt it. He looks like a thug, but his business checks out clean, he's a member of the business association and spent a few years on the city council. Corinne Ariska has served with him, but no friendship there. They are political opposites."

It was 1830 when they sat down for coffee in the fast-food cafe. Coffee was a common but expensive drink at Port Nexus, the beans shipped in regularly from Kratola plantations in the mountains south of the population centers. Carra was supposed to meet them in the cafe, but as the time approached 1900 she still hadn't arrived.

"I better go," said Stefan, taking a final gulp of warm flavor and standing up. "A few deep breaths will calm my nerves down," he joked.

"A very classy lady," said Pavel, "but nice. She treats Carra like a friend. Have fun."

"I'll likely catch a late shuttle back to Alpha," said Stefan.

"I'll be there next cycle late. I might be meeting Zeke again. I'll know by breakfast."

"Okay," said Stefan, and he walked away with his stomach still fluttering around nervously. *Hey, you're not going into combat here. Calm down!* He took four deep breaths before he reached the elevator door. A well dressed, older man was standing there, saw him coming and punched the door open. Penthouse level three required a key, which the man had and used, and the elevator rose.

"The living room is straight ahead, sir. Madam will meet you there."

The door opened; Stefan took two quick steps to escape the rapidly closing door behind him. He was standing in a small foyer with a plush chair and a small table, beyond which was an arch leading to a vast room, and everything was white: carpets, walls, furniture, paintings with some hints of pastel colors. There were no windows, indirect lighting coming from panels in the ceiling, and there was a wonderful, flowery scent in the air.

A semicircle of sofas was in the center of the room around a round, low table, and plush chairs were placed here and there around the circle. The far wall had large double doors on the left and an open door on the right which led to a long hallway.

Nobody was there to greet him. He picked a chair near the double doors and sat down to wait, his stomach fluttering again. He waited only a minute for someone to greet him, but it was not Corinne Ariska who arrived first.

He heard clicking in the hallway to his right, and then an enormous, black animal came out of the doorway and sat down, staring at him with golden eyes. A female, he guessed, coal black, slick coat, short tail, long, slender snout and erect ears, and around her neck was a silver chain done in fine filigree.

"Hi, there," he said softly. He recognized the breed, a Besselhound bred primarily for tracking large animals in the wilderness region of northern Galena. Highly bred, extremely intelligent, they were rare outside Galena and commanded an outrageous price.

The animal cocked her head when he spoke, and then she rose, walked daintily to the double doors and sat down again, her gaze never leaving him.

When she moved past him, his hand twitched instinctively towards his side for a holster that wasn't there. She'd made no threat, but her gaze was unwavering as she studied him, and it was making him uncomfortable.

He was saved by the arrival of his hostess. The double doors suddenly opened, and she was there in a floor length black gown that hugged her tall frame and showed off toned arms and shoulders. Around her neck was a necklace of black stones, a matched pair of ear rings completing the look, and her nearly black hair was styled in an upward sweep that added inches to her height.

"Hello again," she said. "I'm relieved you could come for dinner on such a short notice. I know you've been busy."

His stomach had suddenly relaxed at the sound of her voice. "I had a presentation at the precinct office, and it's close by. The timing was perfect.

And I have to say that you look incredible in that outfit. If I seem to be staring, it's because that's what I'm doing." He smiled as he said it.

"Why thank you, sir. You look pretty good yourself," she said.

Holy krack, what a smile, he thought.

"Have you met Neenee?" she said.

"We haven't spoken yet," said Stefan.

"She's studying you. I have very few visitors here, so she's not used to strangers. She's gentle, but anyone who attacked me would see another side of her that I try not to think about. When she accepts you, you'll know it. Dinner will be in a few minutes. Would you like a drink?"

"Whatever you're having."

"A blue mist for two, Alex," she said to the room, and then sat down in a chair close to Stefan. A moment later, a man in a black tuxedo came out of the double doors, served their drinks from a tray, and left.

"To safe and happy times," said Corinne, raising her glass, and they drank. Stefan raised an eyebrow when he tasted the drink.

"Good, but very strong," he said.

"Slip slowly. I promise not to offer you more than one."

Even with the hound staring at him, Stefan felt strangely relaxed, the stomach fluttering gone.

I have to admit that I've done some reading about your past history," said Corinne. "In spite of a setback or two you've had a successful military career, but you've never married, or even come close to it. As a woman, I naturally want to know why, so you must forgive me for my prying."

"Haven't found the right one, I guess. I was in the field a lot, little or no contact with ordinary citizens, and most of the women in Gan military were medical people and already married. I only met a few women, didn't date regularly with anyone. I like and respect women, and I'm not gay."

"Corinne laughed, and then lowered her eyes and said, "I think you are the most direct man I've ever met." She leaned forward to look at him closely.

"I like that," she said.

"I don't like to pretend I'm something I'm not, even when it means trouble," said Stefan, and looked directly into her eyes. Most people would blink or look away when he did that, but Corrine's return gaze was direct and steady. "Now how about you?"

She smiled. "I dated when I was young, but not recently. There are few older men around here, and most of them haven't had the courage to approach me. The rest are unappealing and crude. I mostly keep to myself, and I have Neenee for company, but there are some moments at the end of a work cycle when I wish to share something privately like we're doing now.

Sometimes I have chats with girls in the dressing room before a show, and I enjoy their gossip. I believe you've met Carra Cozza."

"Pavel's girlfriend," said Stefan. "Can't keep their hands off each other."

Corinne laughed again, head tilted, and it was a beautiful sound. "They are cute together. I envy them. Carra will be Show Manager someday. I consider her a friend, and by the way it was Carra who told me you had interest in dinner with me."

"I've already asked Pavel to thank her for that. They're having their fun tonight."

Another lovely laugh, and Corinne's eyes twinkled. Stefan felt a lightness in his chest, a kind of delight he hadn't felt before, and he smiled at her, chuckling.

Her eyes widened. "I'm glad you wore your dress uniform. It gives you a distinguished look for a man your age."

"And how old do you think I am?"

"Middle thirties I'd guess."

"I'm forty-two. Am I an older man to you?"

"Close," said Corinne, and her eyes said she was teasing.

"Don't worry, I won't ask for your age."

"Even though I'm older than you?"

"I find that hard to believe."

"Well, age difference isn't important," she said, still teasing.

"Something new suddenly occurred to Stefan.

"Wait a minute. You were raised on Gan, and you told me your father entertained members of a group called the immortals. Are you one of them? I'm kidding, you know. I don't believe in immortality."

"So if I told you I'm actually one hundred and fifty years old you wouldn't believe me," said Corinne, her eyes twinkling.

"Afraid not."

"Their founder, Leonid Zylak, died over a hundred and fifty years ago. Some people believe he's still alive in a different form. Others don't. There is a lot of mythology about that group, but their technology is amazing, especially in medicine. They've transferred patents for artificial organs to public domain and have promised more. And they were a powerful force behind the freedom movement on Gan. My father has supported them, and so do I. They are highly respected on Gan."

"And now they're in power," said Stefan. "I wish them well. Stability is long overdue on Gan. The past two governments have brought nothing but hardship and instability. First it was Osman and his taxes, and my parents died early trying to pay them and still have enough money left for seed. I supplemented their income for ten years so they could have enough to eat. And then there was Azar Khalil and his church tether, and his coup for the Bishops."

Without realizing it, Stefan's voice had begun to rise with emotion.

"I have nothing but bad memories from my life on Gan, and I know you've probably read about what happened to me there. I'm lucky to have the job I have, and I intend to do it well. But having said that, I'll try hard not to be married to the job as I did before. It's probably why I've never had a wife and family."

Stefan shook his head. Corinne looked sad, and her eyes were moist. "Wow, I'm talking too much. Sorry."

"You're a very passionate person to open up like that," said Corinne softly.

"I've just met you a couple of times, and I don't want to sound like a whiner. Is your father still alive?"

"Yes, but he's very old, and not well. We don't talk much anymore, and I worry about him. Mother died when I was young, and then I left, and now he's alone in that big house with a few servants who see to his needs and make sure he eats. He's the only family I have left."

The double doors opened, and Alex was there. "Dinner is ready, Madam," he announced.

They rose together and Stefan was surprised when she took his arm as they entered a dining room with a table for six but set for two with porcelain dishes and gold utensils in low light. Alex seated both of them and acted as waiter for the entire meal, bringing them first a potato soup, then a small salad before serving two large steaks garnished with a spicy powder. Food odors failed to mask the flowery scent of Corinne's perfume as she sat across the table from him.

They ate leisurely and made small talk about the dishes and the origins of the food, and Stefan compared them to his diet of synthetic foods on Station Alpha. Corinne was appalled by some of the foods he described. Alex served them a pastry filled with sweet custard for dessert, followed by a city brewed liquor, and then coffee.

"Would you like to see the rest of my apartment?" said Corinne.

"Sure," said Stefan. When he pushed back his chair to stand up he saw Neenee quietly sitting in a dark corner of the room, still watching him.

The apartment was large, with three bedrooms and baths, a commercial-sized kitchen and pantry, and there was an entertainment center with a wall-sized screen and three rows of theater chairs. All of it was lavishly furnished, but somehow cold, and then they came to a smaller room at the back of the apartment.

Corinne smiled and said, "This is my cave. I spend most of my time here when I'm not working,"

There was a small writing desk and chair, a short couch in front of a wall screen and a covered mattress with pillow in one corner. The walls were made with acoustic tiles painted orange, and a thick terracotta rug covered the floor.

"With the door closed I have total silence in here," said Corinne. "I write in my journal and think about my day. It gets me ready for sleep."

"Cozy," said Stefan. "I have an escape place, too, but it's more like a closet. Some days I use it to think things out, You have a nice one."

"You don't think this is unusual?" asked Corinne.

"Why? Everyone needs a place where they can get away from distractions. Of course I'm used to small quarters in the military, and your place here is huge."

"Are you surprised?" asked Corinne, smiling faintly.

"No. You're the owner of a major casino and entertainment center. You've built an empire here, Corinne. That's something to be proud of."

"I am, and it has made me rich, but it was my father who started me out, even though I was going to leave home anyway. I wanted to be in the entertainment business, but both Gan and Galena were so conservative, and Kratola forbid entertainment outright, and then my life at home had become uncomfortable.

"Oh," said Stefan. "I'm sorry. You don't have to—"

"—I love my father very much. He was devastated when my mother ended her life, and it got worse when I got older. He began to think of me as a substitute for my mother, and I just had to leave. He understood why. We don't talk much, and now he's getting old, and I don't know why I'm telling you this. Let's change the subject."

"Okay," said Stefan, "let's do that. I like you, Corinne Ariska. How's that for starters? I liked you the first time we met, and I've had a wonderful time now. I want to see you again. What do you think about that?"

Her eyes sparkled, and she took his hand in hers and squeezed gently. "I like you, too, Stefan, and it's not the uniform. I think I'll need more time with you to figure it out."

"Slow and easy," he said.

"That sounds like a good plan," said Corinne, and she squeezed his hand again.

They walked back to the living room hand in hand and sat down on a couch there, and as they settled back against soft cushions Neenee padded into the room, went straight to Stefan and put her long snout across his legs above the knees, and rolled her golden eyes up at him.

"Well, that's a good sign," said Corinne.

Stefan gently rubbed the hound's head and muzzle. "She trusts me, I hope. I wouldn't want this lady to get angry with me."

Corinne leaned against his shoulder while Stefan petted Neenee, the dog's eyes now closed. "She's very comfortable, and so am I. Can you stay a while?"

Stefan checked his watch. "It's just after 2200. The shuttles run continuously all cycle. I could catch the 0100."

"You could stay over and catch one next cycle. Please?"

"Okay, but we said slow and easy, right?"

Corinne grinned at him. "There are two guest bedrooms in this apartment, and poor sleeping in a shuttle, and we can have a nice breakfast before you leave. What do you think?"

"That sounds good," said Stefan, and Corinne smiled.

They talked for a long time, and slept in separate rooms, and Alex arrived to cook their breakfast when they were up. And when it was time for him to leave, Corinne kissed him chattily on one cheek and gave him a warm, lingering hug. And then she called up the elevator to take him down to a noisy casino, and he was given the shock of his life when the doors opened and Pavel was standing right there with a grin on his face.

"Good morning, sir," said Pavel. "While you've been having fun upstairs, I've been listening to Zeke telling me he thinks we're already being invaded, and that we're going to have to do something about it before it goes too far."

* * * *

She felt giddy after Stefan left, a light, happy feeling she'd rarely felt before. She stood by the elevator door and twirled once, hugging herself. "Oh, he is wonderful," she said. Neenee came out of the living room and looked at her curiously. Corinne knelt and cupped the dog's muzzle in her hand. "You like him, too. I've never seen you act that way with a stranger."

She stood up quickly. "I have to record this. I want to remember this feeling for a thousand years."

Corinne walked to her small, cramped den in the back of the sprawling apartment and took a small suitcase from a drawer in the desk. In it were a circular, leather ring with stubby electrodes that fit snugly at points just below hairline around her head. She put it on, sat on a chair with the suitcase and turned a dial on the device inside it. A red light glowed and she closed her eyes, relaxing. The light turned green for half a minute, and there was a buzz. Corinne opened her eyes again. "Mmm, got it," she said, and put everything back into her desk drawer.

Neenee had watched her again, tail wagging, curious about one of the several routine rituals in the life of her mistress, and sensing her happiness at the moment.

CHAPTER TEN

They left the casino and had walked halfway back to the precinct building when there was a bright flash, and the street buckled beneath their feet. The sound of the explosion was ear splitting.

People screamed and flattened themselves on the sidewalk. Behind them, on their side of the street, but beyond Red Palace, a boiling cloud of flaming debris rose towards the distant bubble ceiling of Pleasure City.

They both thought of it at the same time and looked at each other. "Zeke!" they said in unison and started running. Two police carts and a firetruck, sirens blaring, passed them on the way.

What was left of the Gan Tourism Bureau was a heap of cinder block and twisted metal. Small fires were immediately knocked down by foam. Several officers were setting up a barrier around the debris. They saw Pavel coming and opened up a place for him and Stefan to get through. The explosion had been so intense that most of the debris had been blown into the street, leaving the underpinning composite slab bare.

Stefan saw it first, a metal door set into the slab near its edge, away from the street. He pointed.

Pavel saw it. "Get everyone back here. You two, give us a hand." He beckoned to two officers, and they hurried forward. They stood around the metal door. Pavel leaned over, pulled at it, locked solid. Stefan leaned down, knocked on the door hard with a closed fist. "Police!" he shouted. "It's safe to come out, now."

They waited. Stefan knocked over and over again. "This is Chief of Security Stefan Fechter. We know you're in there. Please respond."

There was a scratching sound, and the door opened slightly.

"It's safe to come out, now, and you won't be seen from the street. Is Zeke in there?" said Stefan.

Now the door opened up, and Zeke was there, standing on a steep staircase. "Did anyone survive up here?" he asked.

"Sorry," said Stefan. "Everything was blown to bits."

"I've lost two men. They were manning the counter. We were actually doing some business here. I heard the telephone ring, and then the world came apart."

Zeke climbed up out of the darkness, and two men followed him. They blinked, and looked around in shock.

"How could they know? There must be a leak from a so-called friend. This will not go unanswered, Pavel. It's going to make life more complicated for you. Sorry about that."

"Are you okay?" asked Stefan.

"Shaken and stirred up," said Zeke, and the others just shook their heads silently.

Officers brought blankets, escorted the men to a patrol cart, and took them back to the precinct building for a debriefing. Stefan and Pavel followed in another cart. In Pavel's office they debriefed Zeke while the other two men were treated for mild bruising and shock.

Most of Zeke's anger was directed at himself. "I should have known they were watching us because of the connection to Gan. We've been watching them every cycle since the terminal regulations were changed."

"Who's them?" asked Pavel.

"Black Diamond Casino, right across the street. There has been a steady stream of visitors from Kratola, all of them young, need I.D. cards, check out of the terminal and haven't returned within several cycles yet. We see every one of them arrive in cabs, inter the Black Diamond Casino, and not one has come out again. Kratola is bringing an army in here, four people at a time. And now they know we know it. They will establish cells first, and that is the time for us to hit them."

"I can't arrest people for visiting a casino," said Pavel.

"But you can for a bombing. You just have to show the connection."

"We don't even know if a bomb was planted or thrown from the window of a passing cab. The investigation is just starting," said Pavel.

"My people can operate without legal constraints unless you insist on it," said Zeke.

"Law and order is for everyone, including visitors from Gan and Kratola," said Pavel stiffly.

"Unless war is declared," aid Stefan, and we're not officially at war with Kratola. We're not even a sovereign state."

"We're supposed to be allies," said Zeke softly. "We saved your asses in the war. Nobody asked then if it was legal or not."

There was a pause, Stefan thinking fast.

"You have a point," he said.

"What?" said Pavel loudly.

"If cell activity is dangerous, it can be treated as terrorism, and outside forces can be invited to counter it. But it's something the Governor must decide on. We have to bring this to her for approval," said Stefan.

"And then I can deal with a war in the streets of Pleasure City," said Pavel.

"It shouldn't be like that," said Zeke.

"More like a gang war, then, and I should stand by and let it happen," said Pavel, sarcasm dripping.

"But if we take it to our Governor, and it's sanctioned, then we take part in it. What do you think, Zeke?"

Zeke glared at Pavel and chewed on his lip, and then, "I have to clear this with our Prime Minister. He might want to be personally involved."

"Okay, do that, and get back to us. Do you have a place to stay?"

"We have friends, and cells of our own. We'll be fine, but you won't be fine if the cells from Kratola are allowed to thrive here. You'll wake up one morning with their gun barrels in your mouths."

"Not if we kill them first," said Stefan coldly.

"That sounds better," said Zeke.

* * * *

Stefan accelerated his program for training a new shock force and talked to Pavel about permanently stationing a single unit of thirty troops at the shuttle field in Pleasure City once they were ready. A barracks could be made available for them there. With specialized training in urban tactics and weapons, even a small force would be a powerful supplement to the city's police personnel in countering terrorist activities, and the recent bombing only stressed the need for it.

A polymer mockup of a partial city block was constructed in the vast gymnasium on Station Alpha, and four units of shock troopers rotated in and out each cycle for their training. No live ammunition was used, weapons equipped with lasers and silhouette targets with multiple optical sensors. Live fire would follow in a similar mockup near the shuttle field in the city. It would also be a trooper's introduction to the use of flight harnesses and the most difficult part of the training. With a range of only four miles, a trooper could drop from shuttle to ground in controlled fashion in or out of formation to a specific target and move at high speed to any part of the city.

Stefan had other plans for his troopers but kept them to himself for the moment. He could dream of the day when his people, suited up for vacuum, could attack from one ship to another in the blackness of space.

He watched the first two groups go through the mockup circuit their first time, and smiled when instructor Janus Hart, a former sergeant he's trained, grimaced at him and shook his head.

First time through, the survival rate would have been a sterling four per cent.

It would get better.

When he got back to his office a call was waiting for his reply, Kira had called, and said it was urgent. *Could it be so soon?* he thought. He returned the call and was not surprised.

"Prime Minister Haig contacted me directly. He's approved Zeke's plan to establish an anti-terrorist unit in Pleasure City if I will give my approval. I'm going to do it, Stefan. I called Pavel, and he's not happy about it. He sees a war coming in the street. Can you talk to him?"

"We'll talk. He's already agreed to a military presence in the city. But his expectation of war in the streets is not unreasonable, Ma'am. The Bishops are attacking us in a more subtle way this time. I'm getting ready for it."

"I'm afraid you're right," said Kira. "Haig is right, too. The only way to stop the Bishops is to destroy them, and in the end we'll have to count on Gan to do it. Our job will be to defend Port Nexus, and nothing else."

Stefan liked the hard sound of her voice.

"How are your boys doing?" she asked. "Sometimes I can hear the racket all the way here from the gym."

"They're learning fast, Ma'am. I have good people training them."

"That's Kira, Stefan. You're getting formal with me again."

"Sorry—Kira. I'll talk to Pavel soon."

"Good," said Kira, and she was gone.

A lady of action. He liked that. He had a sudden urge to call Corinne. She might have been frightened by the explosion only doors from her casino, but she hadn't called him about it. They'd agreed on a contact time after red light, around 2200, had exchanged private numbers, and he wouldn't be back in the city for at least four cycles. Only two cycles since he's been with Corinne, and he was already missing her. *What's happening to me?* He wondered, then, *Whatever it is, it feels good.*

He punched Pavel's number into his phone and called him.

CHAPTER ELEVEN

The gates to the gardens leading up to the palace had begun to buckle inwards when the soldiers arrived. Urged onward by several men shouting over hand-held loudspeakers, the crowd of angry people surged against stout metal and threw stones at the retreating guards there.

Caleb had had enough of it and given the order. The soldiers descended on the crowd from all sides, dropping from VTOL carriers at twenty feet and opening fire when they hit the ground. Explosive rounds tore into the crowd, people dropping as if smashed by a giant fist, blood and gore splattering everywhere. The firing went on and on until nobody was standing. Hundreds of bodies of mutilated people littered the ground in a heap of dead flesh. They were mostly men, but a few women and children had also been in the crowd.

From a palace balcony far above the gore, Caleb Aluna clapped his hands in applause for the work done by his military. Zuhair Pasela stood next to him, looking worried.

"This will only inflame the people," said Zuhair.

"Then we will put out the flames with bullets," said Caleb. "We've allowed this to go on far too long. We've tried reasoning and negotiation, have accomplished nothing because their leaders only want to end our rule, and there has been little progress in identifying and arresting their leaders. Why is that, Zuhair? Intelligence is your responsibility."

'Most of the leaders are Union heads. If we arrest them, there will be strikes immediately. They can shut down the commerce we're trying to rebuild.'

Caleb considered this for a moment, and then said, "Maybe. Well, I didn't see any union placards out there demanding anything, just an unruly mob threatening our safety. Make it clear to the unions we won't tolerate rioting or attempted coups. I don't even think the unions are involved with this. This has been instigated from outside.

"Nothing has come in from Gan except commercial vessels, and the crews never leave the ships. It's all on record."

"Then they're getting in another way. Find it."

"But they can come in only one way."

"We could try banning all commerce from Gan for a while and see if there's an effect."

"But we need the goods, Caleb. Please be reasonable about this. A mandatory I.D. review of the people might help us if we can do it without creating another riot."

"Then do it at the point of a gun," said Caleb. He turned and stalked back inside. "Follow me. We have another mess at Port Nexus to talk about."

"Oh, no," said Zuhair, and followed him back inside.

Galen and Tibor were waiting for them in the big room, perched on their thrones and scowling at Caleb as he seated himself. "You didn't tell us they were going to shoot everyone," said Galen. We could have a full-scale revolution next. The unions are already threatening strikes."

"The message is clear: demonstrations, strikes that threaten our security, any sign of insurrection is now punishable by death. I won't stop until the instigators are gone, and I am chairman here. Do any of you question that?"

There was a long silence before Zuhair said, "If your decisions put our reign in danger, Caleb, you know that any tenure can be terminated, even with extreme prejudice. You are not ordained by The Field, and we have all earned our positions on this council. You must respect our opinions if change becomes necessary."

Caleb softened. "Then give me a year. If my policies are clearly in error, I'll expect you to have a better plan ready to implement. And you can work on that anytime."

Galen and Tibor nodded. "Fair enough," said Zuhair, and a serious tension in the room slowly lessened.

"We do have a new problem at Port Nexus that could affect our plans there," said Caleb. "Our infiltration was planned to be invisible until we were up to strength, but one of our cells has now publicly announced our presence by bombing a Gan commercial office they claim was a spy center. The excuse I'm given is that our cell had been discovered and was about to be attacked by Gan agents. I don't believe any of it. The public will see this as a terrorist act; they will support any police or military action to prevent it in the future. Why don't we just call them up and tell everyone what we're doing? I thought I was working with professional, experienced people. They come from our special forces. How could they do something so stupid?"

They must have been certain an attack was coming. We have informants everywhere in the city, including the police. And we still have friends on Gan," said Zuhair.

"Gan would not attack them without provocation. It is not political.," said Caleb.

"If Gan has cells there, and I'm sure they do, the personnel are from Intelligence. These are the same people who overthrew an Emperor and a President in one generation. They are professional killers, and they are at war with us, even if it's unofficial. Are you suggesting we withdraw our people from Port Nexus?" said Galen.

"Of course not," said Caleb. "We should send more men and fight back when provoked. In the end, it's chaos we want to create. I just don't want to move too fast until we have a sizable force there. We have to get people into the port in higher numbers quickly. My concern is a possible ban on visitation rights for our citizens."

"That won't happen," said Tibor. "Commerce will drop, and taxes pay their bills. This was one incident. We should let it ride and build cells as quickly as we can. Special casino deals for Kratola citizens starved for entertainment, a flood of tourists, lots of agents among them. This is a simple problem."

"Not bad," said Caleb. "You have your business contacts there, Tibor. Get on it, and see what we can do. I'll keep our current cells intact, but with a warning about overreaction. And I'm going to move ahead with document inspection for every human present on Kratola proper, all the way down to the smallest village. I know there are foreign agents here who are behind the disruption. I'm going to find them, arrest them, and kill them publicly. And any future riots at our gates will be treated as they were today, unless, of course, you show me there is a better way."

The hint of sarcasm in Caleb's voice was not lost to any of them.

* * * *

The ambulances came and went, and by evening most of the bodies had been cleared away from the gates. A line of soldiers ringed the area, and three VTOL troop carriers rested just beyond them.

As darkness approached, the civilians who had watched the cleanup from afar had gone home, still shocked by what they had seen. But a hundred miles to the south, with fields of grain nestled within forests of conifers and firs, and connected by narrow, dirt roads, a group of people had gathered in a two story house painted white with green trim and a barn painted in classical red. There were thirty of them from all walks of life: journalists, trainers, computer techs, public relations and military intelligence.

All were citizens of Gan, and their two-year mission on Kratola had come to an end. Now they would be celebrated as patriots, but only in top intelligence circles. News of their mission would never be made public.

There was fear among them. Word had come of the slaughter at the palace gates. They worried about increased patrols, even this far from the city. There was only a faint red glow in the west when someone looked out a window and said softly, "Here they come," and they crowded together to see outside.

A large, bat-winged VTOL descended silently nearby and sat down on a field plowed and ready for seeding. Three small, blue lights blinked on and off several times and went dark. The people filed out of the house in an orderly line, and walked briskly to the craft as a ramp was lowered for them. They entered, and strapped down in seats along the fuselage without saying a word. The ramp was raised, the craft already lifting from the ground noiselessly. They felt a small vibration to accompany the nervous fluttering in sinking stomachs as they rose into a dark sky.

A few minutes later there was a thud, then a muffled roar, and they were pressed into their seats, and now there were a few smiles on their faces showing a sense of relief. There were no windows for them to look outside. They could not see the brown and green planet dropping away beneath them, or the mammoth, strangely shaped ship they were approaching at high speed, a bay door opening to receive them.

They slowed nearly to a halt and were suddenly weightless. There was a faint jolt in touchdown, and bright lights came on, making them squint. The ramp lowered, and a man entered to give them special slippers to slide over their shoes so they could walk and directed them to form a line beside the vessel they had arrived on. They were in a huge bay like a hanger, and the door to outside was now closed. The air was musty, smelled oily and metallic.

Another man came to receive them, did not introduce himself. No names were exchanged, even among the new passengers. All of them were strangers to each other.

"Welcome to Guppy 4," said the man, smiling at them. "Our galley has been preparing a nice meal for you after we make transition. We'll get you seated for that first, and we'll have you home in approximately four hours. Please relax and enjoy yourselves. Prime Minister Haig sends his greetings and thanks for a job very well done, and his congratulations to each of you. Now, please, follow me to the seating area. Transition will be in twenty minutes."

They were relaxed, now, feeling safe, thinking of their friends and family they would soon be with on Gan and Galena, and they followed their host out of the bay and into another level of the great amidship bulge of Guppy 4.

Outside, four hundred miles above the surface of Kratola, the Guppy floated among the satellite debris of a thousand technology years, appearing on radar for only short periods of time. It was noticed a couple of times, but never as a repeatable event. Time was not an issue. It floated there another twenty minutes, and then began to glow green around the forward half of the fuselage and a long, slender snout. For a few seconds the glow became bright, and then there was a flash.

And Guppy 4 was gone, taking its cargo home.

CHAPTER TWELVE

Nathan Czapia was a corporal in Kratola Special Forces when he was chosen to take part in the mission to Port Nexus. His unit still smarted from being left behind in the short war there and had jumped at the chance to show what a small, clandestine force could do in taking control of all operations at the port.

Born and raised on Kratola, Nathan was the youngest of three boys in a blue collar family. His father Ned had been fifty when Nathan was born. He was a sheet metal worker, and now head of his local union, a man proud of both his work and his sons, and devoted to his wife Ellen, who cared for all of them. He had been a young man and a patriot when another democratic government riddled by corruption had been overthrown by religious fervor and replaced by a dictatorship even more corrupt than before.

There was pride, yes, but some dismay when all his sons had joined the military, responding to a call for Kratolan supremacy among the known worlds, and especially the colonies. He cried with pride when his youngest son was elected to the most prestigious unit in the military, but there was no longer any pride for the government it served. Wages, taxes, working conditions for the common people who made the profits for the wealthy few had suffered miserably under the Council of Bishops.

Trouble was brewing, and Nathan was worried about his father when he shipped out to Port Nexus with a forged I.D. card and a phone number to call on his arrival. A strike was being talked about, and demonstrations at the Palace gates were growing every day. His father told him not to worry about it, and kissed him goodbye at the terminal.

His mother cried.

In three hours, he had made transition on a commercial ship with four other men from his unit, picked up by a van at the Port Nexus terminal, driven to a shuttle dock, and flown to Pleasure City in a shuttle crammed with tourists anticipating a good time and behaving stupidly about it.

Another van took the four of them to the Black Diamond Casino downtown where they met briefly with a fat man who directed them downstairs to a basement office where a Kratolan intelligence officer assigned each of them to a different cell and gave them a package of instructions on where to go and who to contact. They were ordered not to share information. For the moment the cells were all sleepers, but orders would come soon.

It was only four days later that he heard about the explosion in the city, but there was no talk about it among the cell members. He was allowed to keep his phone, but it was programmed through a central system to direct only local calls in or out, and he was ordered to never reveal his location. This was okay because he had a school friend who worked at Red Palace just down the street who could now reach him. They could never meet, even though Nathan was now a card-carrying maintenance worker for the Pleasure City Water Department.

He also had six cell roommates in a little apartment building near the terminal.

Life was routine for six weeks, He worked from 0800 to 1700 trenching and pipe fitting, cab to and from, shopped a small store near his room, stocked his own synth dispenser and ate alone. There was no talk with the others. Everyone retired to their own rooms after work, and all of them waited for something to happen.

And then around 1800 one cycle, when he was starved for conversation and had read the few books in his building twice, he decided to call his boyhood friend in the city and maybe talk about old times. He punched his phone, it rang twice and was answered.

"Customer service. How may I help you?"

"I'd like to speak to Damon Barcom, please."

"Speaking."

"Damon? It's Nathan Czapia, a voice from the past. How are you?"

"Nathan? Oh my God, oh my God—"

"Yeah, it's been a long time."

"Nathan, where are you?"

"Can't tell you that. Military stuff."

"Hasn't anybody reached you? They've been calling for two weeks, and can't get through. Your brothers called me, Nathan. Are you here?"

"Can't say anything, Damon."

"That's krack, Nathan. Your family is frantic, and you know nothing. Oh God, Nathan, I'm so sorry."

"What's this all about, Damon?" said Nathan softly.

"Nathan, your parents are dead, and your brothers are about to do something stupid. You've got to talk to them."

"What? What happened?"

"Your father was in a demonstration at the palace gates. There were hundreds of people. The Bishops brought in the army and killed all of them. *All* of them, Nathan, chopped them to pieces. They took your father's body and dumped it somewhere like garbage."

Damon was sobbing, now.

"Your mother couldn't take it. Her heart gave out before your brothers could get home. They're ready to kill the Bishops, said they'll go AWOL to do it. They're crazy, Nathan. They'll die, too. Maybe they'll listen to you. I can try a call if you meet me somewhere. Don't try to tell me you're not in the city. Your brothers told me where you are and what you're here for. I sure don't respect it."

"They're committing treason, Damon."

"They don't care, and neither should you. Those fugging Bishops murdered your parents. What are you gonna do about it?"

"When can we meet?" said Nathan.

"Red Palace Casino, front information desk. I'm on duty for two more hours."

"I'll be there in maybe twenty minutes," said Nathan.

He got there fifteen minutes later after flagging down an empty cab heading towards the shuttle terminal.

When he'd last seen Damon, they were kids, but the man recognized him and waved from behind an information desk.

They shook hands. "Just tried again to call the number your brothers gave me. Nobody answered. Sorry about all of this, Nathan. I didn't know there was trouble on Kratola. People around here are not fans of the government there since the trouble they caused at our port a few years ago.

"Please call again," said Nathan, and heard the quaver in his own voice. His heart was beating hard, and he clenched his hands to stifle the tremors in his fingers.

Damon called four more times unsuccessfully, and on the fourth try there was a click, and the ringtone stopped. Damon listened to a silence not due to absence. A presence was there. He held his breath, said nothing, and then there was another click. He broke the connection. "The ringing stopped," he said, "but someone was listening to see who was calling. Not your brothers, and they knew I'd call back. Man, what have you gotten yourself into?"

Nathan was thinking fast. "I have to talk to the police, the higher up the better."

"God, did you kill someone?"

"Not yet, but I'm thinking about it. I can't leave here, Damon. I'm pretty sure nobody saw me come in. I need a high-ranking police official to come here. Tell them I'm a spy from Kratola, and I want political asylum for my cooperation."

"What? The krack is getting pretty deep, Nathan."

"You know it's true. I'm in Kratola special forces, and I've come to Port Nexus on a mission you didn't want to hear about. Now call them."

Damon scowled at him, angrily punched his phone, and said, "Red Palace Casino calling for Pavel Fiala, please, It's quite urgent."

The call was answered, and transferred in seconds.

"Corinne?" said a voice.

"This is the information desk at Red Palace Casino calling, sir. My name is Damon Barcom, and I have an old school friend here from Kratola. His brothers called to tell him his father was killed in a demonstration there and his mother died, too, and now he's telling me he's a spy for Kratola and wants asylum for his cooperation. He's very upset, sir. I haven't seen him in years, and I don't know what to believe. Yes, sir, he's right here with me at the front entrance information desk. He didn't want to leave the building. Can you—okay, we'll be right here for you." Damon put down the phone and looked surprised. "I think he believed it. He's coming right over, and he's our police chief here. Why do I feel like I'm going to get in trouble over this?"

"I'm sorry, Damon. I didn't expect any of this to happen," said Nathan.

They waited only ten minutes, keeping their eyes on the front entrance, but suddenly a voice came from behind them. "I'm looking for Damon Barcom."

Three men in plain clothes had come up behind them from the rear of the casino. One was Pavel Fiala, who frequented the casino and was familiar to the staff. The other two looked like thugs.

"That's me," said Damon, "and this is my friend Nathan."

"Mister Barcom, please go with my two colleagues for some coffee and a briefing on how you will handle our meeting today. Your friend goes with me. Nathan, is it?"

"Nathan Czepic. I'm a citizen of Kratola."

"And I'm Pavel Fiala, Chief of Police and resident of Port Nexus."

Damon was led away, looking anxious.

"I don't want my friend to be in trouble," said Nathan.

"He won't be if this isn't some prank. He'll just have to keep his mouth shut," said Pavel. "I have a quiet corner in the cafe. Let's get a sandwich and hear your story."

Nathan followed Pavel to the self-service coffee and sandwich shop at the back of the casino, and sat down in a dimly lit corner of the room. Coffee seemed diluted, the synth stuffing old, but the bread was fresh.

"Okay," said Pavel, "tell me all about it: how you come to be here and why, your parents dying, your decision to call us, all of it."

Nathan talked for ten minutes straight without interruption, and Pavel just listened, not writing anything down. By the time Nathan was finished, tears filled his eyes, and he was near sobbing.

"You're serving a failed regime, son," said Pavel softly. "The cruelty of the Bishops will bring them down soon enough."

"We couldn't get back to my brothers," said Nathan loudly, and Pavel shushed him, finger to mouth. "They've gone underground, I hope. Or been arrested. Our parents have been murdered!"

Nathan ground his teeth together. "I don't care about politics. I want the Bishops dead," he said. "I haven't anything against Port Nexus or Gan. I'll cooperate with you as much as I can. I only know my own cell, and we haven't received any orders yet. I could help in the future, but I want asylum on Gan. I will not go back to Kratola, even to find my brothers."

"Okay, okay," said Pavel. He leaned close, nearly whispering. "Would you be willing to meet with our Security Chief? He has to be in on this."

"I took a big risk coming here. If I'm seen with anyone they, I'm a dead man. If we can't make a deal, then arrest me. I'm not throwing my life away for anybody. I'll go to prison first."

"How about if we give you and your friend some machine tokens and a souvenir from one of our shows and send you both out the front door and over to Black Diamond for some fun. We know where you work, we can reach you there when we're ready. You give us something useful I can promise you amnesty, but asylum has to be Gan's decision. We're not a sovereign state here. That's the best I can do, Nathan. I can't arrest you for being a member of a group of foreign nationals when there's no law against it. If I knew you were involved in our recent bombing, I'd haul you off to jail right now. And if you hear anything that affects our safety or security, I'd better hear about it, too, regardless of your own safety. That's the deal for now. Your friend is being sworn to secrecy. I'll have people watching both of you. That's the only protection I can offer. Is this going to work for you, or not?"

"I can live with it," said Nathan. "I wish my brothers were here. I'm sure they've gone AWOL, and they will go after the Bishops."

"I'll bring it up to my boss," said Nathan, "but I doubt we can help with that. We only have a few intelligence people on Kratola now. Okay, we're finished here. Wait for me. I'll get you tickets for a show, and a bucket of tokens to play with. You've been having a good time here, haven't you?"

"I guess so," said Nathan.

"You and your friend leave separately. You can't see him again. You're partying by yourself today in a casino friendly to Kratola. That's your story. Ears open, loyal to your cell, follow any orders you get, even if they're dangerous to us. You aren't any good to us dead. But remember that you're now working against a corrupt government that is responsible for murdering your parents."

"Oh, I'm not likely to forget that—ever," growled Nathan.

CHAPTER THIRTEEN

Everything was going smoothly for Guillermo Corrella. His loyalty to the Bishops was showing real benefits, and the potential for much more in the future.

The messages from Tibor Halmai were frequent and cordial, and the possibility of Guillermo's total control over two casinos and several smaller entertainment centers in Pleasure City was now more than a fantasy.

The ownership of Red Palace had become an obsession for him. He had struggled long and hard to build his business, while across the street a Gan bitch with a rich father had outbid him for a casino larger than his, and then snubbed him rudely when he'd tried to befriend her. There would be a reckoning when Kratola controlled Port Nexus, and his hopes were growing as more and more agents arrived and were sent to various cells. The day would arrive when he would walk into the Red Palace Casino and shoot the Gan bitch in the head, and by Kratolan declaration her business would be his.

The plan to increase tourism from Kratola had been based on his cooperation and generosity. Free coupons for rooms, shows and meals were paid for many times over by the gambling revenue they generated. New, quirky lounge attractions were added for customers using coupons, and specials were suddenly common in all the restaurants.

Guillermo Corrella was becoming a man of extreme wealth.

But it was not enough for him.

He did have some concerns. The bombing across the street frightened and surprised him. Forces were only gathering, and it was much too early for violence. Halmai insisted his people were not involved, that it was some other criminal group in the city. In response, Guillermo had three wide angle cameras added above the Black Diamond entrance, and two guards behind one-way mirrors just inside.

Military personnel in jump boots and blue leather were now being seen off and on in the city. The insignia they wore was a rifle beneath a bat wing shape, and below that numbers from one to three. Mobile ground troops was the talk, hard-jawed and steely-eyed, and not particularly friendly. They walked proudly, and their eyes were constantly moving. Word got around about a training facility out near the shuttle field, and people noticed some shuttle activity over the city, usually near 0200 and later, and occasionally the crackle of muffled gunfire in the distance.

It was all something new and should have been a concern for his Kratolan friends. He reported it to Halmai, who seemed unconcerned and told him not to worry about it.

He was having another good day until early one cycle, around 0900, Pavel Fiala pulled up in front of his casino in a police van with flashing lights and came in with a warrant in his hands allowing him to search all logbooks of new and old employees as well as hotel registries for the past two years.

"This is fugging harassment," he said. "Why are you leaning on me?"

"Signed by the Governor," said Pavel, and he pointed at the paper, "and it's not just you. I'm checking all the hotels, but I do have something extra for you."

Pavel handed him another piece of paper. "That's a list of ninety names we're specifically looking for. They're all Kratola residents and have come to Port Nexus in the last few months. They all got new ID. cards at the terminal, checked out and came to the city. All the people on that list were seen entering this casino after they arrived. They haven't been seen since, and they haven't checked back in at port terminal. That means they're still here in the city, and we want to find them.

"Why? They're just tourists."

"From Kratola, yes, all of them."

"We have special deals here for Kratolan citizens. Tourism is up."

"Nice of you to do that. What's the average stay of a guest? Three cycles? Four?"

"Maybe four. We've had guests for seven cycles, or even more."

"Then let's check the books. Hired workers would still be here. No problems. I have two people with me to do the work. Just show me the books. We have ID. photos to show your staff. They might have seen someone."

"This is still harassment. There's no excuse for it. This is a gambling casino. Registration data is not made public."

"I'm not the public, Mister Corrella. I'm a member of our court, and this warrant is legal. You're going to honor it, or I'm going to haul your ass off to jail. Now show us the books."

"Fugging cop. One of these days I'm going to sue you *and* the governor," he snarled.

He took them to a back office with a barred door. Inside, seven men were machine counting credit notes and bundling them for bagging. There was a screened vault in the back of the room with bags filled for transport and two desks with men working under lamp light. Guillermo pointed at them. "I'll have to let you in there. They can help you. I don't even know where things are."

He unlocked the door, let Pavel and two others inside, then closed and locked the door with a click and looked at them through the close mesh of steel wires and grinned. "Now, there's a sight," he said, then walked away from them, chuckling.

Near 2200, he got a call from Pavel. "We're going home. We'll be back tomorrow at 0800. Tell your people to let us in without an argument."

He did, and they were. One of the accountants called him at 0800. "Are we in trouble?" the man asked softly.

"Don't worry. It's a missing person case. They're looking everywhere."

What could they find? Guys come in and go out, and I don't know where. We're a clearing house, no records. Some staff will remember seeing someone, but so what? In and out, like any other customers off the street. We can't be anything other than clean. They're probing, and this is pressure. They suspect something is going on. I'll have to tell Halmai, but only on our safe line. Krack, what a bother. This could complicate things, and just when business flow is up.

His accountant called him again at 1800. "They just left, said thanks, they found some things, but they didn't seem excited about it. Sure wasted our time."

Pavel didn't call him that cycle or the next. For some reason, that made him nervous. There was nothing to find.

Was there?

* * * *

Stefan watched the three drop craft approaching and remembered his own terror at first drop during his first training days. You are a scared young trooper carrying seventy pounds of gear and wrapped in a rocket harness with nozzles than can burn your ass and legs off in a second if turned the wrong way. Your butt is sore from sitting on a hard metal bench, and when a red light turns green that bench will tilt and drop you out of the bottom of your VTOL and you will have roughly four seconds to ignite your harness and get yourself pointed in the right direction.

There had been more than a few burning bodies slamming like meteors into the ground, and spectacular but deadly impacts with trees and walls and an occasional vehicle in those days, but technology can improve a lot in twenty years. Drops were now controlled by a central computer in each VTOL and troopers were basically along for the ride.

The VTOL's came in at four hundred feet towards a cluster of quonsets laid our in a rectangular grid to simulate a city block. Troopers dropped out the bottoms like loads of bombs, harnessed engines igniting with a collective roar, and three vees of men streaked in a lovely formation towards their objective and landed there running at three programmed points. Stefan had to smile at the ease of the exercise as the young troopers rushed into the simulated urban setting with shouts and gunfire.

He gave the instructor a thumbs up and walked back to a police van waiting to take him back to the precinct station for Pavel's report, but his mind was currently elsewhere. At 1900 he had another dinner date with Corinne in her Red Palace residence. They had not seen each other for twenty cycles, but had talked on the phone every other cycle. He missed her. He missed the sound of her voice, even for one cycle. It was a new feeling for him. Maybe it was age. He had a new life in a new world, and it was changing. He wanted to tell Corinne things he'd never told anyone before. She listened and seemed to understand. He'd never felt so close to a woman, and the feeling was good, and he wanted more of it.

First, there was Pavel's report. The van dropped him off at the precinct building and went away. A VTOL buzzed overhead, and pedestrians looked up, intrigued by the unusual activity.

Pavel was in his office and gave Stefan a sour look when he came inside. "I just finished two days of playing detective, and there's not much to report. Corrella is an asshole, gave us nothing. We didn't find a single name on the list. Nothing on any hotel registry or employee record. We showed ID. pics to casino staff and got a few maybes, but nothing consistent between them, so that was no help. The casino must be a part of a conduit to other locations. I'll bet money Corrella is involved. He was pretty pissed off."

"So he'll know he's being watched," said Stefan. "We know something is up. He'll tell the Bishops. It might slow them down. We need to coordinate with Zeke and his people. Have you heard from him?"

"Nothing," said Pavel, "not since we saw him at the explosion site."

"That's not good," said Stefan. "Call him and see if his line is still active."

"Okay, what do we do in the meantime?"

"Watch Black Diamond red through violet. Let 'em know you're there. Circulate more uniforms inside the place. Check a few ID. cards randomly from Kratolans picking up freebie coupons from the information desk. Anything to rattle Corrella. What are you doing after work?"

"Nothing. Cara has two shows, and I've seen both. I'm going home for a synth feast, and bed. I understand you have plans?" Pavel smiled.

"I do. Dinner with Corinne. It has been a while since the last one."

"I detect a certain lilt in your voice when you say her name," said Pavel, teasing.

"I like her," said Stefan.

"Nice lady. Cara says she's kind of a loner. No past lovers she's aware of. Maybe an old commander like you has a chance with her. You'd never have to work again. Plus, the fact she's beautiful, that's a good incentive if you have ambitions."

"And I do," said Stefan, and he grinned.

"All right!" said Pavel. "Hey, let's try to get Zeke while you're here."

He called the number Zeke had given him and there was no answer. "It rings, so the number is still good. He'll know I called. They must be setting up a new place."

"The traffic has doubled from Kratola. We can't let the cells get too big before we do something. Zeke must be involved," said Stefan.

"We'll do it," said Pavel. "How's the ground force training going?"

"About what I'd hoped for. We have a good bunch of kids in all the units."

"People here are noticing all the VTOL activity. They're asking questions and getting a little nervous. They suspect something is going on."

"Good, then they won't be too surprised when things start to happen. That *is* coming, Pavel.

"Not too soon, I hope," said Pavel.

"And not before dinner with Corinne," said Stefan.

* * * *

Stefan reached the elevator in the Red Palace Casino at 1845 and was greeted by a friendly face, the elderly man who'd previously taken him up the elevator to Corinne's expansive suite of rooms. He stepped in ahead of Stefan and closed the door. "welcome back, Chief Fechter. Madam is looking forward to seeing you again," he said, and smiled.

The door opened, and Corinne was there in a simple, sleeveless black dress with a high collar. "Hi," she said sweetly, and held out her hands and he took them in his as he stepped out of the elevator. "It's been too long, I've missed you," she said, took his arm and led him into the living room.

"Me, too," he said, and looked closely at her, a strange feeling welling up inside him.

"Really?" she said, squeezing his arm.

"Really," he said, and fixed his eyes on hers, so deep brown they were nearly black.

They sat down close together on a sofa. "Alex, could you bring us a couple of Blue Mists?" she said to the room, and there were two clicks from a wall speaker.

"Is he always here?" asked Stefan.

"He's available for me for anything special, or when I'm too busy to cook."

"You cook?"

"Of course. I'll make a dinner for you anytime, when you're not so busy. This is only our second time together. Business visits don't count."

"They count for me. Wish I could promise it'll get better. I'm basically rebuilding the defense force for Port Nexus."

"So I hear, literally. Military craft have been buzzing over our heads for days, now."

"It'll end soon."

"Does it have anything to do with that explosion down the street?"

"No, not directly, but that seemed like a terrorist act directed at Gan at the time. We're still investigating it."

Alex arrived with their drinks and went away. They sipped. Neenee came out briefly to greet them and put her head in Stefan's lap for a petting before disappearing again.

"I know there are things you can't tell me, Stefan, but I was here when Kratola attacked the port, and I remember how frightened we all were at the time. I'm wondering if Kratola is up to mischief again, and I'm hoping you'll tell me if I'm ever in danger."

"Kratola denies any involvement in the bombing, and there's no evidence for it, but I don't think they've given up their ambitions for Gan and Galena, and the Bishops are not our favorite people. That's all I can tell you. But our defenses will be far better than they were four years ago."

"Okay," said Corinne, and leaned her head on his shoulder.

"You smell like flowers," he said softly.

"And you smell like man," she said, and looked up at him, her face so close, lips parted slightly.

He leaned down and kissed her lips softly at first, and she pressed against him. There was no urgency, no hot sense of passion, just two mouths joining two people in a wave of warmth. Corinne made a little sound in her throat, and her breath smelled like mint, and Stefan felt like he was floating away when there was the sound of Alex clearing his throat and the spell was broken.

"Sorry, Madam, sir, but dinner is served. Please excuse me."

The kiss was broken, and they both laughed at Alex standing there blushing red. "We'll be right there," said Corinne, and turned to Stefan as Alex disappeared into the dining room.

"That was so nice I'd like another one, a little one, just to tide me over until later."

They kissed gently again, Stefan enjoying a rushing euphoria he'd never experienced before.

And they were holding hands when they went into the dining room for dinner.

Alex had grilled lamb from Gan for their dinner, and it was the most expensive item on the menu downstairs. The potatoes and vegetables were hydroponic from the indoor gardens of the city, and there were berries for dessert.

They ate slowly, and the conversation became deep. Corinne told him the story about how Pavel and Carra had met, and how sweet she thought they were together. She talked about her father again. He was nearing eighty and in poor health and was rarely in touch with her. Her eyes glistened when she talked about her mother, who had suffered from a mental condition and had chosen to die when Corinne was young. Stefan didn't understand that and asked how it could be possible.

"She also had a congenital heart problem and kidney malfunction that worsened steadily after I was born. She had access to medicine that would have fixed everything, but refused it, always in a deep depression. And one night, she just stopped breathing, and father awoke beside a young wife who was dead and cold. It affected our relationship, too, and I couldn't stand the sadness. I had to leave."

"Did he ever remarry?" asked Stefan.

"No. He does have the three employees who take care of his needs. Work was his life, and he made a fortune with it. That's how he could set me up in business here. Maybe he feels that ended his obligations to me."

"You should call him," said Stefan. "if you don't, and he dies, you're going to regret not doing it."

"I've briefly thought about doing it."

Really? Thought Stefan.

"Father has access to state-of-the-art medicine if he'll just use it."

"So call him. Talk to him about it. You're lucky to have a parent left. Mine died a long time ago."

"Okay, I'll do it, but like I said, we've never been close."

"If he brushes you off, you tried, and no regrets later."

Corinne smiled. "Very astute. I can't say I'm surprised."

"Is that a complement for an old soldier?"

"It is, and you're not so old. Just right, I think. Shall we retire to the living room and get comfortable again?"

Alex made a pot of sweet tea for them before he left, and for two hours they nestled together on the couch, touching, caressing, kissing lightly, dozing a little and listening to soft music in the background. Stefan had never felt so warm, so connected to anyone before, and it seemed surreal, even magical to him. His cares, his concerns, all his plotting and planning for the defense of Port Nexus had disappeared for the moment. Only the person pressed up against him existed. *Is this love?* He wondered.

It was late when Corinne murmured, "I've waited a long time for you, Stefan. Can you spend the night here again?"

"If you'll have me," he said. "Same room?"

"No," she said, and then she kissed him firmly and long, and he was suddenly hard. "With me," she said huskily.

"What happened to slow and easy?" said Stefan.

"It went home early," said Corinne. She took him by the hand and led him to her vast bedroom with a bed big enough for four people, pulled back the covers on one side and gestured to a chair by the bed. "You can put your clothes there. I'll just be a minute."

Stefan stripped down to his shorts, put his clothes on the chair and slipped into bed. Neenee padded into the room, sat down to watch him from the doorway, and yawned. Corinne went into a connecting bath room and closed the door. The lights in the room suddenly dimmed, and the bathroom door opened. Corinne was standing there with a light behind her, and she was completely naked. Stefan took one look at her and was so hard it was becoming painful. She strolled to the bed and slipped in beside him, her hands moving over him until they found his shorts.

"We won't be needing these," she said and pulled them off when he raised his hips for her.

Their love making was gentle at first, then urgent and forceful, then gentle again. And again. At one point Neenee whimpered softly by the door, concerned, but later, when they were at last satiated and dozing, she hopped up onto the foot of the bed and slept there until morning, when they awoke and made love again before breakfast.

CHAPTER FOURTEEN

Interrogating the son of a prominent industrialist was a delicate task, and both Zuhair Pasela and Galen Dietzen were beginning to resent the assignment. They knew full well that if anything went wrong, they would be responsible for the repercussions.

Eckart Zahn was now strapped to a chair, restrained by belts across and around chest, ankles and forearms. An induction crown had been secured to his head, and the nearby power supply hummed a warning in standby mode.

Eckart was a handsome lad at twenty-five, lean and well-muscled, blond and blue-eyed, a man any father would be proud of. Alas, he was also spoiled, arrogant and most uncooperative when dealing with his superiors. His father, Nicholas, was perhaps the wealthiest man on Kratola, a builder of both ships of sea and space, and the corperate head of Zahn Transportation, a company that had designed and constructed most of Kratola's merchant fleet. He was also a vocal supporter of the Bishops' government, having suffered extreme taxation under the previous administration.

But now his only son had been arrested and faced charges of treason.

And Nicholas Zahn did not yet know about the arrest.

"My father will be furious when he finds out about this," said Eckart.

"Your father is a true patriot," said Zuhair. "Our hope is he will not have a reason to be disappointed or shamed by his only son."

"I've done nothing wrong," said Eckart. "I heard a rumor in a bar, and then repeated it to the wrong guy. You seem to have spies everywhere."

"There is a law about spreading lies that can be damaging to the state. You were arrested on legal grounds."

"And the people I heard the rumor from are free. Were they a plant? Are you after my father for something?"

"Please, please," said Zuhair, his heart skipping a beat. "We have nothing but admiration for your father. Why don't you start by telling us exactly what happened last night. What we're really interested in is how such rumors get started."

"Is that why I'm strapped to a chair?" said Eckart.

"That can change in an instant. The straps and head unit have sensors that show your subconscious reactions to our questions. We must have the truth. If we see you were an innocent bystander last night, we'll release you immediately and tell your father you were very cooperative and informative about this incident."

Eckart glanced suspiciously at the humming power unit and paused, then, "Okay, I went to Purple Lights last night to see friends. We meet there once a week, same time, same booth. A couple of drinks, and we go home. We've had the same routine for months. There were four of us. You have their names. They didn't hear anything, just me. And then I said something about what I'd heard to the waiter after my friends had left. It was my turn to pay. The waiter came back with change and a big guy who flashed a badge, put me under arrest and dragged me out of the bar. I'm glad my friends weren't there to see it."

Zuhair glanced at Galen, who watched a monitor screen next to the power unit. Galen nodded. "Good so far," he said.

"So now you must tell us what you heard, and what you know about the people who said it."

"Two men," said Eckart, "in the booth behind ours. The light was low, and they were there when we went to our booth. I didn't notice their faces. I think one man had dark hair."

"That wasn't a good answer," said Galen. "Try again."

"I'm not kidding. I couldn't see their faces. Both had on heavy jackets. They looked like work clothes. I just glanced at their booth when we sat down."

"Better," said Galen.

Eckart visibly relaxed. "It was loud in the bar, and my friends were talking, too, but I was sitting at the outside edge of the booth and could hear snatches of conversation behind us."

"And what did you hear?" said Zuhair.

"A fleet of Kratolan military ships was going through the big wormhole again to attack the Gate exit at Port Nexus. I really started listening after that. I couldn't believe what I was hearing. Mu father would want to know about it. It's part of his business."

"Only if true. That's how the spreading of false information can cause chaos. What else did you hear?"

"There was another battle at Port Nexus, and all of our ships were destroyed by strange looking ships from Gan, and now Gan was coming to make war on us."

"That was all of it?" said Zuhair.

"That was all I heard. The men finished their drinks and left. I didn't dare to turn around for a look. I couldn't believe it, and then when my friends left and I paid the waiter I asked him if he's heard anything about it. He said no and came back with the thug who arrested me. I did *not* do anything wrong, and I'll repeat all of this to my father."

Zuhair looked at Galen again. "All clear," said Galen. "Not so much as a wiggle."

"You didn't hear where the men had gotten such a rumor? Any names or places?"

"No. The noise level was up and down. I only heard a few things when their voices got louder."

"It could have been deliberate," said Galen. "We can check with the bar and see if anyone remembers those two men. They might have planted he rumors all over the city. But Mister Zahn has spoken the truth, and we thank him for that," said Galen.

"Indeed," said Zuhair. He removed the straps restraining Eckart and turned off the power supply before taking the induction crown from his head. "You have our apologies for insulting your integrity, sir. We will also apologize to your father and tell him about your patriotic responses during the interview."

"Interrogation, you mean," said Eckart, still disgruntled, but feeling more relaxed now that the straps were gone.

"We must enforce existing laws to protect the security of Kratola. This applies to citizens of any social status, and I'm sure your father understands that. Please accept our apologies for your inconvenience."

Outwardly, Zuhair was calm, but inwardly he was seething with anger. *Spoiled, arrogant brat*, he thought. *Your social status has come from your father's usefulness to the state.* "One of our drivers will take you home now. We will call your father at his workplace to explain the situation and assure him you have been most cooperative. He shouldn't have any reason to be upset with you. Would you like something to eat or drink before you leave?"

"No thanks. I just want to go home." Eckart pushed back his chair and stood up, anxious to leave.

"Galen will take you to the car. Nice to meet you, Eckart. Your father should be proud of you."

"Didn't seem like that a few minutes ago." Eckart smirked, turned abruptly and followed Galen out of the room without looking back.

Zuhair immediately called Caleb. "Totally innocent, just a loose lip in repeating something he shouldn't have. It could have been a setup. We'll check the bar and see if we can get a trace on the men Eckart heard talking. He really is an arrogant little fugg."

"Ah, well, that comes with privilege," said Caleb. "Actually, I'm relieved. I have some ideas I want to share with you and Galen within the hour. Nicholas Zahn might be an important component in a plan I see coming together as we speak. Meet me in third floor conference as soon as possible. I'll have lunch brought in for us."

"We'll join you as soon as Galen comes back from getting the boy on his way home."

"Fine," said Caleb, and the connection was broken.

In a few minutes, Galen was back. They took an elevator from basement to third floor and went to the conference room adjacent to Caleb's sprawling office. There they waited behind a long table for some twenty minutes before Caleb arrived.

"Sorry," said Caleb. "The cook was on some mysterious errand, and I had to wait. We'll have lunch in a few minutes. In the meantime, I want to go over some ideas I have about protecting ourselves against a very possible invasion from Gan if the Immortals are so inclined. Our move on Port Nexus was ill-timed, and Gan will not likely believe our intentions have changed, but we must make them think so. For starters, I think we need to argue that a full-scale invasion was not our intention in the first place, and we were misled by false information."

"How so?" asked Galen.

"It was Azar Khalil, of course," said Caleb. "His ambitions were his own, had nothing to do with us. When his attempted coup was in danger, he told us the Church on Gan was being shut down, and its parishioners under arrest. We had to act fast to protect the faithful, and our error was in not getting the real facts. We were acting to support the Church, with no other political ambitions on Gan. We send our apologies again for our errors and ask that commerce not be allowed to suffer for it."

"They won't believe it," said Galen.

"Khalil is quite dead. Who is to counter our statement?"

"They still won't believe it. There's been too much talk about us wanting to bring the colonies back into our flock, and just calling them colonies has made Gan and Galena furious. It won't work."

Maybe Gan will dismiss our apology, but it will give the government of Port Nexus pause for thought, and they are our real target now. We must control the Gate before Gan decides to send their ships to attack us. That would be the end; we have nothing that can stand up to their new technology. We cannot allow the Immortals any kind of control over the Gate, and still allow commerce to flow. That means no military attack on our part, at least for now. Port Nexus must be taken from within.

"We already have six cells operating there," said Zuhair. "Pleasure City is a playground for tourists. There's nothing else there besides technicians and bureaucrats."

"You forget the new military, and the new Security chief. He's rebuilding defenses there rapidly, and he's not a fool."

"Unless there are financial impacts, I doubt if the people there will react in our favor to a terror campaign," said Zuhair. "It could take decades to cause enough unrest. We should take control by force, and soon."

Caleb sighed. "So, do either of you have an alternative plan? I can think of one. All of us give up control on Kratola and turn things over to a public vote while we look for a planet that will take us in exile and protect us from being murdered. How's that for a plan?"

Galen and Zuhair both scowled silently.

"No? No plan? I'll give you one day to come up with an alternative. If you cannot do that we will include Tibor and meet to detail the plan I have just given you. If we don't move quickly and boldly, I'm telling you that Gan ships will be hovering over this building, and we will be running for our lives. It might be a year, or five, but it will happen. In the meantime, I will send our highest industrial leaders to Port Nexus to plead for the continued flow of commerce during what they see as a crisis. I've already selected our first envoy. He's loyal, and his son has recently been in some trouble he might see as shameful. I will ask him for a favor to make things even, and he will accept it. Our first commercial envoy will be Nicholas Zahn."

"Didn't his company make many of the original military vessels at Port Nexus?" asked Galen.

"It did indeed," said Caleb, "and he now has a good excuse to seek new business there, at a good price, of course."

Galen and Zuhair nodded in agreement. At least there was one part of the plan they could agree on.

* * * *

Nobody witnessed the arrival of the Guppy. One moment there was only the blackness of space surrounding Alpha and the next instant the ship was there, floating a few miles beyond the giant wheel.

A small, winged craft designed to fly in planetary atmospheres exited the belly of the guppy, carrying the Gan Ambassador and her assistants, and was passed through the lock. It landed at mid-level and taxied to the administrative terminal where it was met by a black van that transferred its passengers to their new homes in Administrative Center. All three passengers were Immortals.

Jilena Uzilac had been selected by committee to be Gan's Ambassador to Port Nexus. She had left a position as Logistics Minister on Gan to assume her new duties, had been an influential officer in the affairs of the Immortals for seventy years, but had the appearance of a thirty-year-old. She was tall and slender. Blond hair worn as a bun on the back of her head, had piercing blue eyes and a quick smile that radiated warmth when she used it.

Her two assistants had worked with her for many years in various capacities but appeared young enough to be interns. Janna Wasabi was an analyst, short in stature, delicate features and a hint of Asian forefathers. Elton Stewart, on the other hand, was powerfully built and had dark features that gave him a dangerous look. It was said that Elton had a variety of skills and was a fixer of difficult problems. He was quiet and was never seen to smile.

They were taken directly to the Governor's office, where Kira Madelia and Stefan Fechter awaited them.

"Welcome to Port Nexus," said Kira.

"A pleasure to be here," said Jilena.

There were introductions, and they all shook hands. Their grips were firm and dry, not crushing, all according to protocol. They sat down around a table with plates and cups and a pot of tea and little sandwiches for nibbling. During the short meeting, Janna and Elton didn't say a single word, but listened carefully and watched faces. Everyone seemed immediately relaxed, which was a good sign.

"Prime Minister Haig sends you greetings," said Jilena, "and wants you to know that six new fliers will be delivered by Guppy to you within the next few cycles. The rest will follow within a Gan month. There will be no charge; the units are being loaned to you without a time limit and can be returned whenever you wish."

"That's very generous of him," said Kira. "We also owe Gan for the appearance of their warships which saved us from a military disaster four years ago."

"It served our own interest. Port Nexus is vital to the flow of our commerce with all the distant worlds, including Kratola. It's only in recent times we've had troubles on Gan, and then the Bishops' coup on Kratola. We should have seen it all coming but didn't. We now take our intelligence efforts seriously, and that will be part of my duties as ambassador."

Kira glanced at Stefan, and he said, "You will have the complete cooperation of my office."

"And mine," said Kira.

"When you're settled, I'll introduce you to Pavel Fiala, who is police chief of Pleasure City. He has already cooperated with your people to start a local intelligence network to sniff out the cells of underground operators sympathetic to the Bishops' wishes."

"We've had experience with such activities," said Jilena. "You have enjoyed some peace, but I fear that things are changing again. We might offer you suggestions for tightening up your security, but it seems you've already done a good job with that. We're here to help, and we will trust your judgments. We consider our work with you to be a partnership."

"Sounds good," said Stefan, and Jilena smiled back warmly.
"And it is very nice to have you here," added Kira.

CHAPTER FIFTEEN

When Pavel finally got an answer to the number he'd been given, an unfamiliar voice answered. "I'd like to speak to Zeke, please." said Pavel.

"He's not here. Who is this?"

"Pavel Fiala. I was told to call this number when I needed to meet with Zeke. When should I call back?"

"Just a moment," was the answer.

Pavel waited a long moment, and then a new, deep voice was on the line.

"Chief Fiala?"

"Yes."

"Excuse the delay. Security check. Are you calling about the situation on Gan?"

"Uh, I'm not aware of a situation on Gan. I have an urgent matter to discuss with Zeke, and that's all I'll say."

"Just a moment, please."

"What the fugg?" said Pavel. It was more than a moment. Pavel's impatience blossomed. "Hello? Anyone? Can I talk to Zeke, please?"

More silence. Impatience was turning to anger when a new voice was suddenly on the line.

"Hello, sir. I see you're calling from your precinct office. There is a bar called Niko's not far from you on second level. Are you familiar with it?"

"Yes, but not in a good way. I've come close to shutting it down a couple of times."

"Go to Niko's by cab and get out at the entrance. A man there will guide you. Civilian dress, and no weapons, please, and come alone. Do not tell anyone where you're going."

"Doesn't sound very secure for me," said Pavel. "I'm not a popular person at Niko's."

"You must trust us, sir, if we're to work together."

Pavel thought for a moment. He had accompanied two raids at Niko's, and the staff knew him well as an enemy. Going there alone was a stupid thing to do. People there would happily dismember him and throw his pieces into an alley. He had to trust in the man who would meet him there to keep him safe.

As if his brain had been scanned, the man he was talking to suddenly said, "We will keep you safe, sir, be assured of that."

"Very well," said Pavel. "I'm leaving now, so it will only be a few minutes."

No answer, and the line went dead.

He changed clothes, left the office without a word to others and caught a taxi on the street outside. It was a six-block ride to Niko's, but traffic was heavy and the ride took more than a few minutes. The front entrance to Niko's had no windows, only a door outlined in pulsing, purple lights, and a dimly lit sign giving the name of the place.

Three swarthy men who looked like thugs were standing on either side of the entrance and gave him a dark look as he stepped from the taxi. Pavel's heart thumped hard twice, in anticipation of something uncomfortable about to happen to him, and he felt naked without his service weapon.

The three men stepped forward and surrounded him. One waved a wand all around his body to check for weapons and electronics. A long limousine pulled up behind him as his taxi left. The man with the wand gestured at the car, and opened a door for him, and he got inside. The windows were darkly tinted, and a panel blocked his view of the front window. His door was closed, and a lock clicked shut. He could not see outside. He heard a front door open and shut, and the car began to move.

"Pretty nice vehicle," said Pavel to nobody in particular, "and I'm not even a high roller."

He was shocked by a voice from a speaker on the panel in front of him.

"We have a benefactor. Traffic is heavy, so you'll have time for refreshments. Press the button on the box to your left."

Pavel did so and enjoyed a cold tea during the fifteen minute crawl to wherever they were taking him.

The car slowed and turned, and there was the sound of large sliding doors opening and closing. They moved again and came to a stop. The back door opened, and he was ushered out into a dimly lit space.

It was some kind of warehouse: high ceilings and side windows, large fans circulating air, a concrete floor mostly empty except for a few crates stacked along one wall. Pavel's guide gestured for him to follow, and the invisible driver remained in the car. Pavel followed the man to one end of the warehouse and up two flights of steel stairs to a brightly lit office. The man opened the door for him, and stood aside as Pavel entered the room.

Seven men sat around a large table there and looked up at him expectantly. Pavel swallowed hard, and said, "I'm Pavel Fiala, Chief of Police for Port Nexus, and I was supposed to meet with a man names Zeke."

"Please sit," said one man, and pointed at an empty chair at the end of the table.

Pavel sat and placed the dossiers Stefan had given to him on the table.

For a long moment the men just stared at him, and there were no smiles, no words of greeting. A man who looked to be the youngest in the group sat at the other end of the table, and was the first to speak.

"Thanks for meeting with us, Chief Fiala. Zeke has another assignment, and we wanted to meet you in person. There are reasons for our security precautions. We don't officially represent any government here, so our status is open to question. You have not done that, nor has your security chief, and so we have reason to trust you both. We do have a question about your superior. We know about his military background on Gan. What else can you tell us about him?"

"Stefan Fechter is a very competent man. He has built a substantial defense force here in just a few months, and with limited resources. His judgments are made carefully, and he doesn't micromanage. I've enjoyed a state of mutual trust with him."

"And his loyalties?" asked his host.

"Governor Madelia, and Port Nexus, in that order."

"How about his home world? He was born and raised on Gan."

"His memories of Gan are mixed. Ask him about it. I won't answer questions about his past, and I'm sure you know his entire history. Stefan Fechter is not a supporter of the Bishops who now rule Kratola. He considers them a danger to Gan, Galena, and also Port Nexus. He should be involved in any business we have to do here. He had provided these personal dossiers for you, and you should consider me as his emissary. We have also been contacted by a possible turncoat you need to know about. His file is also here."

Heads turned towards the young man at the table's head, and Pavel saw a few, small nods.

The man actually smiled. "You are more than an emissary, sir. Your position allows you access to people and places often closed to us. Our interest in your superior relates to his connection to your Governor and his control over security forces. We will need cooperation at all levels in the days to come, and quite soon, I'm afraid. Our intention is to invade Kratola and remove the Bishops from power, and Port Nexus will be a part of that plan."

"We are aware of this," said Pavel. "We both share your goals. I was going to discuss these dossiers with Zeke. There's the turncoat, and some candidates for undercover work. Will these be useful to you?"

"They are copies?" said his host.

"Yes."

"Then we'll keep these and discuss everything later over closed channels."

"So do I contact you as before? I have not been given any names, except Zeke."

"There is one more," said his host. "Petyr is our leader, and the day will come when you'll work with him. There will be no future meeting with our group face-to-face. We are giving you two communicators that use narrow band encrypted channels. One device is for you, the other for your superior. Instructions will be sent to you within a cycle. Any discussions of our mutual activities between the two of you must be done by communicator, even if you are face-to-face. Our security must be absolute."

A man was suddenly standing at Pavel's right shoulder. He appeared without warning, leaned over and put a small metal box on the table. As Pavel reached for it, the man picked up the stack of dossiers, stepped back and left the room.

Two devices the size of a thumbnail were in the box, and looked like normal ear communicators.

"Please always have these in place on your person. If we ever have reason to believe they are in danger of falling into unfriendly hands a signal will be sent to destroy them. You and your superior are being constantly watched, and we are not your only watchers. Both of you should now remain alert for surveillance. We don't know how fast the Bishops might move to oppose the new government on Gan, but it could be quite soon."

"I understand." said Pavel, and he closed the box.

"We are finished here," said his host, and there were a few faint smiles from his still silent companions. "We'll take you back the way you came here. We appreciate your willingness to help, sir. Both you and Chief Fechter are important to us, and we're concerned about your safety. Help will be there immediately for you if the need arises. All our people are trained soldiers."

"Thank you," said Pavel, and stood up as his host sat down again.

"Oh, one other thing," said his host. "It appears that Chief Fechter will not be finished with his social business until tomorrow. Perhaps you can arrange to join him on the shuttle back to Dome Central. If you get a private cubicle, you can familiarize yourselves with the communicators there."

So, Stefan was now being watched, and they would also know about Corinne, and that bothered him. Now Pavel finally smiled. "Thank you for your trust in meeting me. I assure you my superior and I will do our best to counter any plans the Bishops have for Gan."

The mystery man who had given him the communicators suddenly came through a seamless door behind him and led him down a hallway to an outside door and stairs leading down to the limousine he had arrived on. The back door was open, and his dangerous looking escort was nowhere to be seen. Pavel got in and closed the door, and the car moved forward, heavily tinted windows again blocking an outside view.

Apparently, his escort had remained in the car with the driver, for a familiar voice over the intercom said, "Just to emphasize a promise, Chief Fiala, I want you to remember we'll always be around to look after you."

"Thanks," said Pavel. *I hope that's enough,* he thought.

CHAPTER SIXTEEN

Stefan spent another wonderful night with Corinne the cycle after ground training exercises ended in Pleasure City. On the second cycle Corinne cooked their 1700 meal in her industrial grade kitchen, a pasta dish with real chicken loaded with garlic and pesto. She fussed over Stefan while he chopped vegetables for a salad, fearing he might add a finger to the mix at the speed he was chopping. When he assured her he'd had plenty of training with knives, she just gave him a look of mock horror.

They ate early because Stefan had to meet Pavel on the 2200 shuttle back to Alpha and discuss something important in seclusion there. They still had time for a little walk after the meal, and Corinne wanted to show him oldtown and her favorite shops. The downtown Casino area was generally unsafe for unescorted women. Corinne never ventured outside without being accompanied by a dangerous looking security man in her employ, and there were street people who also looked out for her safety because she had been kind to them.

Corinne's favorite boutiques were within two blocks either direction along the block wide band of the casino district, and they window shopped, walking all the way, arm in arm. People occasionally smiled at them admiringly, and Stefan felt wonderment at having such a beautiful woman on his arm. When they reached the edge of the district the street turned sharply and entered a steep tunnel leading down to oldtown at first level, the earliest neighborhood of Pleasure City. Corinne hailed a cab to take them there, and the trip took a couple of minutes before they were walking along a comparatively dark street lit only by overhead violet lights. There were no buildings over one level in height, and most of the modestly priced shops there were already close, windows dark.

"Oldtown is more for locals," Corinne explained, "but tourists do come down for the sightseeing and the bargains. You can find some old treasures in the little stores here, but the place I really wanted to show you is up ahead." She pointed at a brightly lit building coming up across the street. A sparkling marquee announced 'Lubov's' to them. A few people were standing around in front of it, and the street itself was not busy so they crossed it on foot and went inside.

Lubov's was a small casino, but it was crowded. The gambling tables were low-limit and full, and most of the machines were occupied. Bells were ringing often, and everyone had a drink in hand. "Wow," said Stefan. "People are winning money here."

"The machines are set high, the drinks are cheap, and the food is synth. Anyone can afford to come here and have fun," said Corinne. "I wanted you to see it because it was my first business here. It was a dance hall, and I turned it into a pretty good casino I'm still proud of."

"You own this, too?"

"Not anymore. I sold it to one of my managers privately with a loan he could afford and still make a good living. He's done well, and accelerated payments. Another ten years on the mortgage. I still feel I'm part of it. I do have other investments in several other businesses in the city, Stefan. I am a businesswoman."

"Yes, you are, and a rich one," said Stefan, putting an arm around her. "You're a great catch for someone. How fast can you run?"

"Pretty fast," she said, smiling up at him.

"Bet I'm faster," he said softly, and kissed her forehead.

There was a short line of cabs at Lubov's, and they took one back to top level, getting off at the site of the recent bombing there. There was nothing left but a composite slab, and a low, wire fence in front.

"That was horrible," said Corinne. "I heard the boom. Have you caught the terrorists?"

"Is that what people are calling it?"

"Well, it was a Gan government related office, and they do have enemies here. One of them is right across the street."

"Black Diamond Casino?"

"Guillermo Corrella, owner and operator," said Corinne. "He is the head of the Bishops' fan club around here, and a Kratola patriot. I don't know why. He got into some trouble there and fled here."

"Pavel doesn't like him, I know. He sounds like a tough guy."

"Thinks he is," said Corinne, lip curling. "He came here with lots of money and expected to buy the city. He wanted the Red Palace, but I outbid him, and he'll never forgive me for it. And when we were both on city council for a term he propositioned me twice."

For just a moment, Stefan felt he was seeing another part of Corinne he hadn't seen before. There was some iron there. "Well, at least he has good tastes," he said.

"The man is a pig," said Corinne, and it was a snarl.

They walked past the marquee of Black Diamond and down the street for another sweep of shop windows, and then up the other side to Red Palace where Stefan would catch a cab to meet Pavel at the shuttle field.

They were getting close to red Palace when they heard a disturbance behind them and turned to look.

A shabbily dressed man with a long beard was begging at a street corner and had approached a formally dressed man wearing a black cape and beret. The man was offended and pushed the beggar away from him. "Get away from me," he shouted.

"Please, sir, just one coin for an old veteran, that's all I ask."

"Go away," said the man, and shoved the beggar hard.

Corinne and Stefan looked ahead again, and continued walking. "Hard times for some," said Stefan, but Corinne was silent.

Suddenly the beggar pushed past them and stood in their way. Stefan held Corinne back with one arm and tensed, but she put a hand softly on his arm without apparent alarm.

The man smelled like an open sewer and held out his hand to Corinne. "Please, Missy, a coin for old Dirk to help the hunger."

Corinne squeezed Stefan's arm before he could say something and dug in her purse for some change.

And then the beggar said very softly, "Man following you, Missy, black hat and cape."

Corinne handed him several coins. "Thank you, Dirk," she said and smiled. The beggar grinned, took the coins and hurried away.

"Don't look around," said Corinne, when Stefan started to turn his head.

They walked in silence to the entrance of Red Palace, went inside and through the casino to the elevator. Stefan glanced quickly behind them once and saw the black caped man still there, looking at the machines.

Corinne had her own key for the elevator, and they rode it to the top floor occupied by Corinne's suite of rooms. "You do lead a mysterious life," said Stefan, and Corinne just smiled. "Do I have to carry a gun when I see you?"

Now she laughed. "I told you I have my protectors," she said, and put her arms around his waist. "But I'm wondering right now who is following who and why."

The door opened, and Corinne was home again. Neenee padded out to greet them, tail wagging, and gave Stefan's hand a lick when he petted her head.

"I'm wondering about that, too," said Stefan. "there are some things going on that I can't talk about right now, Corinne, and I don't want to worry you, but maybe we shouldn't take another walk in the streets just now. Okay?"

Corinne frowned. "Okay, but remember I'm not a helpless female. I have loyal, professional security people here, and they are armed, and so am I."

Stefan's eyes widened, and he grasped her shoulders. "You have a gun?"

"Small but lethal. It's in the nightstand by the bed, under some things. I'm surprised you didn't find it. I didn't give you enough time to rummage." Now she smiled.

"I'll be," he said. "Beautiful *and* dangerous. That makes me a little crazy, Corinne. A man like me could love a woman like you."

She put her arms around his neck and drew him close. "There's could and should and would. Which is it, soldier mine?"

"All, I think," he said softly.

"Then kiss me and catch your shuttle. Pavel will be very upset if you miss it."

The kiss was long and deep, and then he took the elevator back down to the casino floor.

The casino was still very busy. Stefan looked around, but did not see the man with black cap and cape as he walked outside to catch an auto-cab. He did notice another man who watched him go from the elevator to the cab, a man who then made a call on his earphone.

And neither of them noticed the dark-skinned man seated in a lounge who was observing both of them and then followed Stefan's other watcher out of the casino.

* * * *

Stefan was seated on board the shuttle when Pavel finally arrived and sat down heavily opposite him. "Problems with the cab, and I had to catch another one," he explained.

"You look tired," said Stefan.

"It was an intense day and red light for me. I suppose you slept wonderfully."

"I did," said Stefan, and smiled. "So, how did it go with your meeting?"

Pavel told him everything that had happened. They were in a private cubicle, and Stefan's electronic detector was blinking green.

"Corinne and I found out we were being watched on our way to her place. We only saw the one man. Corinne has her own squad of people watching us, too."

"There are others, I'm told," said Pavel.

"I don't like it," said Stefan. "I don't want to get Corinne involved in any of this."

"You could stop seeing her for now," said Pavel.

"I'm not going to do that. I don't think you realize how powerful that woman is, and the people she has behind her. She would never forgive me for trying to protect her like some poor damsel in distress."

Pavel laughed, then, "That group I talked to today was spooky. One guy talked; the rest stared.

"They're running Gan, now," said Stefan.

"They admitted to me they're going to invade Kratola and bring down the Bishops," said Pavel. "I bet the Bishops know it. We're worried about cells, but the Bishops could come through here with their entire fleet, and soon."

"So, we have to be ready to turn off vacuum state power and destabilize the Gate exit for Kratola. That alone could crush their ships."

"But it would also risk stabilizing the Gate topology again," said Pavel. "It could hang up a lot of commerce between worlds. We need to keep the Immortals informed about what we're planning. They have the only technology that can really help us. Here, I was given these for communications."

Pavel showed Stefan the communication devices he's been given. He lifted them from the box and saw a small card at the bottom. On it were a few key instructions.

There were three channels. Two could be used for communication between Stefan and Pavel, each with a unique code. The third was only for incoming calls from external sources with varying codes. In the privacy of their cubicle they played with the devices, trying all channels, mumbling successfully to each other on two of them, noting only a high-pitched squeal on the third. An additional phenomenon intrigued them. Soft sound coming from outside the cubicle disappeared when the devices were turned on. A field emanating from one or both active devices was forming a sound barrier around them to ensure privacy during calls.

Another piece of technology from the Immortals.

Shortly before their arrival at Alpha, Stefan received his first outside call from the Immortals. A muffled voice thanked him for the dossiers he'd provided and gave him instructions as to where and when the men involved should be sent.

They went their separate ways at Alpha. Pavel went to his office and issued orders to move a third of his force there to Pleasure City for intelligence duties. Stefan met with two wing commanders and dispersed a small group of novas and twelve fast gunships to strategic positions around Port Nexus.

The great force-generating moons at the exit mouths of the wormhole were particularly strategic, but lightly manned and unarmed. Four novas were sent to each moon, twelve in orbit about Pleasure City, and also around Alpha. Six ships remained in government docks at the entry port, the rest of the fleet, twelve crimson fighters and twenty-four gunships, all recently received from Gan, were placed at several static positions between Alpha and the Gate.

Stefan Fechter's preparations for war were only a beginning and would proceed rapidly. Stefan was an intelligent, experienced military leader with only one shortcoming.

He had never experienced a true combat situation with a foreign adversary.

CHAPTER SEVENTEEN

Over a twenty-cycle period, Corinne Ariska called her father four different times and did not receive a reply. This bothered her greatly. Her father was so old and fragile, now, and had important decisions to make soon. Surely, she would have been notified if something dramatic had happened to him. Justin Ariska was the oldest billionaire on Gan, and still active in business affairs. His industrial and mining holdings were highest in the former colony worlds, and his opinions highly valued in the community.

She expected delays with each call. To communicate with Gan, she used an encrypted line to friends stationed some four hundred miles from Port Nexus. The recorded message was then taken to Gan by Guppy and re-transmitted to her father's residence. Since she'd arrived at Port Nexus there had been only two conversations early on with her father while they were doing business together. Both calls had had turnaround times of four cycles. And now she was getting nothing.

Alone, she was getting frantic. When she talked to Stefan at 2200 each cycle, she calmed some. He suggested that she might contact Gan ambassador Uzelac to see if she could get news about a man she'd undoubtedly heard of. He gave her a number to call at Station Alpha.

She had just talked to Stefan and was already anticipating another night with him next cycle when her in-house phone rang, and she received a great shock that momentarily stunned her.

"Hello?"

"It's Max, Ma'am. I have a guy here who wants to come up and see you. He says he's your father, and his ID. checks out."

"What? My father's on Gan."

"And now I'm here. Who do I have to bribe to get this elevator door to open?" said a voice in the background. "Let me talk to her."

Then, "Corinne, it's Dad. I must talk to you, and it's urgent." The voice was gruff, and so very familiar. Corinne's heart was now beating rapidly."

"Ma'am?" said Max.

"Bring him up, Max. Give him any help he needs," said Corinne.

"I don't need anybody's help," said faintly in the background. "And my hearing is fine, thank you."

"Coming right up," said Max.

Corinne waited nervously at the elevator door and then received a second shock when the door opened and her father was standing there.

He looked to be around fifty. "Hi, kiddy," he said, and smiled. "Surprised?"

"Yes, and I haven't heard from you in ages! You don't even answer my calls, and now you go through transition without even telling me! Don't you think I care?"

Justin Ariska stepped out of the elevator, embraced his daughter and felt her body stiffen. "I know you do, hon, and it's been too many years since I last told you I love you. Getting old and crabby isn't fun. It'll be better, now. I feel great, had a choice of thirty, forty or fifty, but fifty has the better memories. What do you think?"

He hugged her, stepped back and gave her a wink.

"I was a little girl when you looked like this, Dad. I worshiped you then. Why don't you return my calls?"

Now there were tears in her eyes.

Justin Ariska smiled faintly at his only child. "I was afraid you might tell me never to see you again. I figured it'd be harder to do if we met face to face. I've missed you, Corinne, not just your mother. The two of you were my whole life. I'm alone in a big house full of servants ever since you moved here. What little business I had left and my work with the freedom party were the only things making me want to live enough to go back for a transition. And now I just had to see you again. Can I stay here a while?"

"Oh, Dad," said Corinne tearfully, and put her arms tightly around his neck. "Of course you can stay, as long as you like."

She led him to a couch, and they sat down. Neenee came out of the hallway, took one look at Justin and quickly retreated to where she had come from.

"You have a dog," said Justin.

"Her name is Neenee. She's very shy with strangers. Give her some time."

"An expensive dog," said Justin.

"I do have money, Father. You helped me get it. I haven't forgotten that."

"I'll take some credit for your business smarts, hon. You built your empire by yourself, just like I did."

"I've done well here, and I'll do better as tourism continues to grow."

"You'd do much better on Gan, now that we have a true democracy there. The freedom party win was a landslide, and the economy is surging again. Opportunities are everywhere. Is there really that much going on here?"

"Not on Gan's scale," said Corinne, "but I'm happy here, and I have friends, and recently a man has come into my life."

"Oh, ho," said Justin. "Are we talking casual or serious here?"

"I think I'm in love," said Corinne.

Her father seemed stunned. "Well—this is unexpected. I'd like to meet him."

"I don't think that's a good idea. I've talked about you. Stefan knows how old you are, and I was worried about your health. If he saw you now, he'd be confused and ask questions I don't want to answer."

"Stefan?"

"Stefan Fechter. He's the security chief for Port Nexus."

Justin's brow furrowed in thought. "Fechter. I've heard that name somewhere."

"He was a battalion commander on Gan for many years but got in trouble with the emperor during the first uprising and was later exonerated. He doesn't have good memories of Gan," said Corinne.

Justin nodded. "That one. I remember him. Our people hid from him for several years, Corinne, when you were a little girl. He was our enemy. Does he know about you?"

"I told him you were a friend of Immortals and entertained them in our home, but he doesn't understand who they are. He thinks much of it is mythology, but he is a supporter of freedom. He supports the new government on Gan and despises the Bishops."

Justin reached over and took her hand in his. "Corinne, I asked if he knows about you, and you know what I mean."

Corinne sighed. "No, he does not, and I don't want him to know. It would just confuse him, and destroy our relationship. Why does he have to know now, Father. Why not later?"

"It's the honest thing to do, if you love him."

"No, I won't do it, not now."

"Are you keeping your scans current?"

"Of course I am. I haven't abandoned our ways, but the man I love is not from the line of Zylek, and I don't want to lose him because of it. We could have a good life together, and he could make his own choices in the future. That has worked for many people, Father," she said, and immediately regretted it.

"It didn't work for your mother," Justin said sadly.

Corinne hugged his arm. "I'm sorry. I forgot again. I was so little."

"No bother," said Justin, sniffing. "I'd still like to meet your man, even if it's brief. When do you see him again?"

"At 2200 next cycle. We'll have breakfast here the following cycle."

"Oh, it's like that already. My, my. Well, I can't stay here with you, then."

"Just for one cycle," said Corinne. "I have seventy hotel rooms here. We could have a restaurant dinner with Stefan. You will be a business friend of my father's from Gan. Please be careful of what you say, Dad. I really love this man."

"Agreed," said Justin, and he patted her hand. "well, this should be interesting, though it's not why I came here for on that smelly Guppy. I wanted to see you again, and tell you some things that worry me about you being here and not back on Gan, if you'll listen."

"This is my home, Father," she said.

"I know. You've already made that clear. But things are looking good on Gan. Our people are finally in charge of things, and the spirit of Anton Zylek is in our Prime Minister. I am very optimistic about the future except for one thing. War with Kratola is being discussed in our legislature, and I fear it has already been decided on at higher levels.

"The Bishops still seek to govern our worlds and prepare for a war that could happen soon. They are foolish men. They have no chance against our technology. Our regular and Guppy forces could wipe them out in an afternoon. They hope to win by a surprise attack not on Gan, but on Port Nexus, is the word I hear. Corinne, you could be in real danger staying here. I wish you would come back to Gan and stay with me until this war issue is settled. Call it a visit. It wouldn't be for long, and you could even return off and on when we feel it's still safe."

"That's not a good way to run a business, Father, even with a good manager. I'm part of the image of Red Palace. My presence here is important. And now there's Stefan to think of. I won't leave over fear of a war. Our defenses are strong, and the guppies can be here with short notice. I'm not afraid here."

Justin sighed. "well, I had to bring it up. I'd feel much better if you were back on Gan. I would not feel good if we had to rescue you in a war. Please think about it."

"I'll do that much," said Corinne, and hugged him. "And I'm suddenly very happy you're here. Now, let's get you a room for next cycle, and you can stay with me otherwise, and then you can meet Stefan and as a business acquaintance tell him what a wonderful man my father is."

"Very happy to do that," said Justin, "but it'll take some imagination, even when it's true ."

He hugged her warmly as he said it.

* * * *

Three bat-winged assault ships and a Nova converged on Moon K at the edge of the nebulous gate leading eventually to the Kratolan system, another Nova already hovering by Moon G to cover the other end of the nexus connecting the two gates. The scenario was a hostile takeover of Moon K, the technicians there having successfully frozen the controls and sequestered themselves in a safe room. One of the two stabilizers, Moon K was a sphere a mile in diameter composed of thinly spaced superconducting sheets drawing forth the energy of the false vacuum and transmitting it to the half mile in diameter ring at the gate entrance to stabilize the opening. Operation was continuous, with a crew of seven men who lived there in four cycle shifts and commuted from Pleasure City.

The exercise strategy was not subtle. There was a single air-locked entrance for the moon, the safe room independently pressurized. The drill had begun with an alarm signifying attack. The crew had frozen controls and gone through the motion of disabling the airlock to space from inside before locking themselves away and suiting up. Once disabled, the airlock would have had to be blown open to gain entrance or exit, and this was not included in the exercise.

The Nova came to a halt a hundred yards from the Moon, all weapons trained on it. The assault ships crowded in closer, bays opened and spewed forth twelve troopers in rocket harnesses that first circled the moon and then came down on it like fine dust, converging at the airlock entrance. They pantomimed the placement of C-12 mines, flew away from the explosion to be expected there, then returned to what would have been an open wound in the moon, now an intact entrance. The airlock had already been depressurized, as had the control room.

The airlock door opened at their touch, and the troopers charged inside, electronic weapons blazing weak laser beams. The crew was released from their safe room and one simulated casualty taken back to a batwing. The elapsed time recorded was four minutes and thirty-two seconds, some forty three seconds faster than the previous exercise. Good enough, perhaps, but one last exercise had already been scheduled.

Stefan had watched the entire exercise on screen in a small command center neighboring the shuttle field outside the city. Four prefab huts were there, including barracks for a full platoon, and two batwings were parked nearby. Janus Stark had watched with him and seemed satisfied with what he saw.

"It can always be better, but that one looked good," said Janus.

Stefan clapped him on the shoulder. Twenty years before, Janus had been a platoon leader under Stefan. Now he was an instructor at the Military Academy on Gan and had volunteered his services to help out an old colleague.

"If it was good, it's because you're a fine teacher, Janus. I don't know how I can ever repay you for what you've done with these young people."

"If it comes to it, just kick some Bishop ass and I'll be happy," said Janus, grinning. "I think you're ready for it."

"I think you're right, thanks to Gan, and people like you. I think we've covered everything important, but you know war, good plans can mean nothing."

"It's coming, Stefan," said Janus.

"I know. But I won't be unhappy if it doesn't happen."

"Yeah, there's that, too," said Janus, feeling the same way.

It was sobering to think about war, but now there was something nice to dwell on. At violet light this cycle, Stefan would be with Corinne again. Now he was certain he was in love with her. How could an old soldier like him fall so fast? He'd had little experience with women his entire life, not a single romantic partner, only the occasional expensive trysts with professionals trained in the arts of entertainment.

What he had now was more than physical. He thought about Corinne all the time, would see her face in twilight sleep, and looked forward to their conversations by phone each cycle. The times they were together were like a dream to him, surely something that couldn't last, not for him, but a dream he wanted so badly that when they were together there was a wonderful ache inside him.

At 1700 he took an auto-cab to the Red Palace Casino, and Corinne was waiting for him in the coffee shop for what she said would be a junk food experience. She was wearing a form fitting business suit in flaming red that emphasized the darkness of her eyes and hair and was chatting with four excited customers when he arrived. Corinne smiled brightly when she saw him, heads turned and there were smiles when they saw him there in his dress blues he had worn to please her.

"Hi," she said simply, and kissed his cheek. The customers stared nervously.

"My friend, Stefan Fechter, chief of security," said Corinne, and then, "Please excuse us."

The customers nodded, smiled broadly and went away, looking pleased with themselves.

They sat down at a corner table, and the coffee shop was crowded. "Now we feast," said Corinne. "Tonight is my naughty night for eating, and I'll order for both of us."

She ordered two chicken pies with rich gravy, potato slices fried in oil, and pastries filled with honey, and added coffee which was the best in the city.

Except for the pastries, all of it was ordinary fare for a military man, except the chicken here was the real thing and not synth.

They waited a short time for their food and talked about their cycle, fingers touching across the table.

The food arrived, and they had taken a few bites when a man approached their table and smiled brightly at them. He wore a white body suit, body slim, late forties or early fifties, looking tanned and fit. "Corinne. Corinne Ariska. I'm Justin Renick, a good friend of your father, and he asked me to drop by and say hello while I was here on business. I'm a broker for him. Anything in steel I can get. I must say I didn't expect to find you in a coffee shop."

Corinne extended a hand, and the man shook it. "How is my father?" she asked. "I haven't talked to him in quite a while."

"The man is too busy for his age. He says hello and wants me to tell you he'll be contacting you soon." He turned to Stefan, extended his hand. "I don't mean to be rude, sir. I'm Justin, and you are...?"

"Stefan Fechter." He shook the man's hand.

"I know the name. You're the new security chief of the port."

"That's correct. Your business takes you a long distance from Gan. I thought anything in steel was fabricated elsewhere."

"Steel pipe for your waterworks is ready made, but I got you a good price," Justin said quickly, and Corinne gave him an astonished look Stefan found strange.

"Did you come here from Gan, Mister Fechter?"

"Yes. I was in Gan military during the turbulent times. I'm glad to see they have a democratic system in place now. We're working with them."

"I'm sure you've heard there is some danger of a war," said Justin.

"We are prepared for it, sir, and we'll defend the interests of both Gan and Galena. Please tell that to Corinne's father so he will not be worried for her safety."

"I'll do that, Mister Fechter, and I thank you for it," said Justin. "Corinne, I just wanted to say hello for your father, and I wish you well. Good luck with your business. I know your father is very proud of you. Good by, sir. Nice meeting you, too."

Justin turned and left them sitting there with now cold food. Corinne looked a bit stunned.

"Well, at least you got a hello from Dad," said Stefan, but I think his friend is a bit eccentric."

"He certainly is," said Corinne, and took a bite of her now cold chicken pie.

The honey pastry, at least, had not lost its flavor.

Their hours together were as wonderful as ever, and next cycle was breakfast, and then Stefan was back on the shuttle to Station Alpha, thinking, *I hope Corinne's father does contact her soon. Maybe I'll have a chance to meet him someday, before he passes on.*

CHAPTER EIGHTEEN

Zeke's current mission was to find and dispose of the people responsible for the bombing of the Gan tourism office, an explosion that had left bits of pieces of two colleagues in the street.

It was a solo mission and had restrictions. For the present there could be no bombings, no public shootings, no obvious acts of assassination that could be noticed by the public. Kratola had made that error in the bombing, either out of fear or premature aggression, and now everyone was aware of the possible presence of terrorists in the community. Invisibility was the order of the day in the building phase, and with a visible approach of war all rules would change. Gan's intelligence service was promised cooperation by the local authorities as long as things seemed peaceful, and it was a kind of contract between them.

Stefan and Pavel had made little progress in the investigation of the bombing. There were no witnesses to the time just before the explosion. An auto-cab had been seen driving away right after it, heading towards the shuttle field. The bomb itself had been a C-8 package sandwiched between metal slabs and a timer likely set for a few seconds at most.

And Zeke's colleagues, Eli and Daniel, were dead, only pieces left to ship back to their families.

Zeke intended to avenge their deaths in an appropriate way.

The explosion had been at 0845. Zeke tracked down the records of all auto-cabs before and after that time and found two that might have been the cab observed near the scene. Both had dropped their passengers in oldtown near the casino, one level down. He then checked oldtown records for properties newly rented near the cycle of the bombing and found three listings. One was far from the stopping points of the suspect auto-cabs and was a rental to a married couple. The other two rentals, both two-bedroom units, had been taken by single men.

Zeke gave a low priority to the married couple's place, even though women were known to work in the intelligence service, and he first focused on the other two. They were a block apart, in sight of a bench across the street by an electrical parts shop, and in a less than desirable neighborhood. From that bench, both houses seemed drab and in need of repair, and were close enough for movement to be seen through the windows.

Zeke chose that spot for his surveillance. He dressed himself in badly worn clothes with a heavy coat and a wool cap and occupied the bench for one to two hours early, middle and late cycle, each time employed in eating a simple meal from a brown, paper bag and grinning stupidly at the few passer-byes. Twice he was accosted by dangerous looking tramps demanding money or food, but both times he simply raised his jacket to show them the heavy gun nestled there in his waistband, and the tramps went away, not to be seen again.

There was activity in both houses, but by his third cycle of watching Zeke was certain that only one of them had more than one occupant. In the house nearest to him, a single, youngish man appeared early each cycle, locked his door and drove away on an electric bicycle, not returning until the beginning of red light, and never in the middle of a cycle. While he was gone, there was no sign of life in the house, no mail delivery, no visitors, no sign of movement at the windows.

This was not so with the second house he was watching.

There were three, perhaps four men in the house. He saw at least three different faces at the windows. There was mail delivery every other cycle or so, but it was in mid-cycle, and someone would retrieve something from the mailbox before that in early cycle each and every cycle. Correspondence was arriving before regular mail delivery, probably during violet or purple light, each cycle, and was retrieved by at least two different men.

Next cycle Zeke returned at 0100 in an auto-cab and waited patiently in a dark doorway not far from his bench. At 0230 he was rewarded when a van with the logo of Black Diamond Casino pulled up to the house. A man jumped out, put a small envelope in the mail box and hurried back to the van. Zeke pressed tightly into the doorway as the van turned, light beans sweeping past him, and drove away. He waited until 0300 and then walked slowly and silently to the porch of the house, retrieved the envelope from the mailbox, and then walked all the way back to the tunnel leading to level two where he was able to hail a cab to return him to his quarters.

Once there he read the printed message inside the envelope. It said "Three men coming 1400 this cycle. Code word is 'execute.' Await further."

Perhaps four men, now going to seven, a typical cell size. It was enough. Were they the murderers of his colleagues? Probably, but not for certain. It was tit for tat, blood for blood, and the beginning of something much larger in scope.

Zeke dressed formally with black coat and tie suitable for any high limit card room in the city. His Hawk 9 with a snubbed silencer fit nicely, loaded and locked, in a shoulder holster. He took an auto-cab to the target house in oldtown, arriving at 1300, and put the cab in standby while he went to the house. He knocked firmly on the door three times and waited, the message envelope in his left hand.

A face appeared in the door's small window for a few seconds, and then the door opened. A young, square-jawed man stood there, one hand behind his back. "Yeah? What d'ya want?"

"New message, short notice, code word 'execute'," said Zeke, he and held up the envelope for the man to see it.

The man looked, began to reach for the envelope.

Zeke drew his gun and shot the man in the forehead at a range of two inches. He crumpled, the gun he'd held behind him clattering to the floor.

Zeke stepped inside and closed the door, stepped over the body as another man came in from another room and said, "Who was that?"

Zeke shot him in the forehead with a muffled pop, and the man slumped down with a thump.

Voices from the adjacent room. "What's going on?"

Zeke stepped inside the room, gun leveled. Two young men were sitting at a table, playing cards. They stared at him in horror and started to move.

"Blood for blood," said Zeke, and shot both of them in the head. "that was for Eli and Daniel," he said as they crumpled to the floor. He threw the envelope on top of one body and left the house without shutting the front door and walked back to his waiting cab.

He was thinking about the surprise waiting for the three agents who would arrive at the house in less than an hour.

The thought amused him.

* * * *

Jule and Jon Czapia had now been AWOL for two Kratolan months. At first they'd been helped by friends who'd hidden them in barns and cellars, but then the Bishops' special forces arrived in their village and they were suddenly all in danger. The force that threatened them was the same force their brother was assigned to. At one time there had been pride in having a son in such an elite unit. Father had bragged about it, but now he was dead, murdered along with many neighbors at the hands of that elite unit and by orders from four cruel men who could now only rule by fear.

It had been coming for a long time. Their father has seen it happening early on, for he was not one of the faithful and only studied the political actions of the Bishops. "They only care about ruling the colony worlds again. It's their only agenda," he'd said. "They do not care about us as workers, and they only cater to the rich who support their course. It's the rich who will benefit from control over Gan and Galena. The resources there far exceed ours."

Still, there had been such joy when Nathan had come home in a black uniform with the crossed lightning bolts and peered proudly at them beneath the shiny bill of his peaked cap. Mother had cried, and even father's eyes had filled with tears.

Now both dead, and Nathan on assignment in Port Nexus, and they had tried to reach him and failed. They'd received no word from Port Nexus before they'd fled from their duties as soldiers, and now lived only to avenge the deaths of their parents. They'd watched from a basement window when the black uniforms arrived, watched their home burned to the ground, neighbors lined up in the street for questioning, two of them clubbed viciously with rifle butts and left to die slowly on the ground.

The entire village was searched, not one house missed. Their neighbor saw it coming, hid them in a storage room in the basement and piled crates in front of the door to conceal it. They huddled in the tiny space when the black hats searched the basement, cursing, smashing small things, all to intimidate the occupants, to terrify them.

Jule and Jon sat in the darkness with their service rifles pointed at the door, ready to kill until the black hats finally went away.

It was dark when the neighbor came to get them. "They'll be back," he said. "They're offering rewards to anyone who will talk, and death to anyone who helps you. Someone will give in soon. You must leave now while they're searching the other side of the village. I can show you the way."

He took them to a drainage conduit that ran to a ditch spanning a large field, now plowed, and hurried home. The boys followed the ditch and others like it meandering between farm sections until there were silos in the distance and a few buildings there, a small holding station for grain, now closed for the season. They broke into one building, found coveralls and other clothing for workers there, and some blankets in which they rolled their rifles and extra magazines and strung them across their backs like bedrolls. Jon's fifty caliber long range weapon, with scope, was the hardest to disguise.

They kept their boots and burned their fatigues to ashes in a barrel. When they were finished, they looked like farm laborers who traveled from farm to farm in season to find enough work for their food. They were careful to dirty their appearances and wear only long shirts under their jackets. Farm laborers were not usually not younger men, and they didn't carry service pistols tucked in the waist band of their pants.

They spent that night and the following day dozing in the building. They traveled at night and minimized contact with anyone. The Bishops' spies were everywhere. They headed east, following rail tracks from village to village nestled in rolling, forested hills. They kept to the trees, which slowed them, but reached a new village every day or so. They gleaned fields and fruit trees for food. They had money, and bought staples from farm family roadside stands whenever they found them. To their relief, they experienced no special notice. Farm people even shared news and gossip with them. In this way they heard that after a three-week search for some missing soldiers, black hat squads had been called back to reinforce troops guarding the temple of First Light and the palace of the Bishops. And there was a rumor going around about a possible war with Gan.

"Wish they could blow the palace up, and leave the rest of us alone," said one man while he bagged some tubers for them. "It can't get any worse than it is now. Did you hear about the slaughter of those people at the palace gate? Not one person even had a gun. It's criminal, and we can't do anything about it."

Oh yes we can, thought Jule, and paid the man for the tubers.

That seemed to be the general feeling of the country folk, they discovered. They had a terrible, criminal government that ruled with an iron hand, and was supported by wealthy barons and merchants, and the common people who made the riches for the rich were only cattle who produced the milk and meat and everything else manufactured on Kratola.

Now it was two months since their runaway, and they were located eighty miles southeast of the Temple of First Light. They were not safe, but no longer actively pursued. They had escaped for a purpose, the killing of those responsible for the deaths of their parents. For two trained soldiers, they reasoned, it was a possibility, and they had a tentative plan. It was not a suicidal plot. In killing the Bishops, even one of them, the loss of their own lives would accomplish nothing, but it did require that they get as close as possible to the palace gate.

They turned north in their travel and stayed away from roads across country that had few villages on a route up valleys and rolling hills covered with scrub and stunted trees.

They walked for five days and part of each night and saw not a single soul. Not even a small shuttle passed over their heads, allowing them steady progress during the day. But as they got closer to Kratola City, and the Bishops' palace there, the countryside changed, the hills more rolling, the trees larger and thicker, the valleys lush and green. Mountains loomed ahead, and they knew they were getting close to their goal. The hills descended to a short plateau ending in a cliff and box canyon, and the iron fence around tall towers and dome of the combined palace and Temple of first Light gleamed in sunlight.

They found a little hollow at the edge of the tree-line about a hundred feet higher than the plateau and settled in. There was a small village on the other side of the hill, and a route through the trees for possible escape if they weren't detected. They unpacked rifles and magazines. Both brothers had achieved fourth level as marksmen, but it was Jon who was assigned the big rifle, and Jule was proud of him for it. Jule loaded his standard service weapon and set it aside. Jon loaded his with re-tipped smart cartridges and sighted on a palace tower. "I can see the balcony, but man it is going to be a long shot."

The scope provided the answer, based on the spread of a UV beam.

"Seventeen-hundred twenty yards, Jule."

"Wow. But your rifle will do two thousand, at least."

"With a good bench rest, maybe," said Jon.

They made one out of blankets and one jacket and piled up brush around the position. Jon sighted in, slid a big cartridge into the chamber and pushed the bolt closed. "A little shaky," said Jon. "I could use a large, flat rock."

Jule rushed to find one for him.

CHAPTER NINETEEN

Nicholas Zahn did not react well to the arrest and eventual release of his son. In a fit of fury he dared to threaten cessation of military ship production for Kratola. This was met with a flurry of sincere apologies from the Bishops along with a subtle reminder that Zahn's business empire had been funded by them and existed at their pleasure.

The foolish gambit at Port Nexus on a pretense of saving the Church on Gan had been sadly transparent. Everyone understood it was just another poorly planned effort to renew control over their former colony worlds. And in the end, Gan had severed several relations with Kratola, and half of Zahn's fabrication market had disappeared overnight.

There had been compensation for his losses. Ships had been destroyed in the port incident, and had to be replaced. The new tension with Gan threatened future war, and the Kratolan space fleet was expanding by fifty per cent. The job had taken nearly five years and was now complete. Nicholas would soon be in search of new markets.

The Bishops seemed to understand this, perhaps regretted what they had done to anger him. And so he was mollified to some degree when Bishop Aluna himself invited him to a private luncheon at the palace to discuss a special mission for him as a sort of ambassador for Kratola.

It was just the two of them at the luncheon, served with a fine wine. Aluna talked about what had happened at Port Nexus years before, and the misunderstanding that had caused it. "Nobody would believe us. Azar Khalil had called for help. We thought the church and all its members were in mortal danger. We didn't know the falseness of it and recognize Azar as a usurper until after the damage was done. Our pleadings for understanding and forgiveness have been ignored. We need a new voice to show the effect this has had on common people and also our business class, people who are innocent of foolish mistakes their government regrets having made. We want forgiveness, Nicholas. We want normal relations with Gan, including trade agreements and exchange of ambassadors. The talk of war must end."

"But Gan has closed its door to anyone from Kratola. How do I go there?" asked Nicholas.

"You don't. We'll send you to Port Nexus to meet with their governor. There is a Gan laison in residence there. You will meet with both of them, ostensibly to discuss renewal of trade relations for the benefit of all our worlds. The request will come from you, representing all business interests on Kratola, but I hope you will also discuss the normalization of all relations with them."

Nicholas thought, a hand stroking his chin.

"Please, Nicholas, we need this. Our people need it. There will be no winner in another war."

"All right. I'll write a request for a meeting and send it to the new Governor at Port Nexus."

"We have written the letter," said Caleb Aluna. "You are certainly free to edit it, and we'll send it along for you. You are doing a good thing, Nicholas. Our feeling is you're the best person to do this for Kratola." Caleb pulled an envelope from beneath his robe. "Here is the letter. Make the changes you wish right now, and give it back to me. It will go to Nexus tomorrow on our next commercial ship."

Nicholas read the letter, short and to the point, a request to formulate business relations and diplomatic discussions with Gan, all of it fully supported by the council of Bishops on Kratola for guaranteed peace in the future. He made a few grammatical changes and handed it back to Caleb. A secretary took it and returned in a few minutes with a new copy. In the meantime, the two men had enjoyed another glass of wine.

Nicholas signed the letter, shook hands with Caleb, and went home to wait. The meeting might or might not happen, and business absorbed his every waking hour.

It was a week before he received a reply to his letter.

* * * *

The shuttle was launched by mag-ramp at noon on a sunny day, and for three seconds Nicholas was slammed back into his seat with terrible force. The acceleration dropped some when the engines ignited. But the next few minutes were still uncomfortable until they were in an orbit four hundred miles above Kratola, white clouds floating over a brown surface.

Nicholas had never been off-planet, and took deep breaths to calm his apprehension, but the outside view held his interest.

An hour later he was docked at Kratola Platform A and transferring to a fusion powered B class cruiser that would take him to the entrance of the great worm hole leading to Port Nexus and beyond. This was the longest part of the trip, a journey to a tiny station at the mouth of something black against a background of stars with twinkling striations of light at its edges. Commonly called 'The Cave', the entrance to the wormhole had been stabilized over time by its interaction with a trio of K-type stars a billion miles distant.

After an acceleration of one gee lasting minutes, Nicholas settled in for a one-hour coast to the station and another hour of docking time. There he boarded a smaller, fusion powered commercial cruiser with fifty other passengers and a cargo of synthetic foods for the trip through the wormhole.

There was little to notice. Time stood still, a brief lapse of consciousness and they were through, a green glow outside his window port.

A delegation of three men met him at the lock, two troopers with rifles and a solid looking man in dress blues who stepped forward to greet him.

"Welcome to Port Nexus, Mister Zahn," said the man. "I am Stefan Fechter, Chief of Security here. We've come to check you through and get you to your meeting."

He followed them to the check-in kiosk where he filled out a simple form, was photographed, and received a photo-ID card to keep on his person at all times. They took an electric car to another gate to board a shuttle to Station Alpha. By this time Nicholas was feeling quite fatigued and yawned.

"Another hour or so and we'll be there, sir," said Fechter. "The meeting is early next cycle. You'll have a room for two cycles, and meals will be brought to you."

"That's very kind of you," said Nicholas, impressed.

He dozed during the flight and awoke during docking at Station Alpha. His escorts had not talked to him, or to each other during the trip. There was another electric shuttle, and then moving walkways through long cylindrical tunnels opening up to a cluster of one-story buildings. Fechter carried his single piece of luggage for him without conversation and pointed out the direction they were to go. The buildings were all plain without decoration, the interiors long hallways with closed doors on either side, the lighting dim red when they arrived. Fechter unlocked a door, opened it, a bright, full spectrum light switching on to reveal a furnished room with bed, table and chairs and a long couch. "this is your room," said Fechter. The room smelled fresh and clean.

There was a small bathroom and kitchenette, a large holo player in one corner and a box of rectangular recordings to play on it. Fechter opened the refrigerator to show him an assortment of drinks and snacks for his use. The phone had one button. There was a food menu beside it. "Just press the button and order what you want," said Fechter. "our kitchen never closes. You should be ready to go next cycle at 1000 and you'll get a call at 0900. The meeting is at 1100, and someone will come to get you."

"I'm overwhelmed by your generosity," said Nicholas.

"Thank you, sir," said Fechter, "and I hope your meeting will be productive."

The door closed, and he was alone, wondering. He'd not expected such a warm reception and was encouraged by it. Relations with Port Nexus were poor at best after the Bishops' incursion in the past. He had expected his reception to be cold and formal, with overtones of hostility. His own attitude was now positive. The Bishops had done a stupid thing, had generated bad feelings about Kratola that were causing economic as well as political problems, and now he had a chance to heal the wounds.

He studied the menu and ordered a light meal, which arrived in fifteen minutes. The meat was synthetic, but tasty, and the bread seemed fresh, the fruit hydroponically grown.

He went to bed at 2300 and was immediately asleep. When the call came the following cycle, bright lights came on and woke him. He dressed hurriedly, had a breakfast of fresh eggs and a sweet bread with coffee so strong it quickened his heartbeat for a moment.

Two soldiers in fatigues came to get him, and he followed them along two moving walkways that led to a neighboring building past a few shops and an eating area to a double door guarded by two soldiers. A shorter hallway had large doors on both sides, and he was now in the administrative section of the station. They left him in a conference room with a long table and chairs, and he sat down to wait. The time was 1052, and at 1100 the door opened, and three people entered the room.

He stood up and smiled as Kira Madelia extended her hand in greeting. There was a second woman, younger but gray haired, dressed in a gray business suit and she smiled faintly at him. The third person was a powerfully built male in formal dress, who immediately stationed himself by the door, arms folded.

"Welcome to Port Nexus," said Kira, shaking his hand, then, "This is Jilena Uzelac, our Ambassador from Gan."

The woman did not shake his hand but bowed slightly with a faint smile.

"Ambassador?" said Nicholas, confused, since Port Nexus was not a sovereign state.

"That is my title on Gan," said Jilena. "Here I serve as a laison to Gan for any matters that concern us. We felt it was appropriate for me to attend this meeting."

"I agree with that, Ma'am," said Nicholas. "I welcome your presence, since my business here also involves the unfortunate relations, or lack of relations, that currently exist between our worlds."

The two women sat down across the table from Nicholas and put their processors in front of them.

"We've read your agenda, Mister Zahn. Would you like to begin?" said Kira.

"I do have a question first, if you don't mind," said Jilena.

"Certainly," said Nicholas.

"Have the Bishops sent you here, Mister Zahn?"

It was like being hit with a closed fist, but it was a question he was ready for.

"I don't believe in deception during any meeting, Ms. Uzelac, and I will be honest with both of you. The idea of meeting with Governor Madelia was mine and was only related to business relations and loss of trade due to our break with Gan. I'd hoped to make Gan contacts, and now here you are. But to arrange this meeting I had to meet with the Bishops for their approval. They were encouraging, since there has been no diplomatic contact between Gan and Kratola since what they see as an ill-conceived and ill-planned incursion on Port Nexus a few years ago. They have admitted their errors publicly, even to their own people. There has been no forgiveness for the incident, all of it due to a misunderstanding and lies by a usurper of power on Gan, but when the Bishops say it again and again, they are not believed.

"We have been isolated from our former colony worlds that have prospered so rapidly. They have provided materials and products that have allowed new businesses on Kratola to prosper. Nearly half of my market was on Gan alone. That is all gone, now, with no end in sight, and our entire economy has been severely damaged by it. It's not just the Bishops, or myself, who want to see the normalization of relations between Kratola, Gan and Galena. We are one people, now separated. In the end, this separation is not good for anybody. My business has suffered from it, and that's why I'm here, but I speak for my planet and all the people there who have also suffered. They are the innocent ones."

Nicholas suddenly realized he was near tears. He leaned back in his chair and took a deep breath to calm himself. "Sorry," he said, "but this is all very important to me, and you need to hear how deeply I feel about it. It's not just about me or my business, It's about all the citizens of Kratola."

There was a long pause while Nicholas breathed deeply, the women across the table looking first at him, and then at each other, with serious expressions.

"You have presented your case well," said Kira. "It gives us a new perspective."

"You might be surprised to hear that I agree with much of what you've said," said Jilena. "Our present situation is not good for anyone, and it should be repaired, but in your remarks, you have left out the real problem."

"And what is that, please?" said Nicholas.

"The Bishops, of course," said Jilena. "They are the central problem that has to be solved before anything good can happen. They have actually been the problem since they first took power. Only recently have things become critical again because of their behavior." She leaned forward and looked closely at him.

"I will give you an example. Recently there was a formal request by a visiting Bishop to allow military ships from Kratola to pass through the gate. This was denied, of course. It was then discovered that a disguised military vessel had brought the bishop here. The ship could have been seized, but only a warning was given. It was a deliberate probe of our security, and for why? Another invasion? We think so."

"I know nothing about that," said Nicholas. "I do know that the law also forbids transfer of any parts of a military vessel, and that is the law that has decreased my company's market by nearly fifty percent. We have not imposed an embargo on any Gan products. What you're doing to me isn't fair. It's purely political."

"That is unfortunate, but correct," said Jilena. "What we sell to Kratola is relatively minor and has no strategic or military value. That will continue as long as the Bishops are in power. We will not support them in any significant way."

"In doing so you are punishing an entire planet," said Nicholas.

"Then the people should demand a change in government. Gan has done this twice in one generation, and with great difficulty, but what we have now is good for everyone. The Bishops were behind both governments that had to go on Gan. And they still want to control us."

"There had been unrest on Kratola. I'm sure you've heard about it. People have died," said Nicholas.

"There was blood in the streets when our emperor fell," said Jilena, "and the second time, when a usurper supported by your Bishops was taken down, it wasn't much different. But sacrifices have to be made, and now we have good leadership."

"Change comes from people with wealth and influence," added Kira. "I personally have no reason to trust the Bishops. We have evidence that Kratolan agents are being smuggled into Pleasure City at an increasing rate to establish cells there. We've had a bombing and are preparing for more trouble. Our defenses are now at full strength, and we have added a ground force in the city. We are planning for another incursion by Kratola, and we are prepared for it. Any disruption of the city will be met with lethal force. Any invasion through the gate will mean total destruction of the invaders. Tell your Bishops that, Mister Zahn. The Bishops are your problem, not Gan or Port Nexus."

"And as long as the Bishops are in power, nothing will change," said Jilena. "Gan has had enough. We are close to a war, Mister Zahn, a war Kratola cannot win. The bishops must go. There is no other way. We are not the enemies of the Kratolan people, only their leaders. You are living under a cruel dictatorship, and part of the responsibility lies with the wealthy class that supports it for their own gain. Frankly speaking, your government is doomed, Mister Zahn. You will have to take sides soon."

Nicholas was stunned, breathing rapidly, hands clutching the arms of his chair. "Do you realize that when the Bishops ask for my report it will be given face to face to all of them, and if I give that report with any accuracy I will probably be shot on the spot?"

"I'm so sorry," said Jilena. "I know you came here with good intentions to improve relations and solve your business problems, but you did not really understand the situation, and now you do. We see your visit as an opportunity for the Bishops to understand their standing in the planetary community, and how dangerously close they are to a war of destruction. If they give up power, it will be a new day for all of us. They must hear this from you. You are an intelligent, influential man on Kratola. You can accuse us of being direct, insulting, and generally unfriendly, tell them what we've said without showing any support for it. Hopefully it will be enough to ensure your safety. We wish you well, Mister Zahn. It's all we can do for you today."

"I understand. Right now, I feel a bit dizzy. Could I have some coffee, please?"

"Elton?" said Jilena. The big man by the door poured coffee from a container on a table in the corner and brought it to Nicholas.

He sipped, the room swimming about him.

"We all want peace," said Jilena.

"I liked what you said about us all being one people," said Kira.

"Unfortunately, I was ill-informed," said Nicholas.

"You'll have another cycle for thinking before you leave," said Kira.

Nicholas was suddenly calm. "I've already thought of something, but this meeting was not what I expected." He made an attempt to smile but failed.

"Is there anything else you wish to discuss?" asked Kira. "Your escort is waiting outside."

"Nothing. I thank you for your time. We've accomplished one thing. The situation is now clear to me, but I can't be optimistic about our future. It's unlikely the Bishops will even entertain giving up power, and my report will not be accepted with gratitude. I was foolish to come here."

"Again, I'm so sorry," said Jilena. "But if there's even a slight chance the Bishops will respond to your report in a positive way your visit here might be very important. Good luck to you, and to all of us."

They stood up and shook hands, and the women left with their burly escort. Two men in fatigues led him back to his room. He ordered lunch and slept for two hours, awoke with his mind whirling, and he wrote some notes, at dinner, more notes, and slept sporadically until his early call. This time, two soldiers came to take him to the terminal.

He was still going over notes for a short and cautious presentation when a stubby shuttle took him back to the surface of Kratola.

* * * *

They were all there in the throne room.

Caleb Aluna brought him in, seated him at a table in the center of the room and patted his shoulder reassuringly. "Welcome back," he said. "From the look on your face, I'm thinking you don't have good news for us."

So, it was obvious. "I'm afraid so, sir," said Nicholas.

"We weren't expecting good news, Nicholas, so relax and tell us exactly what happened and what was said or hinted at," said Caleb, and he seated himself on his throne. "How were you received?"

"Very nicely. Their security chief met me at the terminal."

"Just checking you out," said Tibor. "The man is a hawk."

"Did they ask if we had sent you?" asked Caleb.

"Yes. I said the visit was on my initiative for business relations, but you were supportive and hoped for normalization of all relations."

"Good answer, Nicholas. I knew we could count on you," said Caleb.

Nicholas relaxed with a silent sigh. "They gave me a nice room and good meals before the meeting. I went in encouraged by the atmosphere. I met with Governor Madelia and a Jilena Uzelac who was introduced as a liaison officer from Gan but called herself an ambassador. I could see immediately that the relations between Gan and Port Nexus are quite close."

"We suspected that," said Zahair, "but I didn't know that Gan had a formal representative there."

"I thought their tourism bureau was doing that," said Galin.

"Or spying for them," said Tibor.

"They asked me what I wanted and listened politely while I gave my entire presentation. I addressed our market losses from their embargoes and new laws at the port, reminded them of your apologies for the incident at Port Nexus, known to everyone to be based on misunderstandings and lies from a tyrant losing power on Gan. I argued that refusal to forgive past mistakes was hurting all the people of Kratola, many of whom are related to people on Gan and Galena. We are all one people, I said, and both Madelia and Uzelac nodded as if agreeing with that. I was feeling very confident at that point."

"And then?" said Caleb.

"And then the bottom dropped out of the entire conversation. I barely got a few more words out. Madelia said a few things, but it was mostly

Uzelac who did the talking. They did not act aggressive, or speak loudly, but their words were brutally direct without pause for rebuttal. If I repeated those words in public, I would consider it both slanderous and treasonous. I could understand what you've been up against for the past few years."

"Just give us the gist of what they said. You have a recording?"

"Not allowed. In short, they started with the old lies about the Port Nexus incident. They claim your plans to take control over the colony worlds are still active. They cited an attempt to bring a disguised military vessel through the gate, and—"

"—Krack," said Tibor, covering his face with his hands.

"Madelia accuses you of placing agents in Pleasure City for the purpose of terrorism. What is wrong with these people? They flatly rejected my request for good relations, saying it could not be possible unless one thing happens on Kratola. For me to even say it in private is treasonous, and I will not say it."

Caleb smiled. "You don't have to. There can be new relations only if the Council of Bishops steps down by choice or by force, and disappears forever."

"Yes, sir. And they hinted at war. They politely suggested I tell everything to you when I returned, even though my mission had failed. I'm sorry, sirs. I don't know what else I could have done."

Nicholas awaited his fate. All four Bishops were scowling.

"It clarifies everything," said Galen.

"And I told you so," said Tibor.

"I shouldn't be surprised, but I really thought they would give us another chance without having a war," said Zuhair.

There was what seemed like a long silence, while Nicholas' heart thumped hard, and then Caleb said, "Nicholas, we want to thank you for your service. I'm sure you're very disappointed, but your meeting has clarified our situation, and further attempts at diplomacy will be fruitless. There is to be war, and we will be ready for it, and your company will continue to be an important resource for our efforts. We'll give you our production requirements right away. Gan's Guppies are powerful, but our last conflict showed they can be damaged or even destroyed. We will need C class cruisers to do it."

"We will have to retool," said Nicholas.

"Begin now, today, before sunset. This meeting is over," said Caleb.

In the limousine to home, Nicholas continued to sigh with relief. Leaving the room, he'd first noticed his arm pits were soaking wet. But right now, his mind whirled with the prospect of new business. The manufacture of even a few heavy cruisers would increase his personal fortune by thirty percent, and he anticipated an order for more than a few.

Dark thoughts intervened. The Guppies were said to be the most powerful ships on both sides of the wormhole. If they were allowed to come through the gate nothing could stand against them, not even a hundred C-class cruisers. The people of Kratola might even cheer them when they arrived. It was all because Kratola was ruled by a hated regime that provided high profits for the upper class, including Nicholas Zahn, a regime that wanted to control the immediate galaxy around them and had stirred up the fury of the common people by murdering some of them.

If the Bishops were overthrown, what would happen to Nicholas Zahn and his manufacturing empire?

He didn't want to think about it.

There was retooling to do.

CHAPTER TWENTY

The big merchant ship from Kratola emerged from swirling gravitational mists of the great wormhole and docked at Port Nexus terminal birth twelve at 1800. Only a few passengers were on board, but the cargo manifest was a long one and unloading took until 0500 the following cycle. Most of the cargo was listed as building materials in large bundles or rail car sized crates on their way to both Pleasure City and Station alpha: plasteel sheets, aluminum tubing, bars of plasteel and composite materials for insulation in a level one housing project in Pleasure City. Inspection was routine, by weight, and random. The manifest was passed at 2100.

Materials bound for Station Alpha shipped out the following cycle, but deliveries to Pleasure City remained on dock for two more cycles while transportation was arranged. During that time, someone unknown selected one crate of composites and marked it with red paint on one corner. The mark was only two inches across and was the image of a five-pointed star. In all, there were five crates bound for Pleasure City.

Three VTOL transports arrived to pick up the crates. Two crates each were loaded onto two transports for delivery to Shanigan Housing Construction in oldtown, Pleasure City, the other crate with red marking picked up hours before by a single transport for Pleasure City Water and Power. All crates were taken to neighboring warehouses near the shuttle field outside the city.

It would be several months before the discovery that the crate picked up for Water and Power contained much more than plasteel sheets and aluminum tubing, and, in fact, no such materials had even been ordered by company administration. Indeed, creative packing had been done to insure that crate weight matched the number on the manifest. Boxes unloaded from the crate contained one hundred and fifty T-4 automatic rifles with smartscopes, and pouch belts of two hundred rounds of 0.40 ammunition for each weapon.

The crate was unloaded after 2400 the cycle of receipt. There was an observation of several trucks leaving the warehouse area near that time.

The conclusion reached later was that the rifles were delivered to eight cells of Kratolan elite troops working undercover in Pleasure city and preparing to fight a short, limited but highly focused war in the city streets.

* * * *

Zeke was the first man to contact Nathan after the interview with Pavel. He'd first called Pavel to warn him about four dead bodies in oldtown and explained why they were there.

"I understand," said Pavel, "but I don't want any gunfire in the streets until we're in a real war. Why is it so hard to get hold of you? Stefan and I have both been trying, but he's leaving the local issues to me. A Kratolan turncoat has turned himself in to us, and we need you to see how he can be used."

"Sorry. I had to shut down my communicator while I was doing my nasty deed. It had been planned for a while, and I'm free now. Who is this guy, and how can I meet him? "

"Nathan Czapic is the name he gave us. Kratolan Special forces, assigned to Port Nexus underground, has a cell, but doesn't know much yet. No orders. They're all just waiting. He says his parents on Kratola were murdered by the Bishops. Has two brothers in the military; they've gone AWOL there and want revenge. We were able to check his story. The brothers haven't been found yet, but villagers were killed in an attempt to find them. You'll have to judge for yourself.

"He has a labor job with the water works, and they're doing some pipe replacement at the shuttle field right now. You'll find him there. Sorry I can't be more specific. His brothers' names are Jule and Jon, if that helps. I don't have his parents' names."

"I'll get on it," said Zeke, "but there's one thing you'll have to understand. If I'm not satisfied with him, he will not live another cycle."

"Wow," said Pavel. "You are extreme, Zeke."

"It's my job," said Zeke. "Understand?"

"Yep, and Stefan will too. He's a bit like you."

"Good. I'll let you know when I have something," said Zeke.

And now it was time to meet an undercover Kratolan special forces trooper who claimed to be a turncoat.

Zeke dressed in work clothes and boots, complete with hard hat. Gan had a friend who worked with Water and Power and had been used by Zeke before. The man had a brother in Gan intelligence and had a vague knowledge of what was going on.

Zeke went to the work site at the shuttle field, where a long piece of ten-inch plumbing was being replaced onto a rack one foot off the ground. Several men were working on it. He went to the prefab office, found the man he was looking for, a heavy man with graying hair and a short beard.

"Hey, Darrell," said Zeke.

Darrell eyed him suspiciously but smiled. "Been a while. What's up?"

"I need to speak privately with one of your workers out on the pipe. Nathan Czapia. Do you know him?"

"Yep. Is he in trouble?"

"Not at all. Tell him it's about his brothers."

"Okay, I'll get him. There's a little storage area in the back of the office. You can talk there. Be quick about it. Super will be back from lunch in half an hour."

"Thanks, Darrell. 'Preciate it."

Zeke went to a small niche in the back of the office and sat on a stool. In minutes, Darrell was back with a hard looking kid with a square face and jaw and a hostile look in his eyes. "Make it fast," said Darrell, and left them.

"Nathan Czapia?" said Zeke.

The kid leaned over and looked closely at him. "That's me. Now what about my brothers? Are you Gan Intelligence, or do we fight now?"

Zeke smiled. "You don't want to try it, son, but yes, I'm with Gan Intelligence. Your brothers went AWOL and intend to assassinate the Bishops."

"I know all that."

"They haven't been found yet. Some innocent people have been killed in the search."

"More reason to kill the Bishops," said Nathan.

"And we agree on that. We want you to help us do it."

"Nothing I can tell you yet. My cell is up to eight men. Two of us have jobs, the others just sit around and play cards all day. We have no orders except to wait. None of us are happy about it."

"No weapons yet?"

"Just the sidearms we brought off ship with us. They don't even scan passengers here."

"Yeah, well, that'll be fixed," said Zeke. "For now, it's information we need from you. Tell Darrell when you need to see me; he knows what I'm doing. He'll call me and tell you when and where, face to face."

"That's it?" said Nathan.

"For now. I don't have to tell you what'll happen to you if you do one thing I think is suspicious."

"Yeah, I know. But tell me what you hear about my brothers. They'll all I have left of my family."

"Got it. We're done here. I'll promise another thing. If you do good for us, and war happens, we'll try to get you out of here alive."

"Right," said Nathan, and Zeke heard the doubt in his voice.

He made it back to his cab before the work site supervisor had returned from lunch.

* * * *

Light years away on a bright sunny day, two men hunkered down in a dugout with a well-supported sniper rifle pointed at the Bishop' palace a mile away. They had been there for two days and their water was running short, their food supply down to a few sweet crackers. Jule had dug a trap shelter for them inside a tight cluster of three trees and covered it with branches and debris with the one trencher he and Jon had kept with them. Right now it was the only place they could hide if there were boots on the ground to search them out. Muzzle flash could be a problem, muzzle blast not so much. A baffled choke on the end of the big gun directed much of the gas upwards, greatly reducing forward sound at a distance. They had done what they could to survive but knew the odds for that were not good.

But it would be no matter to them if one Bishop or more could die at their hands.

It was only an hour later when their preparations and patient wait were finally rewarded. Jon was looking through the scope when two figures appeared on a tower balcony overlooking the dome of the tabernacle. At this distance their faces weren't identifiable, but their robes told him enough. It was two Bishops who stood there in the morning sun, and they could be gone in seconds.

"Fire in the hole," said Jon, and Jule leaned away from him, saying nothing.

The big rifle was loaded, bolt locked, an extra cartridge near his trigger hand as he sighted. There was no vibration in the sight picture, his two targets standing so close together they were overlapping. He aimed at their center as he took a breath, let out some, held, his finger gently squeezing the trigger.

The sound of the explosion was deafening.

Jon ignored it, loaded and locked the second cartridge with a practiced flick of his wrist, his finger beginning the squeeze before he was sighted in. the targets were still there, struggling with each other, and the big gun went off when the crosshairs were centered on them.

He looked again, saw nobody on the balcony, then a face in the doorway there, and a man ducked down.

Jule was throwing sand on him, beginning to fill their shallow dugout. Jon grabbed his rifle and an empty cartridge case, swept aside the rock and debris parts of his shooting stand in all directions. They stayed low, below sight from the palace complex, filled and smeared over the dugout, crouched over and stepped from rock to rock to their hiding place a few yards away, checking all the way for any marks in the sand. In another minute they were in their four-foot-deep trap shelter and covered with a weaving of branches, brush and small rocks, prepared for a long wait with only a few ounces of water and four crackers to sustain them.

* * * *

Caleb had breakfast with the man he still regarded as a mentor, though recently they often disagreed on matters of policy. Zuhair had been prime minister two decades before, but times had been simpler then and the use of force with the people had been unnecessary. Caleb still liked the man, and listened politely to his advice, even when he didn't agree with him.

They discussed whether war was still uncertain, or now out of control. The report by Nicholas Zahn had been depressing, and supported Caleb's position of preparation and first strike. Zuhair was still arguing for one more attempt at diplomacy, and worried about their clandestine activities at Port Nexus.

Breakfast over, they retired to the tower balcony for a few moments of warmth and sunshine. It was a beautiful day. Zuhair turned his face up towards the sky. "Lovely," he said.

And then Caleb felt something strange, a sudden shock bristling his hair, and Zuhair jerked beside him, grunting. From far away there came a little popping sound.

Zuhair was falling, and Caleb turned to grab him, struggling for balance, and he felt something warm in his left hand, and then another shock, a searing pain along the right side of his head at the hairline, and his vision went black. He was falling, Zuhair beneath him, and he was conscious of slumping to the floor and a guard at the door, screaming.

"Shooter! Shooter! We're on the tower balcony. Get a med team here. Turn out the guard, all stations. Move!"

Caleb felt hands on him, heard a soothing voice, and tried to talk.

"Wha—can't see—where?—"

"Easy, sir. Shallow wound, but a lot of bleeding. Reverend Pasela is wounded badly. Stay still. Help is coming."

Caleb blanked out for a moment, and when he awoke, he was being lifted onto a stretcher and there were voices all around him.

"Better hurry. This looks bad. Large caliber. One shot, probably the second one, went off the doorway, and I see a hole where it hit the wall. I'll dig out the slug."

"Did you hear anything?"

"Nothing. Long distance. Two quick shots."

"Krack. I bet it's military."

Caleb drifted off again, and not for a short time. When he awoke, he was in the infirmary, a thick bandage like half a turban stuck to the right side of his head, and he was hooked up to a dozen machines. A male nurse looked down at him and smiled."

"Good evening, Reverend. Glad to have you still with us. It was close, but you'll be fine."

"We were shot," said Caleb, still groggy.

"From very far away. They've sent out drones and a VTOL, and a search party is on the ground. They'll get them, Reverend. Your job is to relax and get well for us."

"Bishop Pasela was hit first. How is he?"

"He's still in surgery, listed as critical. The wound was quite extensive."

Caleb sobbed in despair. "If he dies, I will avenge him. He is my friend."

The nurse looked at him strangely. A guard at the door cleared his throat for attention and said, "Excuse me, Reverend, but you should know that we have retrieved the bullet that struck you. It is fifty caliber, composite jacket. It is a military bullet, Reverend, used in our T-50 sniper rifle, bolt action, very accurate. The rifle is only issued to your guard and the Black Hat units. Every soldier will be accounted for and questioned."

Shot by my own military, thought Caleb.

This is not a good sign.

CHAPTER TWENTY-ONE

War was no longer just possible, but certain.

Kira called Stefan early in the cycle to inform him of a required meeting.

"It's direct from Prime Minister Haig and relayed from Gan. There has been no declaration of war by the legislature. The public has gone through two civil wars in recent times and is just now showing some confidence in their new government. It's felt that a unilateral declaration without a new provocation by Kratola would endanger that confidence. They're certain such a provocation will happen soon. Their plans for an invasion of Kratola are complete and include ships coming through the gate. It violates the rules, but we are allied with Gan, Stefan, and those rules can be suspended in a time of war. Prime Minister Haig has asked that you meet with his field general charged with prosecuting the war. His name is Petyr Vlasok, and the meeting will be on a Guppy docked four hundred miles from here. It will take an entire cycle of your time. Can you do it next cycle?"

Stefan checked his schedule, felt relief noting it was two cycles before he and Corinne had planned to be together again.

"It's open. What time?"

"You leave on a Nova at dock two promptly at 0600. You should be back by 1700. I will be honest, Stefan. I know I've earned Gan's trust, but they still seem to be a bit uncertain about you. These people are representing the Immortals, or the freedom party as they like to call it. There was a time on Gan when you were their enemy."

"That was true, but not now," said Stefan.

"I'm just saying that this meeting is an opportunity for you to convince them you're a reliable ally. You certainly don't have to convince me. But I think most of the meeting will be about their attack plan."

"Okay. I'll get it done, Ma'am."

"Stefan, how many times do I have to tell you."

Sorry—Kira. It's my military brain that does it."

"Good luck," she said, and was gone.

He managed to clean off his desk by 1600, had an early, synth dinner from a machine, then talked to Corinne for an hour and went to bed dreaming she was beside him. He was up at 0400 and at the dock at 0530 where a trooper directed him to a sleek Nova, the bottle-shaped weapons platform that would take him to his meeting. It had been years since he'd been on this fighting ship now designated for the protection of Alpha Station and the Gate's guardian moons.

The trip was mostly acceleration, deceleration and docking, and was just over an hour in time. He sat with the crew, had a good view screen to enjoy, could see the depot when it was only a point of flickering red light. As they drew near, he could see the Guppy docked there, an amazing vessel, but probably the ugliest ever conceived. He always thought of a fish with a long, pointed nose that had either swallowed a much larger fish or was pregnant with many of its own kind. But under that sharp beak bristled countless ports for missiles and rail guns, and inside the beak was the magic projecting a field that could make targets simply disappear, and then there was the big secret he and Kira had been entrusted with. Inside that pregnant belly was another magic of the Immortals' technology, a device enabling it to do the work of wormholes and jump many light years from point to point in the blink of an eye.

They docked next to the Guppy and were dwarfed by it. Stefan was ushered through the lock to a tunnel with a moving walkway to the next lock at which the Guppy was attached, and they went through it. There was an escalator rising at forty-five-degree angle to the entrance lock at the Guppy. When he came out of it a man was there to greet him, a tall man flanked by two men with holstered sidearms. And the man looked very familiar.

Stefan had worn his dress blues for the occasion. His host wore fatigues, smiled, looked him up and down and extended a hand.

"Welcome to Guppy Four, Chief Fechter, and thank you for coming so promptly. I'm sure you're very busy these days. I am Commander Petyr Vlasok, and this vessel is my flagship."

"Awesome to see, and I've heard what it can do. Very impressive," said Stefan. *Where have I met this guy?* he thought.

"Staff has prepared a snack for our meeting. Please follow me."

Using hand holds, Stefan drifted with him to an elevator, which seemed to rise forever, and the doors opened on a small area with four narrow branching halls with handholds in the walls, and Stefan was again an ape swinging from one hand hold to another.

They reached a room with a table and chairs and little dishes of assorted foods, and he could smell coffee, and suddenly his feet were solidly on the floor.

"Gravity?" he said.

"A little trickle from our power plant," said Petyr. "We use it locally when it's convenient."

A clue about a Guppy's engine? Thought Stefan. "More magic to me. You people are amazing."

"We have some very bright people," said Petyr. He sat down at the table and reached for a plate of food.

There were little sandwiches with synth meat, dried fruit and decent coffee. The men munched for a moment, and then Petyr spoke.

"You were in the Gan military for many years and grew up there. We have a complete file on your service. You were a searcher, and at one time our people were hiding from you."

"All true," said Stefan. "I was a soldier following an emperor's orders, and once again after his overthrow, and then one day my orders conflicted with the oath I'd taken in the academy. That should also be in my file."

"It is," said Petyr, "and it was all well known when you were hired at Port Nexus, but one thing was left out, Chief Fechter. On one of your searches you killed a man, one of our people, and he was very young."

Finally, thought Stefan. "The man had shot two of my troopers and was holed up in a basement. When he came out of the basement with two guns blazing, looking right at me, I shot him in the head. It still haunts me, and I've had regrets, but I am still alive, and persecution of your people ended several years ago. We are now free to do better things with our lives."

Petyr thought for a few seconds, then, "I like that. Past is past. Unfortunately, the same is not true for the Bishops of Kratola. Do you agree?"

"I do. The battle at Port Nexus was only a setback for them. Their strategic goals have changed, perhaps, but they are still a menace as far as I'm concerned."

"How do you think their goals have changed?" asked Petyr.

"Their goal was to take direct control of their former colony worlds by invasion, and they had to capture the Gate to do it. If it hadn't been for your Guppies they would have done it and continued on to attack Gan."

"Okay," said Petyr. "and?"

"The Guppies obliterated their forces. The Bishops learned from that, and they are not stupid men. If they ever attack Gan, it is a suicide mission against your Guppies. They cannot do it and will not. But they can still do something that could lead to positive negotiations with you by its effect on commerce. They can invade Port Nexus and with help from within the port they can close the Gate on the Gan side of the Nexus. Kratola would still have wormhole access, and you would not. They would occupy Port Nexus and cut off your commerce. It would hurt them economically, and anger some wealthy people, but they could survive it. And they would have a good starting point for a first strike on Gan in the future by opening a gate again. All it takes is damaging or repairing a stabilizing moon for the one gate."

"It won't work," said Petyr. "Our Guppies can come through without a gate and destroy them."

"They don't know that," said Stefan. "It's supposed to be a best kept secret."

Petyr frowned. "Oh—you're right. But—unless—unless they saw the Guppies come in when they invaded the port. If they saw them suddenly appear they'd know the gate wasn't used."

"I've never heard talk about that," said Stefan. "We've heard nothing to indicate the Bishops know that secret. But if they knew it, they would not be infiltrating forces into Port Nexus and setting up cells there. That smells like an internal takeover to me. It might happen very soon and kill a lot of people, and it has nothing to do with an invasion of Gan."

"Do you support our planned attack on Kratola?" asked Petyr, and his dark eyes had narrowed.

"Absolutely. It's the timing that bothers me. I hear you will not consider a first strike because of political pressures, and you will wait for some incursion by Kratola before you strike."

"Our people are sick of war. If we're to become invaders and strike first the people will not support it, and we are a new government. Even a small incursion would be reason enough."

"A small incursion in Port Nexus, you mean," said Stefan softly.

"I don't know where else it could be. Our guppies would be there to defend you in the blink of an eye."

"In my experience, a lot of people can die during the blink of an eye. The first strike in your war against Kratola will be in Port Nexus, and it's my people who will suffer from it."

"The war is for the continued freedom of Gan and Galena. You are still a citizen of Gan," said Petyr.

"For legal purposes," said Stefan. "My people are on Port Nexus, and some are more than family to me. I want them to be safe." It was a near whisper when he said it.

"Ah," said Petyr. "We both want that, and war always has a price, but the Bishops must go. In the end, Gan will also have casualties."

"The Bishops fear you," said Stefan. "They've heard talk of an invasion and so have their people. At this moment, they're not on the attack, but see it as defending themselves, and they have to move before you do. Their attack on the gate could come in hours or cycles. We'll only have some warning when Kratolan ships gather near their entrance to the wormhole. When they attack, I expect an immediate battle inside Pleasure city where they've established cells, and we've only identified a few of them."

"Gan sent people to counter that, didn't they?"

"About twenty, and not enough. We estimate two to three hundred Kratolan agents are now there. I've established a ground force of three hundred in the city, and they're ready. We're all ready for war, sir, when it comes. And we hope the Guppies will come quickly."

Petyr smiled, leaned over the table and clapped Stefan on the shoulder.

"We're soldiers, you and I. The best thing we can do is to be prepared for war and know that plans and strategies must often be changed during the fighting. I promise you we'll do our best to aid your defense of the port. But that is only the beginning, and our reaction to it will be instantaneous and with approval of our legislature."

"It is necessary that the Nexus gate on the Gan side not be allowed to become unstable."

"So Moon G must be heavily defended," said Stefan.

"And fighting in the streets or buildings or even the terminal will be yours to do. Our Guppies will destroy any Kratolan ships that appear, and then go directly to Kratola for the main attack, but over a hundred of our regular fighters and light cruisers will follow immediately and they will come through the nexus and use both gates without pause for even a second. The gates must remain stable, even while fighting goes on within the terminal or the city."

"We can handle that. Our space force, thanks to Gan, is up to full strength. I'd feel a lot safer if you left one Guppy behind. When you hit Kratola the bishops might launch a second attack on the gate. It takes a lot of fighters and even Novas to go up against a Class C.

"We'll bring in a Guppy or two for that purpose, It's not a problem," said Petyr.

"How many of those things do you have?" asked Stefan.

"Enough," said Petyr. "Production has been continuous for six years. Awesome power can mean quick surrender and fewer casualties."

"I remember that from the Academy," said Stefan.

Both men were relaxed, now, each feeling that nothing had been left out and they were indeed allies in a common war.

Stefan finally said, "I met your Prime Minister before his position was official. I know he's said to be an Immortal, and I'm assuming you are, too, being a field general and all. Has anyone ever told you that you bear a striking resemblance to him? Are you related to him?"

Petyr smiled. "Yes, some people notice the resemblance. We're not directly related, but we share one thing. The spirit of Leonid Zylak is in both of us."

The answer was vague and incomplete for Stefan. "Okay. I don't think I'll ever understand why people call you immortals."

"Someday," said Petyr. "It's not anything dark, we just don't talk about it."

"Let's just hope we both come out alive at the end of this thing," said Stefan.

"I can agree to that. Good hunting, Chief."

"You, too."

They shook hands, and the meeting was over.

And in three hours, Stefan was coming into Pleasure City, where he would soon be with Corinne again.

* * * *

They'd made leisurely love, and then dozed, awakened again when Neenee jumped up on the bed and curled up near their feet. When they opened their eyes and looked at her she wagged her tail twice and then closed her eyes.

"Your dog is watching us again," said Stefan, and pulled Corinne snugly against him.

"Our dog, you mean," said Corinne. "She loves you, and so do I."

"Good. I love both of you, too," said Stefan, and kissed her forehead.

Corinne murmured something and pressed her face against his bare chest when he squeezed her gently.

"Do you think you might consider spending the rest of your life with an old soldier?"

"Hmm, It might be an effort, but I could try living with that," she said softly. "You're not so old. I'm older. I told you that."

"That's hard to believe, Madam, unless you are very well preserved. You sure you're not an Immortal?"

Corine ran a finger lightly over his chest hair. "I never said I was or wasn't. You'll have to guess. I hate that word, anyway. Immortals are just normal people who have developed incredible technology, including medicine."

"Yeah, I've heard that before. I met another one in a meeting before I came in last cycle. Looks normal, from Gan, talked about having the spirit of Leonid Zylak inside him. Gan's Prime Minister said the same thing when I met him before he even had the job. Sounds religious to me, and weird. The two of them look exactly alike."

"Leonid Zylak was the founder of the freedom movement on Gan," said Corinne. "He's been dead for nearly two hundred years. My father once told me that Leonid Zylak was the first Immortal. Believers say he still lives in altered form."

"Do you believe that?"

Believers don't ask for proof, darling. Father taught me to believe in science. I'm hoping the Immortals help my father. I finally heard from him through his friend you met, the businessman from Gan? He came back later with a message for me."

"Is your father better?"

"Yes. He's undergoing treatment by Immortal doctors, and is much better, but now he won't come to see me. He says war is coming here soon, and he wants me to come to Gan right away to be safe."

She touched his face, looked up at him with concern, and he kissed her forehead lightly again.

"Well, I wouldn't like it, but it might be a good idea. I can't say how, but things are heating up here and it's not looking good. You could go to Gan to visit your father, get together again. It does sound like you've drifted apart. Stay a month or two, see what happens."

"But I have businesses to run, and you'll be here. I can't be gone for more than three cycles without creating problems."

"You have managers, and I can wait. If bad things happen, I'll have plenty of things going on at the same time. A war does that."

Now Corinne looked angry. She pulled away from him and grasped his neck with one hand.

"Well, I won't do it. I will not run away from my business or my man. I will not be chased off by a stupid war, either. I have a large staff, including security people who are former police or military. Anybody who tries to invade my Red Palace will find themselves in a firefight, even without your help, Mister Soldier. And I will be there when it happens."

Stefan could not contain a euphoria that washed over him. He grabbed her hand, pressed it to the pillow as he rolled her over and grinned down at her. "Okay, warrior woman, you'll get your way, and it's not possible for me to love anyone as much as I love you."

He kissed her long and deep, and Corinne was ready, and they made love again, this time with considerable enthusiasm, and when they were finished, they saw that Neenee had been watching again.

"What do you think of that?" Stefan asked the dog.

Neenee wagged her tail vigorously, got up and pushed hard to get between them, and they all went to sleep together.

CHAPTER TWENTY-TWO

The size of Kratola's underground force had grown to over three hundred men by Guillermo Corrella's estimation, with anywhere from eight to fifteen men per cell and weapons were finally coming in for them. There was one master cell, location unknown, that informed the others of new orders or weapons arrivals and places for distribution. Communication was by written notice, delivered by a van provided by Guillermo, the driver a member of the master cell.

Guillermo had been entrusted with providing a railway from port terminal to pickup locations for men being distributed among the cells, and he had photographed all of them. He'd been promised rewards for his loyalty and services, both money and new power in his takeover of Red Palace, which he had coveted for so long. A successful occupation of Port Nexus would be the ideal, of course, but Guillermo did not count on it. He was a realist, had lived through the previous attack on the port, had closely watched the defensive improvements made by the new security chief, and was well informed about the close relations between Port Nexus and Gan.

The chances of a complete takeover of the Gate or even Pleasure City were minimal at best. The war would likely be short and fierce, but if the Guppies arrived that would be the end of it, and the new ground forces were certainly large enough to defend the city.

His plan only needed a short war, regardless of winner, a battle in the streets fought with rifles and handguns, men in uniform and street clothes, a horrible mix of friend and foe not easily identifiable by each other. His own team would be ten men who had worked security for him many years and had also handled unpleasant and sometimes messy business tasks outside their normal duties.

At the height of fighting in the streets of Pleasure City, Guillermo would lead his civilian clothed and masked team to the Red Palace Casino where they would commandeer the elevator upstairs to the office of Corinne Ariska, and she would be dead when they left. His dream was to shoot the bitch himself, but no matter if someone else did it. When the smoke cleared, Red Palace would be his, or he would have another chance to bid on it, and anyone who threatened to top his bid this time would suddenly die.

The plan had a requirement if the Bishops' forces were to be the losers in the war. His people must be equipped with Kratolan weapons like those coming in for the cells. The death of Corinne Ariska had to be at the hands of foreign infiltrators using standard T-4 rifles. Guillermo's little force was supposedly defending Black Diamond and nearby businesses including Red Palace. And any T-4 rifles they carried could be explained as being taken from the dead bodies of their enemies.

To actually do that was too chancy. He had to have T-4 rifles before battle day. And the underground seemed reluctant to give them to him. Knowing that a second shipment of rifles had been received and another was expected, his request for ten weapons was being ignored, and his patience, never long, was running short. When a courier arrived with another message, he demanded a call from someone in charge if they wanted his continued loyalty and cooperation.

The call came an hour later.

The voice was not familiar, and not friendly.

"Are you threatening us, Corrella?"

"I'm not threatening. You're leaving me out of things. I was supposed to get rifles. My people only have handguns."

"So what? We're doing the fighting, not you."

"That wasn't the plan."

"The plan was yours. We don't care about that."

"I have to defend my casino, so they don't suspect I'm involved with you. That was the promise, direct from Kratola."

There was a pause, then, "How many do you need? We're getting barely enough for the cells, and that's if everything gets through."

"Ten rifles, at least forty rounds each, that's what I need."

Another pause, then, "Five now, with ammo, the rest later if I can, but no promise."

Krack. Fuggin' Kratolan trash, thought Corrella. "Okay, send it, and we'll try to make do if we have to, but I don't like it."

"We don't care what you like, Corrella. Your help is useful, but we can also make do without it. Don't threaten us again. We might decide to blow your ass off with the rest of them."

Click.

Maybe went too far, thought Guillermo, but even five rifles will be fine as long as one of them is for me.

* * * *

Zeke had a brief meeting with Nathan and hurried back to his room to call Stefan on the communicator. The call was short, and terse. Zeke was angry and made no effort to hide it when Stefan answered.

"It's Zeke. I have some bad news for you."

"Oh, oh," said Stefan.

"Yeah, oh, oh. You and Pavel aren't doing your jobs. I just talked to our turncoat kid. His cell is now armed and ready with T-4 rifles and ammo delivered by Kratolan ships and shuttles to the city. Your security isn't worth krack."

"All cargoes are inspected, and ship holds are scanned."

"What kind of inspection?"

"By weight. We look at density variations."

"Krack, that's not even any good in peacetime. You should be scanning everything. The guns are in crates of plasteel and composites. They just change the packaging. Where to you find the fools who run your docks?"

"I'll talk to Pavel right away," said Stefan quietly.

"Don't talk about it, *do* something. Start scanning this hour. More guns are coming in soon, and one more thing."

"There's more? This is bad enough," said Stefan, obviously embarrassed.

"You've got people from Kratola walking in and out of the terminal without a scan. They just show an I.D. card and they're gone. All these people are coming through with handguns on them, and you don't even see it. That is just stupid, Chief. Fix it!"

"Done," said Stefan, "and within the hour, Zeke. Thanks for the heads up," he said, and clicked off.

"Okay," said Zeke, putting his communicator down. *No argument, no excuse, admit the error and fix it. I like it*, he thought.

But on Station Alpha, Stefan was calling Pavel, who was in Pleasure City.

"Got a call from Zeke, and he just gave me a new asshole."

"What's up?" asked Pavel.

Stefan told him.

"Oh, krack, the dock super is supposed to handle all that, and he knows we're on war alert."

"We're in charge of security, bud. We blew it. We need to scan everything, including passengers.

"They'll hate us for it."

"Put it where it hurts the most. It starts now. Make the calls. Really sorry about this, Pavel. I should have seen it."

"Yeah, me too," said Pavel, and ended the conversation.

And within half an hour, two new laws were in effect for all ships and passengers coming in from either Gan or Kratola.

* * * *

In hospital, Zuhair Pasela remained critical, and near death. A large portion of his chest on the right side had been blown apart by a single fifty caliber bullet fired at long range and flattened to a thick disk on impact. The exit had been ghastly.

Caleb's wound was much less severe, but ugly. "Two inches to the left and your brain would have been blown up," said a doctor. A bloody trench seven inches long and scalp deep above an ear and at hairline had taken a lot of needle work and bandaging, and then there were pills for a severe headache that made him see spots in front of his eyes.

Now he felt somewhat better, sitting up in bed, looking like an ancient shaman of The Field with the great lump of bandage wrappings around his head. Galen and Tibor had been in to see him in the morning, had listened to his ravings until the normally submissive Galen had become assertive.

"We have been attacked by one or more members of our military community. I would have both battalion commanders taken out and shot. They have to be behind this."

"Be careful," said Caleb. "It could be anyone: a Gan spy, an angry citizen with access to a military weapon, even a drunken trooper."

"There has been a terrible, quiet unrest among our people since the shootings at our gates," said Galen.

"Question every trooper, both guards and Black Hats. Threaten torture of their families. I don't care how it's done, but find the people who shot us, and anyone who knew about it. I want them all tortured and publicly executed in our courtyard. But at first, we will blame the attack on Gan spies."

"Caleb, please listen," said Galen. Things are being done. A search is underway on the ground and in the air. The shots likely came from a hill a mile from our gates, but we've found nothing there. A small village on the other side of the hill is now being searched. It really could have been a Gan assassin like you say. There's a lot of empty land out there. The shooter could have come in on a small shuttle at near ground level and then escaped on it. I've ordered questioning about any sightings of such a thing. I've also ordered a list of any military personnel who have recently gone AWOL. I know this has increased of late, just after the shootings at the gates. We went too far with that, Caleb. Our citizens are really angry. Please don't anger our military with threats or accusations right now. Let me handle this, and you focus on getting well."

There was fervor in the man's voice, and Caleb was impressed. Galin was making some sense, and it was not a common event.

Now Caleb felt a kind of sadness. "Zuhair is not just a fellow Bishop to me, he is a friend. We go back a long way."

"I know," said Galen.

"He was a lecturer when I was in seminary," said Tibor. "He is a wise man. First Light burns within him."

"As it should in all of us," said Galen.

"I need Zuhair for several reasons," said Caleb, "but I fear First Light will now solve our problems. I might be losing both a friend and advisor." He began to feel the sting of tears in his eyes.

"He is grievously wounded," said Galen. "We must be prepared for the worst. Tibor and I will do all we can to give you strength, Caleb."

Caleb shook their hands gently, tears now blurring his vision. "I think the shots they've given me have left me with a kind of depression. I need to sleep. Please visit me in the morning and let me know what's going on. I should be feeling much better tomorrow."

Galen and Tibor returned the next morning, and their faces were long and saddened. Caleb was sitting up in bed. Eating a light custard, and immediately sensed the news was not good.

"Zuhair Pasela passed on to The Field early this morning," said Galen. "He is now part of the infinity of past, present and future, and will return to us in new form."

It was said like a benediction.

"So shall it be,", said Caleb, and felt tears gush, filling his eyes and running down both cheeks. He put down his custard and spoke softly.

"If you don't mind, I would like a few moments alone to compose myself before our discussion."

"Of course," said Galen, and both he and Tibor left the room.

Caleb Aluna cried over the loss of his friend, mentor, advisor, a man who had understood his weaknesses and impetuousness, and had managed to keep him from always making judgments not well thought out. The comfort of new birth was no help. Zuhair as information stored in the entropic infinity of The Field was lost forever to Caleb and would not return to him in any form. Caleb cried for a long time, sobbing, holding his face in his hands, shoulders shuddering in grief.

And when he was finished, he called Galen and Tibor into his room, and they sat down next to his bed.

"Please prepare a memorial service for our dear Brother in the Faith," he said. "And I expect to officiate."

Galen nodded, and Caleb folded his hands over his stomach.

"Zuhair's wisdom will be missed, but now we must move ahead, and quickly. I want us to formulate our detailed preparation and strategies for our first strike on Port Nexus."

CHAPTER TWENTY-THREE

Stefan received an ominous call from Petyr on the communicator provided to him by Zeke.

"Big news from Kratola," said Petyr. "There has been an assassination on Kratola. Bishop Pasela is dead, and Aluna nearly had his head blown off. Unfortunately, he's quite alive. Looks like it was a military hit."

"The military is turning on them, maybe?"

"I doubt it. That would be too easy. Aluna is our biggest concern, and he's half crazy. I think this will push him into moving ahead faster against you, and then us. It's anger that controls that man. I'm putting out an attack alert right now and getting in some practice. Do you have access to a viewscreen?"

"Here in my office."

"Switch to the outside view channel."

Stefan did so, saw stars in the blackness of space, a twinkling colorful and distant star that was Pleasure city.

"Okay. Nothing new here."

"Yeah. I'm calling from the fuel station. Keep watching."

Stefan looked—and looked.

Suddenly there was a green flash, and a Guppy was there, blocking out stars with its bloated shape.

"Whoa!" said Stefan.

"Back again," said Petyr, and he sounded amused. "It gets better. Keep watching."

A longer wait this time, maybe thirty seconds, and then there were three bright flashes of green and four Guppies were now filling his view-screen.

"Hoot, hoot!" shouted Petyr. "Right on the button, Chief. It's all in the computer. My three companions have come straight from Gan in a single jump, and the echelon formation they started in has not been disturbed."

"More Immortals' magic," said Stefan in awe. "I wouldn't mind if you could leave two of those ships here. I'd even settle for one."

"You'll get a short loan when the time comes, Chief. I've been around for a long time, but I'm no scientist. Things still have to be explained to me."

"Like how a ship can open up its own wormhole?" said Stefan.

"Part of it. Half of Guppy is a current generator. There's a force from a coupling of magnetism and gravity that pushes us into another space where light speed is really high. Five minutes transit from Gan. It does boggle the mind. Nanoseconds for my ship, didn't get an eye-blink in. those scientists of our are really good, but I was worried about the timing. My companions could have overshot by a lot of light years. And the trip isn't over yet for one of them. I hope you are confident now that we can get here in a hurry when Kratolan warships start coming through the gate. My flagship is always nanoseconds away. Might be two of them when the attack comes."

"It'll take me a cycle-plus to move all my ships around to where I want them. It would be easier for us to destabilize the Kratolan side of the nexus right after their first ship comes through. That could stop the rest of them."

"Do *not* do that, please. Let the guppies handle it. We can't take chances on stabilizing the gate again quickly before our ships come through the entire nexus at high speed. Our destruction could be total."

"Okay. I'll put Novas by both Moons to protect both gates. The one leading to Gan will be their first target."

"Agreed," said Petyr. "And you'll need to know exactly when that first Kratolan ship is going to come out of the wormhole. I'm working on that, but it's not something we'll be able to do exactly. I'm sending one of the Guppies here to a place near the gate at Kratola until the attack happens. At that point, they will be joined by most of our Guppy fleet to destroy the Bishops' ships before they can even entire the wormhole, but some are certain to get through. Politics again. Kratola must strike first before we can retaliate. Our Guppy observers will get back to us with a warning when it looks like the invasion is about to begin."

"That could be very soon," said Stefan.

"The observer is leaving sooner," said Petyr. "Just watch."

And only a minute later there was a bright green flash, and one of the guppies had disappeared.

"Good hunting," said Stefan softly.

"And to all of us," said Petyr. "Without politics we could have done more. I'm sorry about that, chief."

"Me, too. When Kratolan ships begin assembling near their gate I want to know it. I'll be closing Pleasure City, and sending all the tourists home in both directions. The Bishops will probably know we're expecting their attack."

"No matter. They'll come. They're fighting to survive, and now the assassination will rattle them even more. It'll be soon, Chief, very soon. And we're going to be the victors," said Petyr.

"At a cost," said Stefan softly.

"Yeah," said Petyr. "that, too. Good luck, chief."

"That's Stefan, Petyr."

A chuckle. "Chief fits better. Now let's get this thing done."

The connection was broken before Stefan could reply.

Stefan sat and stared at the viewscreen for several minutes. One by one, the Guppies disappeared. The last one flashed lights before fading, a kind of farewell, probably from Petyr's ship already docking a the fuel facility four hundred miles away.

There was a beep from his console, another call coming in, and maybe from Pavel.

"Hello?"

"Oh, Stefan, I hate this war talk. It's making people crazy!"

It was Corinne. "What's wrong?" he asked.

"It's my father. He's throwing his weight around again. I just got a call from that ambassador woman from Gan. She wants to have me evacuated if there's any fighting in the city, and I'm not being given any choice in the matter. We talked about this, Stefan. Is there anything you can do?"

"I can talk to the Governor, Corinne. That' all. I don't think they can force you to leave, but I think it's a pretty good idea when we're having a war in your streets. You will not be safe there. It wouldn't be for long, a few cycles maybe. When things start popping, I'll feel a lot better if I know you're safe."

"Well, you're not much help," said Corinne, seething.

"And I'd go through life with that if you were killed and I wasn't there to defend you. At least consider it, love. Please?"

There was a long silence, then, "I'll think about it if you call the governor and find out who started all of this."

"Done," said Stefan. "Love you. I'm busy with war stuff. See you in two cycles."

"Too long. Wear your blues, please, for a real good time."

"Also done," said Stefan, laughing at the little joke between them, and they broke the connection.

He didn't call the governor, just waited to see if Corinne would remind him.

Stefan got out a small notebook and turned it on. In it was a detailed outline of defense structure for the port. He made several calls to wing officers on Alpha Station, port terminal and the city, and arranged a seat for himself on a C-class fighter to follow distribution of forces. In one hour he was in a co-pilot's seat, looking out through thick titanium-glass a mile above Alpha station, talking to all his people on the same line. "Alpha Station, I want four Novas to form two pairs and assign them to a Moon by each gate in the nexus. Watch will be continuous, and close proximity. Some backup personnel if you have them. If you don't, call me. I want two

Novas on point where I'm now located at all times, another above the terminal, and one orbiting Pleasure City. No Novas are ever to be grounded, even if damaged. The remainder should set up near the terminal and be ready to attack anything big that comes through the gate. Run in and out as fast as you can. Your targets will probably be heavy cruisers. If things work out properly, the guppies should be here before you have to make a second pass. Questions?"

"Fighters, sir?"

"Form an echelon above Alpha Station. I'm expecting cruisers, not carriers. If one comes in and dumps fighters, attack them in a single group. Set aside four to hover near the locks on alpha and also Pleasure city. You can use the two C-4's inside the city towards that. All shuttles will be grounded unless used by military personnel. I want military control over all the locks, in or out. I will provide troopers for it, not your concern. More questions?"

There were none.

"Then let's get to it."

The rest of the cycle, and all of the next one, he followed the placement of forces from his snug seat in the small fighter. The ship interior had not been designed for cycles of flying. There was an adequate supply of tepid water and synth bars, mostly tasteless, all of it standard fare for combat personnel. He shared it with them without complaint or comment and managed to doze an hour or so during the entire exercise.

Finally, it was finished, He sighed, and the young pilot grinned at him. "Satisfied, sir?"

"Never, but it's the best we can do. You ever been in combat, son?"

"No, sir. I'm one of the new guys, fresh out of the academy.

"Name?"

"Ronald Abel, sir."

Stefan leaned over and shook the man's hand. "Stefan Fechter, lieutenant. We're gonna win this thing, you know."

"Yes, sir. All the guys are saying that." Abel smiled. "They seem to think you know what you're doing."

"That's nice to hear. Now if y'all are correct, this war should go without a single hitch, and no casualties."

Abel sensed his sarcasm. "That doesn't sound like a war, sir."

"Indeed," said Stefan, "but it's worth trying for."

He dozed the rest of the way back to Alpha and the docking there, and went straight to his office to call Pavel, who was setting up the ground defense of the terminal and Pleasure City.

"Coming together," said Pavel. "How about those special troopers?"

"I'm sending you another platoon. The rest will stay on Alpha until the threat of attack is gone there. If we still have luck and you're still fighting, I'll send them in with rocket harnesses.

"I wish I knew exactly what we're up against. Zeke has dug out locations for only four cells, even wiped out one, still working on that, but we think there are probably twenty-five cells out there. Add it all up, and the sides are even. I'm not crazy about the odds."

"Kratola is counting on surprise. They won't get it," said Stefan.

"Okay," said Pavel. "Have you talked to Corinne?"

"Yeah. She isn't leaving and won't argue about it."

"Same here," said Pavel. "I offered to provide a guard for Carra, and she turned into a screaming banshee. She showed me a gun, and a target she'd shot with it. Arm of steel, man. Forty-five or fifty caliber, that thing. She says she'll hole up in her apartment when things get bad and shoot anything that comes through the door."

Stefan could hear the pride in Pavel's voice. "Kinda sexy, isn't it?" he said.

"Yeah, it is," said Pavel, "as long as she stays alive."

Stefan was startled by a sudden thought. "Whoa, I've got another call to make. Almost forgot it. Talk to you later."

"Okay," said Pavel, and was gone.

Stefan called Del. "Patch me through to Moon K and tell them who's calling, please."

He waited a minute, and his console buzzed.

"Hello?"

"Daniel Geranios, sir. I'm lead operator, Moon K. What can I do for you?"

"I have a question, Daniel, and your answer might affect the outcome of this little skirmish coming up soon."

"Doesn't sound little to me, sir."

"That's because it isn't. Look, my question is about the performance of your Moon. I know what it does, but I need some details."

"Ask away, sir."

"What instabilities are the Moon dealing with?"

"The vortex mouth at each exit tends to change shape, even pinch near closure in a random way. The Moon provides the energy to keep the shape constant. If the mouth gets smaller than your ship you come out in pieces. Early travelers found that out the hard way. And once you're in the wormhole you can't stop and wait for a safe exit."

"So if you turn off Moon power, the instabilities return. How quickly?"

"A second or so before a big one. After that, don't try to exit, don't even enter the wormhole."

"And how fast can you restore stability?"

"Oh, I'd give that a few seconds, sir, just to be sure."

"Okay, here's the last important question. If we were in a battle, and I call and tell you to destabilize the gate, will you hit the button and do it instantly without question?"

"I will, sir, and I think I know what you're up to."

"We can save a lot of lives, Daniel. But it must be done instantly when I call. The harder part comes later. Moon G will be the prime target of the attack. We'll do everything we can to defend it. When things quiet down a whole mess of warships will be coming through from Gan and on their way to Kratola, and both Gates will have to be open. If they're not, we'll have the disaster of a millennium."

"I understand, sir. You call, I hit the button again but give me another ten seconds to be sure."

"Thank you, Daniel. If we're still alive when this is over, I want to meet you face to face."

"That would be my pleasure, sir."

Well, I've done it, thought Stefan. But I'm the one in charge of Port Nexus safety, not Petyr. Kratola is not attacking Gan, they might only send one or two cruisers through, but I don't think so. Warning Petyr can take seconds and Guppy travel more seconds. How many heavy cruisers can come out of the Gate in twenty seconds? We must let one through, or there's no incident to declare war over. Two, maybe. More than that will be a big problem unless the Guppies are here. Petyr will really be pissed, after telling me not to do it.

Tough krack.

CHAPTER TWENTY-FOUR

Twenty-three invited guests attended the memorial service for Zuhair Pasela beneath the great dome of the tabernacle. There were a few senior military officers, and priests from the larger towns, including Kratola City, but most attendees were the wealthy captains of industry who had held up the Church of First Light during the gradual decline of public support.

They sat in straight backed chairs in sunlight streaming through transparent panes in the domed ceiling far above them. Soft, abstract electronic music was barely discernible, encouraging meditation on the life of a great man cruelly murdered by a distant enemy.

Caleb Aluna officiated the service from a portable podium and wore a black turban to cover his wound dressings. Galen and Tibor sat behind him in large, padded chairs. Beyond was the great window fronting the chamber of glowing, red plasma representing The Field, the place of infinite entropy and hidden energies, where past, present and future dwell together, creating new life from old in different form. Zuhair Pasela was now returned to The Field for renewal, and he would live again.

Caleb talked fondly and emotionally about his friend and colleague, their early days in seminary, Zuhair as teacher and mentor and a time of peace and prosperity as First Bishop when the colony worlds were in their infancy. But then the mood changed, and his voice rose in pitch and in passion as he talked about the growing corruption in the colonies, and the rise of rulers who persecuted the Church, and a failed attempt to rescue the faithful who, through lies and manipulation, were about to bring war to Kratola. And the assassination of Zuhair Pasela and near death of Caleb at the hands of Gan agents was just the beginning of it.

There were some nods of agreement from the audience, but their facial expressions said otherwise. Senior military officers were facing execution if they could not find the few AWOL troopers who were likely involved in Zuhair's murder. And the industrialists, already briefed on war plans, were anticipating huge profit losses when the gate was closed. Nicholas Zahn and his son Eckart were sitting in the front row now, and both were scowling at him.

"The time has now come for action," said Caleb loudly. "Our enemies seek to invade and rule our planet, and we can lose everything to them, living by their will and not our own if we do nothing. We cannot defeat their technology, but we can eliminate their ability to use it against us. Listen, now, for our response."

There was a long moment when there was nothing to hear, but then a hint of a vibration of the floor beneath their feet, and a faint sound, deep and distant, like waves breaking on a distant shore.

In seconds, the floor was shaking violently, and sunlight came and went from bright to dark as if blocked from view. People were holding onto their chairs and looking around to find the nearest exit.

"Do not be afraid," said Caleb loudly. "We send our warships to the gate leading to the nexus and on to the colony worlds, and when we are at the nexus, we will destroy the gate leading to both Gan and Galena, and Kratola will be safe from them forever."

Caleb raised his arms in benediction. "Blessed is the light that creates and nurtures us, and The Field that gives us new life, forever and ever. Be it so."

Only a few people remained to thank him for the service. The rest got up and rushed outside to watch the Kratolan fleet of ships rise slowly through the atmosphere before streaking away on a mission that could bring them peace instead of war.

Several miles away, two young men stood outside a friend's ranch house where they'd been hiding in a basement and watched the stream of warships climbing into the sky. "Think we started this?" asked Jule.

"Maybe," said Jon. "Wish I could take back that second shot and move it a tad to the left."

"I'm worried about Nathan. Don't know if he got our message."

"He'll be right in the middle of things. Best he don't know about mom and dad," said Jon.

"Yeah, I guess. We're not exactly safe here, either," said Jule.

* * * *

The Guppy hovered near the surface of a lone asteroid little bigger than itself at three hundred miles from the Kratolan gate. It watched with both optical and radar, with infrared detectors as well, and followed the stream of ships coming up from Kratola. There were ten C-class cruisers and seven B-class troop carriers in the little fleet, a good size for their intended mission, but pathetic in the presence of the Guppies that would wait for them.

Hours later, a second fleet of twelve cruisers came up from Kratola and spread out in a great arc around the planet, providing an additional shooting gallery for incoming Guppies/

Still more hours later, Kratolan ships had formed a line of ships, closely spaced, which now moved slowly towards the gate mouth, and it was time for warning.

The green flash of transition was mostly obscured by the asteroid. The Guppy appeared a hundred miles from Alpha Station. The message was delivered. The Guppy waited, and locals enjoyed a spectacular light show when nine more of the mammoth warships arrived near it.

There was a truly blinding flash of green light when the ten of them left on the jump to Kratola, and a battle with the Bishops' fleet there. And morale of the crews was high.

* * * *

"They're coming, Kira," said Stefan. "We don't know exactly when, but a fleet has been assembled near Kratola and is heading towards the gate entrance there. Our informant estimates the size of the fleet at a third of what the Bishops can use against us. We can put up a good fight, but there's no way we can defeat a force that size. We'll need the Guppies."

Kira frowned. "Have you heard from Petyr yet?"

"We haven't even heard from the local cell yet," said Stefan. "We don't have a direct line to them anymore. They must call us first. I don't like the arrangement. All wings are assembled and at station. I've scattered our troops among all the stations, with enhanced forces at the Moons. If there's any ground action, it'll be in the city. Their main targets will be the gate and Alpha Station."

"We knew peace wouldn't last," said Kira.

"Afraid so."

Kira struck her desk softly with the flat of her hand. "Well, we're going to deal with it. If nothing else, we can inflict a lot of damage on them before the Guppies get here."

"So let it be done," said Stefan, and he smiled. "Pavel is shutting down Pleasure City and getting everyone off the streets. We can find a safe place to hide you there until it's safe."

"Not likely, sir," said Kira. "I have my own burrow to hide in right here, and you're the one who equipped it. That's where I'll be. I'll want to know about everything going on."

"I'll respect that, but I'll also have a plan to get you out of here if any ground forces invade Dome Central, and I will not hesitate to implement it with or without your approval."

Now Kira smiled. "Understood," she said.

They parted ways with a firm handshake. Stefan went back to his office and called Pavel on the encrypted device he's been given."

"How is she doing?" asked Pavel.

"Ready for war. Our governor is a strong woman. Anything new from the Immortals?"

"Not since the warning about the Bishops' fleet. They seem to have feelers everywhere."

"Kira got a call from Petyr Vlasok assuring her again of military help from Gan when we're attacked," said Stefan.

"Ah, hah. That guy is an Immortal big wig. When I hear his name, it's spoken with a kind of reverence. Are we ready, Stefan? Do we have any chance against that fleet?"

"I'd be lying if I said we did, bud," said Stefan. "What we *can* do is cripple their forces some. The rest is up to the Guppies."

"So we wait and worry, and do our jobs."

"Heavy hangs the head, as Corinne would say."

"How's she doing?"

"She's in her office, and refuses to leave, but she knows a Gan embassy team is coming to evacuate her if the fighting spreads to the streets. Last time I saw her she showed me her gun, and it's not a little one. I'm worried about her, Pavel. I'm worried about you, too. Be careful."

"I have a precinct building full of cops here," said Pavel. "Watch your ass, Chief."

"And yours, too," said Stefan.

CHAPTER TWENTY-FIVE

Their first warning came with a public announcement of the coming attack, shop closures and an imposed curfew on both levels. All the glitter on level two was gone, and there was only the soft glow of streetlights to navigate by. Ground taxis were shuttling disgruntled and scared tourists back to the hotels, but they did so willingly. The blaring warnings from police vehicles about a coming invasion had frightened people badly. Even though dark cycle had ended on level one, red light conditions remained in the dome and transportation within it had become scarce.

Ramon Dion had heard reports from travelers early in the cycle about the movement of military ships beyond the plasteel shell surrounding Pleasure City, and the sudden presence of armed troopers on second level.

He wondered how the Bishops' plan had been discovered so quickly.

And as lead officer of the cells operating in Port Nexus, it was his duty to warn them.

He finally found a taxi driver whose shift was ending, and he was returning to home on first level. After Ramon's fast talking and some lies about a sick mother, the driver agreed to take Ramon home for double the usual fee. The driver never realized how fortunate he was that Ramon wasn't carrying his sidearm at the time. Ramon would have happily killed him for the overcharge, and also because he was an enemy. And the thick screen between driver and passenger in the taxi prevented strangulation as an option.

Ramon did not dare to use his communicator. All lines were probably being listened to during the emergency. He hadn't heard from either Tralyn or Vafar since before the chaos had begun. He could only hope they were at their safe house when he arrived. One quick message to a shuttle still cleared to leave the gate and the Bishops would be warned. And that hidden, single channel could be operated remotely from the safe house. If Tralyn or Vafar were there, in fact, the message had probably already been sent.

He heard otherwise when he arrived at the unassuming little house not far from the industrial district on level one. He waited until the taxi had gone away, then walked up to the darkened house and knocked on the door four times. He waited ten seconds, and then knocked twice again.

The door opened, and Tralyn beckoned him inside and closed the door behind him. "We have a bad situation here."

"Have you sent a warning to Caleb yet? There will be no surprise attack here."

"We tried," said Tralyn, "but the channel didn't respond. We have a connection, but there's no recognition. Something has gone wrong, and we'll have to go there to fix it."

They entered a dark room dimly lit in one corner where a man was hunched over a table and a box the size of a bread loaf.

"Any luck, Valfar?" said Tralyn.

"Nothing," said the man. "when I put in the first three numbers everything is looking fine, but when I put in the fourth it gives me a red light. The connection is fine, but the code has gotten scrambled. We must reprogram manually."

"The relay is only a mile away," sid Ramon.

"In the dark, and there are some police vehicles cruising around to enforce curfew," said Valfar.

"They'll never see us," said Tralyn. He went to a desk and pulled out a heavy caliber pistol. "If they do, it'll be unfortunate for them." He pulled out two smaller weapons.

"Each of you take one of these. We're all going."

Ramon stuffed his weapon in a coat pocket. They turned out the light and left by the back door. The relay was hidden in a locked storage room in a warehouse for electrical machinery less than a mile distant. They had traveled to and from the place several times by foot without being seen. They went down back streets and alleys and along a canal pipe filled with factory effluent to the backside of the warehouse, squinting in weak amber light from streetlamps along the way. A small door there was padlocked, and Tralyn unlocked it. Inside, weak yellow light came from bulbs hanging from a high ceiling. A few crates were scattered around the floor, but the place was mostly empty, and shadows filled all the corners around them. They went straight to a small, locked door near some crates, and unlocked it. Bright light from a lamp there made the squint.

The relay was the size of a large suitcase, with several switches on a flat front panel. A green light pulsed there. Vafar took out a screwdriver and began work to remove the front panel.

"Well, at last we have a chance to meet," said a voice behind them.

All of them jumped, and turned around, their hands reaching for the weapons they carried.

Four men, faces dark in the gloom, stood in a semi-circle in front of them. Faint light gleamed from things they had in their hands.

Vafar never had a chance to reach his weapon and brandished his screwdriver. Tralyn and Ramon pulled their guns and were fumbling with triggers when the warehouse lit up in a blaze of light and the sound of rapid gunfire was a loud buzz that went on for seconds.

Vafar, Tralyn and Ramon collapsed to the floor in bloody heaps with dark pools of blood oozing out from beneath their bodies.

"Three less to worry about," said Zeke.

"What about the relay?" said another man.\

"Bring it along. It might be useful for the strike on Kratola."

The men took the relay, left the bodies where they'd fallen, left the warehouse, and locked the front door behind them.

* * * *

Stefan had his usual meeting with Kira during the last two hours of red light, had a cafeteria synth breakfast and was back in his office when his special communicator buzzed in his ear.

"This is Stefan Fechter," he said.

"This is Petyr. A fleet of Kratolan warships has approached the gate. The attack will be within hours now. They are leading their attack with heavy cruisers. We have approval on Gan, and I've designated two Guppies to help in your fight. The rest will head to Kratola. We're experiencing some delays in getting this all together, but we'll try hard not to be late. Have faith in our coming support, Chief. Together, we will prevail."

There was a chirp, and the encrypted line went dead.

Sounded like a recording, thought Stefan. So, the battle for control of Port Nexus was about to begin, and Stefan Fechter was in charge of its defense. There were reasons for confidence. He had a lifetime of military schooling and leadership. He had acquired expertise in the strategies of war during a long military career. But there was that one negative that now chewed at the edges of his self-confidence. In all those years of study and experience he had not once led an entire military unit into combat. School was over, and it was time for a final examination.

And Stefan felt confident about passing it.

He called Pavel, and found he'd received the same message at the same time. The defense plan was in place, their forces at assigned stations, the wing commanders briefed on the strategies for defense. Stefan had anticipated an initial thrust from ships with heavy weapons, and had added torpedo launching Novas that might hopefully clear the gate exit from damaged or destroyed vessels.

A total shutdown of Port Nexus went into effect minutes after Stefan and Pavel had been warned. Red light conditions prevailed everywhere. On Alpha, all non-military personnel went to emergency bunkers on first level where there was food, sanitary facilities and oxygen supplies that would last for several cycles.

Hatches were closed and locked on the great Moons that controlled the stability of the Gate exits. Inside, technical crews of only a few souls were now separated from their families and in charge of a monumental system of charged plates and magnets that manipulated the fluctuating vacuum energy fields of creation to fine tune the shape of spacetime fabric around the gate exits.

Within an hour, there was general panic in Pleasure City and Pavel had his entire force on the streets to maintain order and force people to places of safety. The shuttle port was closed to all but military vessels, and many tourists found themselves suddenly trapped in the city. All casinos and entertainment centers were in the process of closing and the windows of many shops were grilled shut. Suddenly there was no place to get a meal, and it was the tourists who panicked. Most of the local residents had already reached their homes where there was a standard safe room sealed off and stocked with provisions in case there was ever a break in the great plasteel sphere surrounding the city.

Hotels herded their guests into safety bunkers in basements and the accommodations were soon full and cramped. Tourists without hotel accommodations were chased down and rounded up by the police and taken to large public shelters in several places around the city. There were no beds, only water and oxygen, and a limited supply of food was brought in later.

They all knew war was coming, and all of them were terrified.

But by the end of the cycle, all were in a safe place, and all of Port Nexus was a dark void beyond the greenish swirls of the Gate towards which a terrible force was moving. With only hours left before the battle began, Stefan was taken to a command ship stationed beyond Alpha to oversee the operation. Pavel remained in his precinct office to look after the safety of Pleasure City. Alpha Station was occupied by a company of heavily armed troopers, and a governor who kept in touch with everyone through open channels to her basement bunker.

And then, just thirty-six Gan hours after they had been warned, the great, greenish swirl of spacetime at the wormhole exit began to glow brightly. Something big was coming through there.

CHAPTER TWENTY-SIX

The vee-shaped snout of a Kratolan heavy cruiser rushed out of the swirling mists of the wormhole exit and sent a cloud of missiles and torpedoes towards Moon G. Totally surprised by the rapid targeting, Stefan screamed "Return fire!" to whomever was listening, for he had open channels to every position in his defense force and at the fuel station some four hundred miles distant. "Petyr, we're under attack. Send the Guppies!"

An audible click was a response. As the cruiser cleared the Gate, it was hit by missiles from the Novas by Moon G and there was a satisfying ball of fire near amidships as it turned. The missiles it had fired were aimed with high accuracy and all struck the Moon at the same time. Most exploded with little effect against the densely armored surface of the Moon, but one made a direct hit on the entrance lock and blew open a hole a hundred feet square, beyond which there had once been a control room manned by five souls.

Stefan stared in horror as the Gate leading to Gan and Galena suddenly flared brightly and began to boil.

"Moon G, anyone there?" yelled Stefan, with hope that the backup crew in the armored safe room had somehow survived.

There was no reply.

Another cruiser was coming out of the Gate, now met by fire from four Novas, while the first one, showing fire in the interior, turned left from the Gate and fired a single torpedo into the terminal platform of Port Nexus. The explosion was blinding, shards of hot metal thrown out from fire become plasma, and the ship turned again, heading outwards from the gate as a third cruiser rushed out of the wormhole.

"Moon K, copy?" yelled Stefan, "At my command?"

"Ready, sir," came the reply.

Three cruisers already facing them, and more coming, the situation was already marginal. "Where are my Guppies?" he shouted.

`A short reply this time. "Hang on, we're coming!"

Two more torpedoes struck the first cruiser and Stefan's view screen was overloaded by a brilliant orange flash as the ship detonated like a fusion weapon, leaving little in the way of debris, but now two cruisers were rushing past where it had been on their way out towards Stefan's position near Station alpha.

A fourth cruiser came out of the Kratolan Gate and right behind it a boxy carrier ship covered with rotating missile domes, and that was enough for Stefan.

"Moon K, close the Gate!" he screamed, and felt satisfaction when the Kratolan Gate almost immediately began to boil, but he did not expect what happened next.

The Gate instability was quickly extreme: boiling, changing shape, pinching together in places, and within a second there was an explosive eruption of fire and seared metal spewing forth from the wormhole to fill half of the nexus between Gates with flaming debris until suddenly ceasing.

Much more had been coming at them from inside the wormhole and at incalculable speed but had arrived in flaming pieces and gas.

And there would be no more attacking forces coming at them from Kratola.

Still, three cruisers and a carrier were enough, and now they were heading towards Alpha, leaving behind a ruined terminal and an unstable Gate closing traffic to Gan.

"Moon G, answer!"

His heart leapt when there was a reply.

"Here, sir. Our door was blocked, and we're suited up. We have five dead, and the control console is really messed up."

"I need the Gate stabilized as fast as you can do it!"

"We'll try, sir. Out."

Back on his screen, three cruisers were still coming at him, now chased by two Novas, and then two more Novas rushed by his vessel to join the fight. But behind the cruisers came the blocky carrier ship, and a dozen missile domes were now concentrated on the pursuing Novas, and then there was a hit, and another, and one of the Novas was veering away in flames.

And then the bowels of the big carrier opened, and a swarm of fighters came out like angry insects to reinforce the attack on Alpha Station and the administrative center for Port Nexus.

Within a minute, the fighter squadrons from Alpha came to greet them in what would become the bloodiest encounter in the battle for Port Nexus.

The fighters came out of the carrier like a spreading fan. He estimated over a hundred, all with seasoned pilots. Stefan's pilots were all young, recently schooled, and had never flown in combat. But the one thing they were not short on was courage, and they flew at the attacking Kratolan ships like suicidal zealots, and Stefan heard the screams and curses of their wing commanders as they fought—and died.

For Stefan, it was a terrible thing to hear, a thing that would not leave his dreams for years to come.

Flashes of fire in the blackness of space, each flash the death of a pilot, a young man with a girlfriend or a family, maybe on Kratola, Gan or Galena, like two swarms of bees having come together in a dance of death. But as the battle went on, Stefan was surprised to see that they were holding their own, though the losses on both sides were terrible. The fight had been going on for nearly half an hour, and still no Guppies had arrived to help him. The three remaining cruisers were getting closer to his position, close enough that one had chanced an early missile launch of just one weapon, and it was now racing towards them.

"No sweat, sir," said the pilot. "We've time to intercept, but when they get close, it's the multiple shots that'll take us out."

A missile streaked away from his command ship, and thirty seconds later there was a satisfying flash of light when the incoming missile was destroyed.

For a fraction of a second, Stefan's confidence wavered. *Blast it, Corinne, I wanted to marry you*, he thought

"Retreat, sir?" asked the pilot.

"Not likely," said Stefan, now furious, and then, "Damn it, Petyr, *where are my Guppies?*" It was a shriek, and he pounded a console with both fists, and then heard a voice that made his heart stop for a single beat.

"Here, Chief," said Petyr.

* * * *

One by one the Guppies arrived in Kratolan space until there were twenty of them in a tight formation near the single Guppy that had been watching the Kratolan Gate. The watcher had done its first job of warning Port Nexus of the coming attack, and then returned with companions for the attack on Kratola itself. If all went well, forty light warships from Gan would be coming through the wormhole to clean up after the Guppies, but the plan for that had been made in three distinct phases. First, attack and destroy any Kratolan warships in the vicinity of the Gate on the Kratolan end of the wormhole. Second, destroy all ships defending Kratola from strategic positions around the planet, and three, destroy the Bishops' palace, the Tabernacle of First Light, and any major military positions in Kratola City.

Twenty-one Guppies were now in position for phase one.

The distance to the wormhole was too short for a dimensional jump with any accuracy, so the Guppies had begun to move when warships were observed entering the Gate. Flight time was estimated to be just over a minute, but a few seconds into their flight a strange phenomenon was observed. The tight cluster of Kratolan ships at the Gate suddenly scattered in all directions as an explosion of matter and flame burst from the wormhole, debris catching two smaller ships and smashing them to pieces. It was several seconds before the eruption ceased, leaving the Guppies' intended targets scattered in all directions and at low density. The plan to intercept them in a tight cluster and use a combined transport field generated by twenty-one ships to send them to places unknown was suddenly dissolved.

For a Guppy, using missiles, torpedoes and rail guns was always the hard way to do things.

They were coming in fast, and the reaction of their targets seemed sluggish and disorganized, perhaps due to the eruption they'd just experienced coming out of the Gate. There were three echelons, with three commanders. Petyr was not one of them. The echelons came in as a vee, and loosed missiles and torpedoes simultaneously in a widespread, but each weapon locked on a specific target.

There is no sound to hear in space, no medium to transmit the screams of the dying.

Thirty-four Kratolan ships exploded simultaneously and produced a spectacular light display that could be seen on the surface of the planet. The rest of the ships streaked away towards the planet, and the Guppies gave chase.

And phase two was not so easy as the first one, as the Guppies soon experienced in a terrible way.

As the enemy ships sped ahead of them, The Guppies slowed for observations. Commander Enid Stark had taken Petyr's place at the last minute when the first reincarnation of Loenid Zylak had decided to personally fulfill a promise to the defense chief at Port Nexus.

He studied the scans and saw the heavy cruisers in orbit above Kratola as a primary line of defense. In numbers, the enemy ships had an advantage of two to one, but such a number was meaningless when dealing with the Guppy technology of the Immortals. Guppies could be damaged by cruiser fire; such had been shown in the skirmish at Port Nexus some years ago. But their size and armor and weapons platforms were simply overwhelming to any ship known to Gan's military science. His ships would each select a pair of targets and then attack them individually, and their weapons alone would overwhelm any cruiser.

It was an oversight that would haunt him the rest of his life, for it was based on an agreement between Gan, Galena and Kratola from centuries past, an agreement that was about to be broken by the Council of Bishops at their own doorstep.

The Guppies plummeted towards the orbiting cruisers, spreading out to their respective targets, and coming within missile range without bothering to use projected transport fields requiring high energies.

The cruisers responded with missile fire that had little chance of penetrating nose armor of any Guppy.

The missiles impacted with the first three Guppies that reached their targets.

And it seemed as if the very light of creation suddenly filled the universe, overloading every Guppy viewscreen in the fleet. Communications were in and out for nearly a minute, and computers spoke in strange tongues before recovering from the horrible pulse from the nuclear explosions.

"Fusion weapons! Turn on your fields! They're using fusion weapons!" screamed Stark over and over as all electronic systems struggled to revive themselves. Only a Guppy could have withstood such a pulse.

But three Guppies were gone, a few pieces of blackened metal floating from the planet. And fifteen hundred men had been vaporized.

"Take them out with the field! Don't let them flank you," screamed Stark. A missile was headed towards his ship, but his field was now on, a greenish bubble projected some thousand feet in front of a long, pointed snout.

The missile reached it—and vanished.

All the Guppies were now lit up in green, all on collision trajectories with their targets.

The cruisers fired their ordinance, and watched it vanish, and then the Guppies were on them.

In less than half an hour there were no cruisers left in orbit around Kratola, and the smaller ships had fled back to the surface.

The Guppies regrouped. There was no cheering among the crews. There was only a seething anger.

Stark's brief message was piped to all crews. "We've suffered a terrible loss today at the hands of evil people who are without honor, but now it is our turn. When we get to the surface, our targets are the Bishops' palace, the tabernacle and the military installation nearby."

He paused, then, "I have only one wish when we get there, but Petyr will have to decide it when he returns to lead our attack"

"Nobody lives."

The hoots of thousands were his reply.

* * * *

Stefan's viewscreen lit up brightly as the approaching cruiser was struck port side by a tight stream of missiles and a single torpedo that penetrated deeply to the magazine before exploding, and the entire ship was now a ball of plasma hurrying towards his command ship. His pilot swerved to avoid it and nearly ran into one of two Guppies that were suddenly in their midst, snouts glowing green and all weapons ports firing.

The two remaining cruisers veered away, and within seconds were ripped to pieces by railgun and missile fire by the Guppies.

"I thought there were more," said Petyr.

"There were. They were coming in fast, and I had to stop them without the Guppies being here. I closed the Gate to Kratola, Petyr. The instability destroyed the rest of their ships. That's where all the debris in the nexus came from."

"Damn it, Chief! We talked about that!" yelled Petyr.

"I've been assured we can turn it back on quickly. That's not the problem. The first cruiser got in a fatal shot on Moon G, and the Gate to Gan is also down. A backup crew is working on it. The controls are badly damaged. Whoa!"

Stefan winced as a flaming fighter narrowly missed his ship, carrying a dead pilot to his grave in outer space.

"Hope it wasn't one of ours."

"It wasn't," said Petyr. "I saw a crown emblem on it. We can't help with the fighters without endangering your people, but we're going after the carrier right now."

"I'll call Moon G and get you an update. Good hunting."

Stefan called, got an immediate answer.

"How's it going?"

"Not as bad as it looks. The entire console is junk. The computer was scrambled, but we have a backup cube, and the program should be up in a few hours. We just found one of the leads to the field generator, but there are two others buried in all this krack. It'll be at least a few hours, Chief, unless we find those leads pretty quick."

"The Guppies have smashed the attack, but we still have a firefight here. Gan will be waiting to bring their big fleet through the Gate to finish off Kratola. As soon as you're up, I need to know it instantly."

"Got it, sir. We'll give it all we've got."

"Who am I talking to?" asked Stefan.

"Aaron Silver, sir, Tech 4."

"When this is over, I want to meet you, Aaron."

"Yes, sir."

Stefan called Petyr to tell him what he'd heard and suddenly saw a huge ball of orange and blue fire expanding not far from the Kratolan Gate.

"What's that new explosion from?" he asked.

"Carrier. Guppy 3 got it with two rail projectiles and a torpedo. Let's see how Kratola's fighter pilots react to *that*. They have nothing to go back to."

Maybe it'll stop the dying, thought Stefan. He told Petyr what he'd heard from Moon G.

"That is not good news," said Petyr. "I have much of our fleet waiting at the Gan Gate. I'm not going to tie up a Guppy running back and forth with news. One message, and quick, when everything is ready. If something goes wrong, you and I will be living with it the rest of our lives unless the grieving families kill us first, and Gan won't have a war fleet anymore except for Guppies."

"We can start by cleaning out the nexus. That's going to take some time. I'm reassigning our Novas to help with the enemy fighters."

"Okay. I'll talk to our pilots. We can use our transporter fields and clear the Nexus, but carefully. If we get too close to a Gate, our fields could interact with the wormhole, and that would be interesting only to a scientist, which I am not. But I don't think it'll take long, and we'll get right to it."

Stefan called the Nova pilots and sent their ships against the Kratolan fighters. A Nova had the advantage of heavy armor and carried much more ordinance than a fighter.

The fight continued for nearly another hour. The Kratolan pilots, without a carrier to return to, fought bravely to the end. Many died with their weapons killing, others when they ran out of fuel or ammunition. There were no escape pods on a fighter, and no mercy shown by the pilots of Port Nexus. In the end, it was the fighters for Port Nexus that limped back to Station Alpha with a casualty rate of eighty percent, and the Kratolan ships were all gone.

Stefan called Pavel to hear what was going on in the city and got no answer. The man was probably engaged in a firefight. More people dying, and it was now up to the defensive forces he and Stefan had placed there.

Like colossal vacuum cleaners the Guppies worked their greenish transportation generators one at a time to clean out the debris in the two-mile space between gates and send it all to parts unknown in some universe. Everyone's heart stopped for a beat or two when the Gan Gate suddenly stabilized, and then was roiling again when a Guppy was dangerously near. This happened several times as the Guppies finished their task after nearly three hours had passed.

The wait was terrible. Stefan and Petyr both thinking about all the things that could go wrong, a collision with unseen debris in the Nexus, the destruction of a fleet and the deaths of thousands in a sudden disturbance in the wormhole again.

And then the time came. Stefan received the call just short of four hours after repairs on Moon G had begun.

"Got it, sir," said Aaron. "It's not pretty, but it should work. I have the board in my lap here. Watch the gate. Power on…"

The Gan Gate of roiling spacetime suddenly brightened with the focus of residual gas and debris, and the roiling ceased as if stopped by a great hand. There were hoots from Moon G, and a sudden call from Moon K.

"Ready to turn the Gate back on, sir."

"Do it," said Stefan, and held his breath. His worry was unfounded; the Gate to Kratola was on and totally stable within a few seconds. But how long would it all remain stable?

Petyr was thinking the same thing. "I'm supposed to send my fleet through when a guy has the control board sitting in his lap? Once the guys at the other end get the order, there's no turning back."

"Better do it quick, then," said Stefan, and felt a bit impatient about it.

In the space of ten seconds, Guppy 3 flashed green and was gone.

The wait was short, but even more terrible than before. Once inside the wormhole, transit was instantaneous, but it was two minutes before their senses were reeled by what came through the Nexus.

The Gan fleet came through nose to tail, out one Gate and into another, a high velocity stream of vessels, ordinance and fighting men. Stefan lost count in only a few seconds, and all the time Petyr was screaming in his ear, "Go, go, GO!"

The Nexus was suddenly empty, and Stefan's chest hurt.

For a minute or so, he'd forgotten to breathe.

"Good job, Chief," said Petyr.

"There's probably fighting in the city. I haven't heard from Pavel."

"I got one report early. It started at the shuttle field, and the people you had stationed there. That was hour ago. I'll check again."

There was a flash of green, and Guppy 3 was back, only now it was hovering near Pleasure City.

Petyr came back. "There's fighting in the streets. Guppy 3 has orders to pic up evacuees from the city. Sounds like it's getting wild. I'm leaving, chief. Have to get back to Kratola."

Petyr's ship left with a brilliant flash of green.

Corinne, thought Stefan. *Be safe, my love.*

He was still thinking this as his command ship passed near the city on his way back to Station Alpha. A shuttle popped out of the big lock above the city proper and headed straight to Guppy 3, entered a bay in the belly of the ship and disappeared.

Guppy 3 flashed green and vanished a moment later.

But as his ship neared Station Alpha, Pavel finally returned his call and gave him the news about the fighting in Pleasure City.

And for Stefan, the news was life shattering.

CHAPTER TWENTY-SEVEN

The wait had been long and monotonous, but orders had finally arrived. The attack was set for 0700 and a truck would be there to pick them up at 0645. Their target would be the shuttle terminal with one other squad or two. Fortunately, they were given a full cycle's warning, and Nathan had had a chance at work to pass a message to Zeke. He'd only done it twice before, when his cell was up to strength at eight, and when their rifles and limited ammo had arrived.

Cell morale was not good. Before arrival they'd been told there would be three hundred of them going up against less than a hundred police, but that had all changed. They'd watched maneuvers of highly trained troops dropping with rocket harnesses from VTOL's flying over the city and counted well over a hundred of them.

Receipt of their weapons made it worse. The T-40's were good rifles, but two generations old, and a per man supply of ten magazines was ridiculous for extended fighting.

For Nathan's squad, from the grumbling he'd heard, their little skirmish at the terminal was likely a distraction from action elsewhere, and its proximity to the nearby military installation could easily turn it into a suicide mission.

The men were up and dressed at 0500. The uniform of the day was civvies with heavy jackets and black stocking caps to cover their faces. The black bands on their jacket sleeves identified them as Black Hats of Kratola in service to the Bishops, and proud of it.

But that had been the feeling when they first arrived.

They were ready at 0600 and waited in silence, each man lost in his own thoughts. Nathan's were focused on survival. He was being sent into a battle he had worked to subvert, for a government he hated for the murder of his parents, but he had a strong desire to be alive when it was all over.

He did not think the Black Hats would be the champions of the day. He would have to avoid being killed by both sides while trying to avoid killing *anyone* himself, and this would not be a simple task.

In battle, shooting himself in foot or leg would be too obvious, and his own squad leader might shoot him for that.

A fall, hitting his head on an obstacle, was a possibility once inside the terminal. Getting there would be a dodge running game to stay alive.

In battle, he could blaze away randomly and empty his magazines. Then hide out and give up when it was over.

But stay alive.

They waited—and waited. 0630 came, and 0645, and no truck was there for them. Men looked at each other nervously and gripped their rifles tightly.

"Something's wrong," said one of them.

"I don't hear any shooting," said another.

Suddenly a truck pulled up outside, and the men all jumped to their feet. Men with black hoods jumped down from the truck and came towards the house.

There was a pounding on the door, and Nathan's squad leader didn't hesitate to open it. "You're late!" he yelled, and then reached for his side-arm. "No arm bands!" he screamed.

A burst of automatic fire drove the squad leader backwards against a wall as five men rushed through the doorway, carrying black, compact assault rifles.

Men hurried to unsling the T-40's they carried. Nathan made a move towards it but hesitated.

Gunfire cut down four of the other men who were with him.

One of the house invaders stepped up to Nathan and smacked him hard on one side of his face with the butt of his assault rifle.

Nathan saw lights flashing and fell to the floor with a moan.

"Don't shoot! Please!" said someone.

"Get them out to the truck," said another.

A very familiar voice.

Nathan looked up, the room still spinning. One side of his face was numb, and his speech was slurred.

A man looked down at him, the muzzle of his weapon held six inches from Nathan's nose.

"My fugging jaw is broken," mumbled Nathan.

"Yeah, but you're still alive, and we'll send you home that way. Now get up on your feet."

"Truss 'em up, get 'em in the truck and deliver them. We've got a fight to finish."

Nathan was jerked to his feet, hands tied behind him and led outside. Only three men were left alive in his squad. He groaned as hands lifted him up onto the bed of the truck, and then had another shock when he saw the bodies of eight dead men there.

How many are left to attack the terminal? he wondered.

In answer, he heard gunfire coming from the direction of the terminal as the truck pulled away from the house.

* * * *

Elton Stewart had been sitting in the van for six hours, and now he had to wait some more while the rest of them got their armor on. When you're an ambassador's hired gun, he mused, you're expected to put up with stuff, but the original assignment was getting more complicated by the hour.

Evacuation of important people before a firefight is no big deal, van to shuttle to Guppy and back again. But then one client, whose father is paying part of the bill, including my salary, refuses evacuation until there's fighting at her front door. Procedure unchanged, now bullets are flying around. Pay is better by three for a combat situation, but now I can get my ass shot off earning it. Then Ambassador Uzelac wants our severely wounded people evacuated, too. Pay goes up again, but now I need two med techs, two vans and six troopers, and here I sit, waiting for the troopers. There *is* an upside. I might get a chance to kill a Kratolan terrorist or two.

It was half an hour before the troopers arrived, all puffed up with their armor and fancy assault rifles like his strung across their chests, and they squeezed in behind the drivers of the nine passenger vans from the ambassador's office. The vans were parked by two shuttles, one of them assigned to Uzelac and sporting an R-53 canon in the nose that could cut a large truck in two in seconds. A pilot had been seated, and the engine was now gently warming.

Over two cycles a concrete block perimeter had been established around the shuttle terminal and adjacent military barracks, and the vans were parked well inside it. Troops and heavy auto-fire mounts were scattered around the perimeter and had been in place for ten hours. Any attack was expected to come from the downtown area.

And it occurred at 0710.

At a distance, a line of large trucks was observed coming towards them at high speed along the main road from downtown. All trucks were packed with standing men, and rifles bristled among them.

One pass with an R-53 and this fight won't even get started, thought Elton.

"Hold fire for maximum kill," murmured a trooper behind him.

Two hundred yards out the trucks veered and spread into an arc centered on the barracks without reducing speed and were nearing the barricade of concrete blocks in seconds.

"Ready to fire," murmured a trooper.

We gonna shake hands with them? Thought Elton, and then, only thirty yards out the trucks came to screeching halts to dump their cargoes of armed men who fired as they ran towards the barrier, screaming like banshees. They wore civilian clothes with heavy coats and black cloth bands on the sleeves.

"Fire!"

Defenders crouched and opened fire, and blossoms of flame burst from heavy weapons along the barricade.

Even for a gun man, watching the slaughter was difficult. The defenders were young, newly trained, but their trainers had given them more than lessons in marksmanship. A screaming man coming at you with a weapon and death in his eyes at a distance of thirty yards leaves you with no time for thought, no pause for reflection. And the young troopers of Port Nexus paused only a fraction of a second before squeezing off a hastily aimed shot or sweeping their forward area with a burst of fire.

Dead or dying men crashed into the concrete barrier and lay still. A few leaped over the barriers and sprinted towards their objectives as the defenders turned around and sighted more carefully.

Three men made it to the front doors of the terminal, where they were shot dead by four policemen stationed inside. Seven reached the front steps of the barracks before being gunned down from the barricade.

The entire action lasted three minutes, with no defenders killed and five wounded.

Ninety-two terrorists would never see a sunrise again, and thirty three would be taken from the field with serious to critical wounds and then pose a problem for the limited hospital facilities in Pleasure City.

And through all of this, the evacuation vans waited with frightened occupants hunkered down to avoid a stray bullet coming through a windshield and looking for a signal to begin an evacuation.

And it was only several more seconds before they got it.

There was a distant boom, and a small shock wave passed beneath the van. A large, roiling black cloud of smoke and debris rose above the central part of the city.

"That's us!" shouted Elton. He started the van's engine and turned on the headlights while swerving right to get around the barrier near the terminal building. The other van followed behind him.

They raced back to town along the main road. The trucks that had brought in the assault force had quickly fled during the brief firefight and were nowhere to be seen.

As they came nearer, the debris cloud seemed to be rising from the middle of downtown and they could see flames far ahead of them. They were passing through an old residential area, but nobody was outside.

A small truck was on fire in the middle of the street, and there were two bodies sprawled near it. The column of smoke boiled from a nearby building frontage now crumbled and blackened by soot, and Elton recognized it with a shock.

"They bombed the police station!" he shouted, and saw two men running towards the van, wearing black arm bands and aiming rifles at him. He veered the van as shots rang out from a nearby building and the men dropped on their faces in the street. Another group was across the street, sliding from door to door, heading towards the Red Palace Casino where a man was carrying a ladder inside while another held the door open for him. The terrorists shot both men and headed towards the open door.

"They're attacking the casino. That's where our client is!" Elton swerved across the street, up on the sidewalk. The terrorists saw him coming and rushed inside.

Both vans stopped together at the front entrance, and everyone jumped out, Elton screaming commands.

"Follow me! Troops first, med tech last."

There were two sharp explosions inside the casino, and people screamed.

Elton rushed through the open door, troopers on his heels. A man was on his knees, hands clapped over his ears. Several people had crowded under tables in terror. There was another explosion at the back of the room, and then a burst of gunfire and more screams.

No powder smells. They were using flash bombs for concussive disorientation, ordinarily used by police. In a crouch, Elton led his troops to the back of the room. An elevator was there but was not operating. The door to a stairwell next to it had been blown off its hinges by gunfire. Elton could hear boots on stairs above. He leveled his weapon. "Shoot anything that moves." he said and went up the stairs with eight people crowded in behind him. He heard a scream, and a door slamming, and then a man yelled, "Come out of there, bitch!! Break it down!"

As he reached the top of the stairs there was a sound of a door splintering, and then two shots from what sounded like a pistol and a woman screamed, "You!"

It was a reception area, an open door to an office beyond. Two men lay on top of a broken door in the doorway. Seven men were in the reception area, turning as Elton came through the entrance with his weapon on full auto and the first three troopers behind him opened fire, all of them spraying the room with death.

There was an explosion of rifle fire from the adjacent office. Elton saw a man there with a rifle and shot twice until his magazine was empty, and the man fell to the floor on his knees.

Elton pushed through the doorway ahead of the others and was the first to see the tragedy there. There was a desk, and beside it a woman was sitting on the floor with her back up against the wall. Her right chest was covered with blood, and blood spattered the wall behind her. A pistol was still tightly gripped in her right hand, and her head lolled to one side, mouth open, skin ashen.

"Medic!" screamed Elton. "See to the woman! One minute *sooner*! She's our evacuee. Medic!"

The medics pushed past him and knelt down by the woman. "Still alive," said one, "but it's bad. We have to get her to a Guppy fast. The locals can't handle this."

"Call the shuttle!" Elton beckoned to a trooper who was already doing it. "Take the second van and kill anyone who tries to stop you. You and you go with the medics and the patient. The rest of will deal with this piece of krack shooter here."

"Looks like she got two of them before they got her," said a trooper.

The shooter was on his knees, a shattered rifle lying in front of him, and his hands were clasped together behind his hooded head.

Elton reached down and ripped the hood from the man's head. A bloated face with swollen lips and greasy black hair glared up at him.

"A little old for a terrorist, aren't you? Retired military? Look at you, fugger. Broken rifle, and I broke it. You're not even shot, but you assume the position to keep it that way. Well, I might kill you right now."

Elton put his rifle muzzle against the man's forehead. "What d'ya think, asshole?"

"Coming through," said a medic. The two men had lifted the woman up and were in a hurry to leave the room with her."

"Wait a damn minute!" screamed Elton. "She was supposed to have scans with her, and some other things. Where are they? We *have* to have the scans!"

One medic pointed behind the desk. "A little bag and a metal case are over here."

A trooper stepped over to retrieve them, picked up a small cloth bag and an aluminum case.

"Check the case," said Elton. The trooper put the things on the desk and opened the unlocked case. "Here it is," he said, "crystal disks in plastic sheets and a portable scanner, all in one case. Wow, this is expensive."

"Take it. Guard it with your life," said Elton. "Now get her out of here."

"Shuttle called," said another trooper. "They're ready for her and have four other criticals stacked up and ready to go."

"Go, GO!" shouted Elton, and the woman and her possessions were carried out of the room and down the stairs to the casino where a small group of people was anxiously waiting. There were cries of dismay when they saw the medics and who they were carrying. Both men and women were sobbing, and one woman cried out, "We love you, Corinne" as they reached the front entrance and the van waiting to rush them to the shuttle and on to the Guppy hovering above the city.

Upstairs, Elton poked the forehead of the shooter with his assault rifle. "Name, rank and serial number might save your life."

The shooter glared up at him in silence.

"No talkie, no livee," said Elton.

The man smirked at him, and Elton poked him hard with the gun muzzle.

"No? If it was up to me, you'd be dead right now, but the security chief here will probably want to question you, so we'll just hand you over to the locals and get back to cleaning up the mess you poor excuses for soldiers have made here."

"They have holding cells in the precinct station," said a trooper.

"Call them now. Tell them what happened here, and what we've got."

The trooper went into the outer office to make the call.

When Elton looked down at the shooter again there was fear showing in the man's eyes, but he remained silent.

"Feeling the heat, are you? Good. I really hope they kill your ass, even if it goes counter to the rules of war. Killers of woman, children and puppies should be exceptions to those rules.

A minute later the trooper returned after calling the police. "They patched me through to the Police chief and I told him what happened, and he got pretty excited. He asked me to describe the shooter, and I did it, and then he got really pissed and said he's shoot anyone who left this room before he got here in a few minutes, and then he hung up on me."

Now the shooter's eyes were wide with fear. Elton looked down at him, and grinned. "Oh, that doesn't sound too good for you, does it? I think we'll just hang around a bit to see what happens."

CHAPTER TWENTY-EIGHT

Pavel and his police force of forty men were well positioned for over an hour before the attack occurred. Everyone had agreed that the shuttle terminal, military camp and precinct station would be the primary targets in the city. Pavel emptied the station of all personnel except for the officers who remained in the well-fortified holding cell area in the back of the building to handle prisoners if the need arose. The rest he dispersed in pairs at many points within the casino district on second level and at two places in old-town to watch for terrorist movements.

The focus was on two blocks either side of the Precinct Station. Ten snipers looked over the area from second story windows while others huddled in ground floor shops and cafes. Everything in the street was covered by crossfire.

Black Diamond Casino had gated up its front entrance and Red Castle would soon be closed. Pavel had called to check on Corinne, and she was in her office, ready to defend herself but waiting for the evacuation team to arrive. She'd sent her secretary home and had Alex guarding her locked suite and taking care of Neenee. She was very worried about Stefan, and asked Pavel to please be careful, too.

Pavel felt very responsible for her at that moment.

He would not be connected to Stefan except through an emergency channel relay from Station Alpha with approval of one of Stefan's adjutants during the fighting. An auto feed from Alpha would provide him with continuous updates on the battle going on outside the walls of Pleasure City, and a mini monitor hung from his belt as he made a final round of inspections of his defensive positions.

He was coming down the street on the way to his own position in a second story room facing the Precinct Station when he first heard rapid gunfire coming from the direction of the shuttle field. He rushed upstairs to join three men aiming automatic weapons from the windows. "Gunfire!" he shouted. "It's coming!"

And the wait was not long for them.

A lone car, and then two of them, came racing down the street towards their position, engines roaring. They were old model cabs, four door, well used and unpainted, but with real power under the hood and crammed with people.

Pavel was surprised and hesitated in reacting. The roar of the engines numbed his mind, but only for an instant.

The two cars skidded to a sliding, screeching stop in from of the station. Doors flew open, and men with rifles jumped out and opened fire at the building while one man ran towards it and threw a heavy package underhand with great effort to land against the front door.

"Fire!" screamed Pavel, and thirty high caliber weapons roared in unison, but only for three seconds.

The explosion was ear splitting, the charge somehow shaped to direct the blast primarily inwards towards the structure.

Windows shattered everywhere, Pavel and the others flattening on the floor to avoid shards of glass but recovering quickly to resume fire. Their first volley had cut the man down who had thrown the bomb, and a few others in the street. Now they were shooting at shadows in a roiling mess of smoke and dirt and rocky debris. The engine of one car roared again and then faded in the distance. A flame appeared in the street, then a loud whoosh and a fire was there to accompany the tracks of heavy tracer fire streaking across the street from all directions.

Pavel detected no movement below him. "Cease fire!" he called. "Cease fire, I said!", when the response was slow.

There was a long, horrible silence as the street slowly came into view again. One car was gone, the other on fire with the driver slumped over the wheel of a car perforated with bullet holes. Several bodies lay in the street near the car.

Pavel listened, heard no distant gunfire, but then the sound of another vehicle coming towards them, and this time there was no hesitation.

"Load up. More coming. Fire at my command."

Magazines snapped into place, and bolts rammed in first cartridges.

It was an open bed truck with slat sides and a load of hooded men with black arm bands and armed with T-40's, coming in to finish a job.

"Fire!" screamed Pavel.

The truck drove straight into the crossfire. Men began jumping off and rolling to their feet, only to be cut down where they stood. A dozen men never made it off the truck, which kept going, the driver still alive, but bullets still followed, a rear window shattered, and one block down the street the truck slowed, veered left and lightly collided with the facade of a building there.

They listened, heard some distant popping sounds off and on, a muffled boom, deep, sound of distant, scattered fighting, but now the worst seemed to be over.

"Hold your positions," ordered Pavel, and finally checked his monitor. The news was good, and a surprise. The fast-paced battle for Port Nexus was essentially over. The Guppies had arrived, and the heavy enemy ships destroyed, but the Alpha Station fighter group had sustained heavy losses.

The space battle was won. The fight in the city had been a diversion, perhaps, or based on expectation of Gate takeover, which could have happened if they'd not been so well prepared, and the Guppies had not been there to help them again.

Victory felt good, and they were coming out of it with minimal losses overall, and Pavel was grateful for it as he crossed the street littered with bodies to check in with his people who had been shaken but not injured by the explosion at the station entrance. He didn't notice the two vans newly parked by the entrance to Red Castle two blocks up the street, had not heard gun shots and muffled explosions coming from there sometime earlier.

Pavel climbed over debris to get to the holding cell area at the back of the station. Two officers waved to him from behind the short concrete block barrier they'd erected, but then one held up a phone and pointed to it. "Call for you, sir. It's urgent."

Pavel took the phone, and his world suddenly changed.

"Chief Fiala?"

"Speaking."

"Trooper Ferris with the Ambassador's Evacuation Team, sir. We're in the office of a Corinne Ariska, owner of Red Castle Casino. A squad of terrorists attacked the casino and Ariska has been seriously wounded. We have the shooter here, but he needs to be locked up. Can we bring him to the Precinct Station now?"

Pavel felt his heart thud hard, and then stop for two beats before resuming a pounding. "What? Is Ariska alive?"

"Yes, sir, but the wound is serious. We're evacuating her to a nearby Guppy right now. She's being carried from the building as I speak."

"Your evacuation was late, Mister. I can be there in five minutes, and I'll shoot anyone else who tries to leave the building with that prisoner. Got it?"

"Yes, sir. We'll wait."

Pavel scrambled over debris to get out of the building and pointed at four officers standing at the ruined entrance.

"You two, with the minis, follow me. There's been a shooting at Red Castle, and a shooter's in custody."

The men nodded and followed him at a fast trot down the street to the casino two short blocks away. The casino was dark inside, but people were there, looking grim, a few teared faces, and they pointed the way that Pavel already knew. The elevator was off, the stairway door blown from its hinges, and he charged up the stairs with the two officers right behind him.

The room air was heavy with smoke from gunfire in a small space. Troopers turned to look at them, and a man in civilian clothes was hovering over another man kneeling on the floor with hands clasped behind his head, but the first thing Pavel noticed was the big blood stain on the wall by a desk.

The man in civvies turned around and said, "Elton Steward, chief. I'm running the Ambassador's evacuation team."

"Running late, it seems," said Pavel. "She shouldn't have been here." He pointed to the blood on the wall.

"When the big explosion went off we were here in a couple of minutes and saw these guys shooting their way in," said Elton, and he pointed to the dead bodies on the floor. "We were right behind them all the way up, shot 'em all right here, but that guy on his knees got in one rifle shot that hit the woman. I shattered his rifle with two snap shots, and he gave up quick."

They all looked up as the ceiling shook, and there was a roar from overhead.

"Shuttle to Guppy 3. She's on her way. Chest wound, and the bullet went through her, and here's the guy who did it," said Elton.

Pavel looked down at the man, and felt heat on his face, his right hand moving to the butt of his holstered pistol.

"Corrella," he growled. "Guillermo Corrella, you bastard, why aren't you dead?"

Corrella looked up at him with an ugly smile. "Bugger you, cop," he snarled.

"Working for the Bishops, are you? I doubt it. This was personal. Blame it on the Kratolans, right? You piece of krack. You're a dead man. I call Chief Fechter right now, and he'll come down here and blow your frigging head off, and you know it."

"I have rights," said Corrella.

"This is a war. You have nothing."

"Chief," said Elton, sensing a dangerous mood, "he can probably answer some important questions for us."

"He can't do anything for us, except die," said Pavel softly, and he looked at the rifle on the floor only one foot from Corrella's knees. "Hey, krack face, is that rifle still loaded? The stock is the only thing broken on it."

Corrella's eyes were widening, and his smile faded fast. He glanced at Pavel's right hand resting on the butt of his holstered pistol.

"Chief, please don't," said Elton softly.

"Why don't you just save us the bother, and kill yourself for us," said Pavel, and the look on his face was now a menacing thing, his eyes narrowed to slits.

"Here, I'll help you."

Pavel took a step and kicked the rifle hard enough to bounce it up against Corrella's knees.

The man's hands were a blur as he grabbed the rifle.

Pavel jerked out his pistol and shot Corrella in the forehead at a range of one foot. Brain matter sprayed the floor, and the man fell over on his back, eyes open.

"That was for Corinne," said Pavel.

"I wish you hadn't done that," said Elton, but two of his troops were grinning.

"A prisoner of war tried to escape," said Pavel. "He shot a female civilian, and you're a witness."

"Yeah, okay," said Elton.

Another explosion shocked them as Pavel fired another round into Corrella's heart. "And that's for Stefan, who couldn't be here."

"We have to go," said Elton. "We have a second shuttle loading up with wounded. What do we do with this guy?"

"Leave him with the rest of the krack. We'll clean it up later."

"I'm really sorry we didn't get here sooner."

"Yeah, well, you did the best you could, and that's all any of us are doing."

They all went downstairs to the casino, and Elton's squad headed outside to a waiting van. People there had heard the shots, and looked at them fearfully, but out of the corner of his eye Pavel saw someone coming at him fast and he turned.

It was Carra, in a robe, coming at him with arms outstretched and he caught her in a tight embrace. She squeezed him tightly and buried her face in his neck. "I heard," she sobbed. "People said she looked dead. Why would they do that to her?"

"It was Guillermo Corrella who shot her. He dressed up like a terrorist to do it. I just killed him, Carra, but it won't help Corinne."

"She's my best friend, Pavel. She's treated me like a sister, and I love her, and now she's gone."

"She was still alive when they took her out of here. There's still hope, Carra. She'll be treated on a Guppy with Gan medicine, and we can't do better than that. But now I have to call Stefan and tell him what happened."

"Oh," said Carra, and tears ran down her cheeks.

"Is there a quiet place here for a call?"

"The restaurant is dark and empty," she said, and led him to it. They sat down at a corner table, and Pavel made the call, his heart full of dread.

Stefan answered instantly, was excited about the expected victory he had overseen, and then he asked how things had gone in the city.

Pavel told him.

There was no outcry, no gasp, no angry shout. There was a long silence and then Stefan asked, "Is she alive?"

"Yes, and on her way to Guppy 3, probably there now. Gan medicine on board, Chief. Can't do better than that."

"What about Corrella?"

"Well—I got him to go for his gun, and then I killed the fugger, Chief. All the people in his little strike force are dead."

"I owe you a bullet," said Stefan softly.

"You owe me two," said Pavel. "There's hope, Chief. Don't lose it. The ambassador's office should be abler to get updates for you. Let me know what you hear. Carra says hi. She's worried sick. Corinne's a very important person in her life."

"Yeah—mine, too," said Stefan softly, and then he broke the connection.

"Is he okay?" asked Carra.

"He was until I talked to him. Now he's not okay at all," said Pavel, and his eyes began to burn with tears.

CHAPTER TWENTY-NINE

Caleb Aluna, First Bishop of Kratola, watched the beginning of his end from the tower balcony high above the dome of the tabernacle. A receiver in his right ear kept him up to date on all the happenings above his planet, and the news had been bad from the beginning.

The sudden gush of metallic debris from the mouth of the wormhole had been the fatal sign. Something had gone wrong inside the thing, a pinch, closure or an instability at the other end. He wondered if even one of his ships had gotten through to Port Nexus, and if they had, why hadn't he yet heard back from them?

A second fatal sign was the appearance of the Guppies in numbers he'd never imagined possible. They had not come in through the wormhole, but by some other way independent of the existence of the Gates at Port Nexus.

The attack on Port Nexus had served no purpose at all.

From his balcony, in the dark of night, Caleb could see the Kratola Gate as a faint nebulosity with a tight cluster of flickering stars that were his ships. When the Guppies were spotted, and the report came to his ear, Caleb could not see them, for they first appeared in a more southerly part of the sky and were moving rapidly northwards. He found them a few degrees south of the Gate in a crescent formation and a few minutes later they engaged his ships with withering missile and torpedo fire the likes of which had never before been seen in the annals of space warfare. The explosions were like mini-novas in a rainbow of colors until there was nothing there except for the Guppies, which now turned sharply and were heading straight for Kratola.

Hope waned in the breast of Caleb Aluna, but did not disappear, for his first line of defense had been planned for a worst-case scenario when there was only one last chance for survival. His ships could not stand against the Guppies, but the big ships from Gan had suffered damage when extreme firepower had been directed against them before now.

Kratola possessed such power in missiles hidden away after a humanitarian ban on weapons of mass destruction decades before Caleb and his fellow Bishops had taken power. In preparation of his orbital defense force Caleb ordered one megaton thermonuclear weapons to be placed on every heavy cruiser and two hundred kiloton weapons for each of the smaller ships.

Caleb saw this as one final effort for survival and felt no guilt about doing it.

So it was that on the following evening, as the Guppies approached the orbital fleet above Kratola, Caleb was on his balcony again to see what might happen. Galen and Tibor waited fearfully in the throne room, arguing escape strategies through tunnels beneath the tabernacle. Caleb had no such illusions of escape. If the Guppies arrived at his doorstep there would be no escape, and no mercy.

The first orbital encounters occurred in the night sky far to the east, and Caleb had to shield his eyes three times as night turned to day with a fierce glow over the horizon. Caleb's heart leapt with sudden hope. He could imagine the total destruction of three Guppies, but there were nearly twenty of them coming in.

He waited an hour, then two. Three red and orange nebulae in orbital space came over the horizon, and then a crescent formation of bright stars. Among all the other scattered stars in the sky, nothing moved.

His communication had clicked on as the nebulae had appeared, but there was no sound. Nobody was there. Nothing was now in orbit above Kratola, except for a crescent of bright stars. And the crescent was breaking up as the stars began their descent towards the planet's surface.

Caleb went inside to the communication office and made the necessary announcement to his commanders with a heavy heart, but with the directness and courage of a head of state.

Our orbital defenses are destroyed.

We are defeated.

The Guppies will be here within hours, and I expect no mercy for myself and my fellow Bishops.

Save yourselves. You have served well and deserve to live.

Throw down your weapons and get as far away from your base or station as you can.

Gan's fight is with your government, not the people of Kratola.

What happens is written in the Field, past, present and future. It cannot be changed.

Your Bishops have done what they thought was best for Kratola.

(signed) Rev. Caleb Aluna, First bishop.

The message was sent, and minutes later Caleb heard the blaring of an alarm coming from the military base only a mile distant from him. He decided to talk to Galen and Tibor, to lie a little, try to ease their fears and avoid any cowardly display in a fruitless attempt to escape what he knew was coming. He went to the throne room, and they were still perched on their thrones, still arguing.

"We are defeated," he said softly. "our ships are destroyed, and Guppies are now descending to the surface around a hundred miles south of here. They'll likely be here in a couple of hours."

Both men gasped, hands to their throats. "We have to leave now," said Galen. "Both of us have packed a few things."

"Don't be absurd," said Caleb. "We are the leaders of this planet. We're not going to run away like frightened animals."

"But they'll kill us!" said Tibor.

"Nonsense," said Caleb. "They have formally declared war on us, and the rules do not include killing without trial. Gan is a civilized society with ancestors who came from Kratola. Some still have relatives here. They will not support a slaughter of any kind. We must negotiate a truce and discuss reparations to bring peace again. When the Guppies arrive, an emissary will be sent, and we can expect to be placed under arrest. So, calm yourselves, and forget about running away."

Both men looked at him suspiciously. "So now we wait?" said Galen.

"We wait," said Caleb. "I will go outside to be seen when they arrive."

"Well, we will not be there with you," said Galen.

"Then stay here, but we must be together for any negotiations."

Caleb left them there and returned to the communications office near the tower balcony to await a call he was certain would come when the Guppies arrived at his front gates.

And it was nearly three hours later when the call came in.

Caleb had sensed their presence before the call. A subtle vibration in the floor had begun minutes before. The temperature in the room had dropped enough to chill him, and light streaming in from the balcony doorway had suddenly disappeared. Emergency lights in the con room went on automatically, bathing the walls in red.

Caleb stood and walked to the balcony doorway. Outside was blackness, and there was no sound. He stepped onto the balcony and looked up. The sky was blacked out by the presence of three ships of unimaginable size hovering between a hundred and a thousand feet above the palace gates, noses a few hundred feet from the tower.

"Kratola Palace, this is Petyr Vlasok, commander of Guppy 4, Gan Expeditionary Force. Please respond."

"I am here," said Caleb calmly, "and I know your name. You were once Leonid Zylak, a founder of Gan. I am Reverend Caleb Aluna, first bishop of Kratola, a sovereign planet and home-world to its colonies."

"The spirit of Leonid Zylak is within me," said Petyr. "The colonies you speak of do not exist. Their independence goes back before the time of your coup on Kratola, and your efforts to take control of both Gan and Galena have been ceaseless since that time. Your most recent activities have resulted in the loss of many lives through civil wars and attacks on the gates still connecting our worlds, and your reign on Kratola has been both harsh and cruel. This ends today. We are here to end it, and surrender is not an option."

"You are judge, jury and executioner, acting without a trial. You Immortals think you are Gods, when you are not, and all that happens in life is written in The field," said Caleb.

"What we do has been approved by our senate, and is supported by our people, and despite your efforts we do not worship The Field"

"Then you are ignorant of the truth," said Caleb.

"And you will die for what you have done," said Petyr. "I will give you half an hour to prepare for it."

There was a click, and the call was ended. Caleb stood on the balcony for a short time in deep shadow looking at the array of weapons ports on the behemoths above him, imagining how quickly death would come, and then he turned and walked slowly downstairs to the throne room where Glen and Tibor anxiously awaited his report.

"The Guppies have arrived. Three of them are hovering above our gates in a most intimidating way. I've talked to their commander. An emissary will be sent to discuss the terms of our surrender. The wait will be short."

Caleb sat down on his throne.

"What will we say?" asked Galen. Tibor seemed frozen in shock.

"What they want to hear," said Caleb bitterly. "Now let us be silent and await our fate."

It was not long before there was a distant rumble, and then a vibration beneath their feet and the walls began to shake and the ceiling shuddered, and the rumbling became a roar.

"What is happening?" shouted Tibor, staring up at the ceiling.

"The emissary has arrived," said Caleb.

The walls of the rooms collapsed, and simultaneously the ceiling bulged and burst downwards, and the avalanche of megatons of rock and shattered concrete crushed the three of them to bloody smears on their shattered thrones.

* * * *

Outside, three Guppies opened up simultaneously on the palace and the Tabernacle of First Light. Missiles, torpedoes and tree-sized rail gun projectiles tore into the structures, pulverizing them from the top down over a period of minutes, and emptying all weapons in the process. Miles away the roar was deafening, the monstrous Guppies themselves enveloped in a thick cloud of dirt and concrete dust. And when the roaring ceased, there was a long, horrible silence as the cloud slowly dissipated and a mountain of crushed rock and concrete came into view, all that was left of the Bishops' palace and the Tabernacle of First Light.

That, too, would not be allowed to remain.

One Guppy backed off a thousand yards and waited while the other two dropped lower to the ground and moved in closer to the great pile of debris.

The noses of the Guppies began to glow green.

The glows brightened, greenish spheroids spreading outwards to touch the pile of rock and concrete as the Guppies inched forward. A dusty vortex formed above the debris, air sucked inwards towards the ground and making a loud, whistling noise that could be heard a mile distant. Again, the guppies themselves were cloaked within a thick cloud of swirling dust.

The whistling sound stopped, and the Guppies backed away, and in a few minutes the dust cloud had settled again.

Where once a palace and tabernacle had stood, there was only a modest box canyon with a smooth floor of glistening, polished rock.

The three Guppies slowly ascended together to a hovering position several thousand feet up, and were joined there by two others that had been assigned to the destruction of the neighboring military base, but were called back when it was discovered the base had been abandoned.

"Their soldiers have given up, are unarmed and scattered all over the eastern plains by the look of it. There's been enough death," said Petyr. "We'll need the base facilities to house those troops until they can be debriefed and mustered out. Our occupation force will not be happy if we blow things up. No more deaths. We've done what we came to do. We're not at war with the people of Kratola."

By late afternoon the Guppies had all gone into high orbit around the planet, but for the soldiers and private citizens of Kratola things were just beginning, for the skies were soon blackened by many ships that had been in orbit, but now dropped to the surface to occupy the planet. There were many gunships, light destroyer class for security, and dozens of carriers loaded with Gan troopers, and several merchant vessels and their shuttles to provide food and other supplies for the operation.

The occupation of Kratola had begun.

CHAPTER THIRTY

Stefan would later remember the day Pavel called as the worst day of his life. Corinne had been shot, the injury critical, and she was being treated on a Guppy with Gan medicine, and that was supposed to be reassuring, but it wasn't.

The pig who'd shot her was dead. Stefan was satisfied by that, but a dark part of him resented a lost opportunity to kill the man himself. If it hadn't been for Corrella and his hatred, Corinne would now be safe and healthy on a Guppy, and not in a critical state.

He had work to do: the recall of ships, damage assessments, checking on Moon G repairs and digging out the remaining pockets of terrorists who had fled to oldtown. His orders had been simple. Kill anyone who resists. They had taken only a few prisoners, and Zeke had put himself in charge of them for questioning.

Half of his mind wouldn't leave Corinne, refused his other tasks. He had to have news. He had to know hour by hour how she was doing, or his mind would be horribly tangled. He called Petyr's number, got no answer, and then remembered that Petyr had led the final attack on Kratola and was still there.

Gan ambassador Jilena Uzelac would know something. Her office had been involved in arranging Corinne's evacuation. He called her office and got a secretary.

"Chief Stefan Fechter here, calling for Ambassador Uzelac. A good friend of mine has been severely wounded and taken to Guppy 3 for treatment. I need to find out how she's doing. Is there a way I can contact the Guppy?"

"I'm sorry, sir, but that won't be possible. Guppy 3 is gone again. It made another jump back to Gan a little while ago."

"What?" said Stefan softly.

"Yes, sir. They had more critical patients onboard, and decided it was best to treat them at the medical center on Gan. They should be there shortly. They called Ambassador Uzelac about it. Perhaps she can tell you something, but she's in a meeting right now. I'll give her your message, and I'm sure she'll call you right back. You were on her list of calls."

"Then I'll wait, thank you."

He was on her list of calls. Somehow that was not reassuring. Corinne's condition, and that of others with her was demanding treatment at possibly the finest medical center in the local universe.

His mind was now hopelessly muddled. The room blurred as he stared at infinity, and his heart was racing. *Corinne, my love, don't leave me, not now. I've never loved anyone before you.*

He shuffled papers on his desk, and got nothing done, and it was the buzz from his console that shook him out of his reverie as he answered it.

"Yes?"

"Jilene Uzelac here, Chief Fechter. I'm so sorry I didn't get back to you earlier. You know about her departure on Guppy 3, and I really do understand your concern for Corinne Ariska. Her evacuation was our responsibility, and everything possible is being done, but I'm afraid the news I have for you is not good."

Stefan swallowed hard, a constriction in his throat.

"And what is that?" he croaked.

"Corinne Ariska's heart stopped twice during treatment, and they were still trying to revive her when they made the jump to Gan. That's all I can tell you now, chief. I'm so sorry. Guppy 3 will be returning, and we should know more then. I know it looks bad, but there's always hope with Gan medicine.

His voice was now a whisper. "Thank you," he said, and punched off the connection.

There was pain in his chest, and his hands were clenched into fists. Tears exploded from his eyes and ran down his cheeks and he had to breathe through his mouth, making faint grunting sounds. He sat like that for several minutes, and then things began to change. The tears stopped, his breathing deepened and the pain in his chest was replaced by a tightening, a flow of energy that reached his face, his cheeks flushing red, a horrible anger boiling to the surface.

He wanted to kill, to mutilate. He could see himself taking a heavy ax and dismembering Corrella's body into pieces and burning them in gasoline. He saw Corinne's grinning face in the fire, and shot it fifteen times before it disappeared. And with one motion of his arm, he swept everything on top of his desk onto the floor, stood up, and with one mighty heave he lifted his heavy desk and rolled it over onto its side with a crash. The big chair went next with a heave that sent it into a wall and left it hanging there by a leg.

Rage dissipated, Stefan sat down on the overturned desk, gasping for breath.

The office door flew open, and Del was there, horrified as she looked around the room.

"Are you all right, Chief?" she asked timidly.

"Not at all. I got bad news and lost it."

Now there were tears in his eyes again.

"Corinne just died on Guppy 3," he croaked.

"Oh, no! Oh, Chief, I'm so sorry. Can I get you a drink or anything? I'll call engineering and have them clean this all up. You should take a break and get some rest."

"Yeah, maybe I'll do that," said Stefan.

Now he felt numb, and in a kind of dream state. There was a little coffee closet near his office, a little place with only a couple of tables and low light. He took his handheld and went there, ordered a large one, high stim, and sat in near darkness, his mind slowly quieting, but then a call forced him to start over again.

It was from Governor Madelia. The call was short, and to the point.

"It's Kira, Stefan. I just heard about Corinne. If you want to talk about it call me anytime and I'll be there. Please don't try to get through this by yourself. Do you hear me?"

"Yes, Ma'am," he said, "and thanks."

And Kira broke the connection.

He finished his coffee and wiped his eyes dry. His office was ruined, but Del's had two desks, and he could work from there. The port was still officially in a state of war, and there was a lot of cleanup he had to oversee as Chief of Security.

But anger still boiled deeply inside him, along with a terrible grief as he went back to work.

* * * *

His work pushed the grief deep inside him. In doing so, he indirectly shared the grief of others by cosigning many condolence letters to the families of fighter pilots killed during battle. Two of those letters were delivered to Kratola. Hardest to write was one he added to, a letter to Gan for the parents of Lieutenant Ronald Abel, killed in action after destroying five enemy fighters.

There was a note from Zeke. Troopers had found eight Black Hat terrorists hiding in a basement apartment in oldtown and, due to Zeke's request, had been spared when they didn't resist arrest.

The concrete block barrier around the military camp was torn down and replaced by a ten foot wire fence, behind which tents were erected to house the few Black Hat terrorists who had survived the fight. What would happen to the prisoners depended on the progress of occupation activities on Kratola. Eventual emancipation was expected when and if a new, friendly government was established.

Construction was underway on the facade of the precinct building and the streets in central city were cleaned up. The filling of bullet scars on building walls was put off for later. The city was still closed to tourists but was scheduled to be open again in fifteen cycles. The casinos were still closed, both of them without living owners, but staff worked every day with optimism about reopening, even with paychecks in doubt. The smaller shops used the time to reorganize their displays and would be ready when the tourists arrived again.

All of this was especially encouraging to Pavel, for Pleasure City was not just a workplace for him, it was his home. He and Carra met every day for lunch. Carra was grieving Corinne, who had been like a sister. Alex oversaw the casino, and also looked after Neenee in the owner's suite. Corinne's father, a silent partner, was expected to arrive soon and determine their future. It seemed unlikely the casino would be closed.

Stefan was invited several times to join Pavel and Carra for lunch, and he finally accepted it on a day when he would have normally come into the city to be with Corinne. He joined them at Red Castle coffee shop in the back of the casino. The machines were all silent, but there were plenty of hammering sounds as workmen replaced the heavy security door and repaired damage from several flash bomb explosions.

When Stefan entered the coffee shop Carra rushed up with tears in her eyes and gave him a crushing hug, then looked up at him and said, "She would want us to be strong."

Stefan smiled and sat down with them. There was no fresh meat, and they ordered synth sandwiches and coffee.

"The city is coming together again," said Pavel. "You did a good job for us, Chief."

"A lot of good fighting men did the job," said Stefan.

"But we were prepared," said Pavel.

"Yes, I think we were, but in the end the Guppies gave us the edge we had to have. We have a lot to thank Gan for."

Carra's eyes filled with tears. "We started rehearsals for a new show yesterday. Corinne would be furious with us if we even delayed an opening. We're dedicating this one to her."

Pavel put a hand on her arm. "Carra, please," he said softly.

"That's okay," said Stefan. "I feel it, too. Dedicating the show to her is a nice thing to do."

Stefan felt relief when the sandwiches arrived. They were hungry, and ate in silence for a few minutes until Stefan suddenly asked, "How's Neenee doing? Is she always alone upstairs?"

"Alex is with her early and late in cycle, and fixes her meals," said Carra. "He says her eating is good, but all she does is curl up on the foot of the bed in the bedroom, and the look in her eyes sometimes makes him want to cry himself. Alex is a fine man. He was Corinne's right hand from the very beginning."

"Could I talk to Alex today, while I'm here?" asked Stefan.

"Of course," said Carra. "He's in the office now. Let me know when, then I'll call him, he can meet you at the elevator."

"Right after lunch?"

"Okay."

"Now?"

Carra took out her handheld and made the call. "Chief Fechter is here. He wants to talk to you. Do you have time? Okay. Ten minutes."

"He'll meet you at the elevator in ten minutes."

"I'd just like to see how Neenee is getting along," said Stefan.

Carra smiled. "I'll bet she likes that."

Ten minutes later he stood in front of the elevator as the door slid open and Alex was standing there.

"Chief Fechter, so nice to see you again. Step inside, please."

Stefan did so, and the door closed. "What can I do for you?"

"I wanted to see Neenee again, to see how she's handling all of this. Corinne has been gone for several cycles now."

"She'll be glad to see you, Chief. I'll take you right up."

The elevator rose quickly and stopped at the top floor.

"We're all still in shock here," said Alex softly. "How are you coping with this?"

"It's difficult, and the feeling of loss is terrible. I feel kind of numb now."

"Perhaps Neenee is feeling the same thing," said Alex, and the elevator door opened.

"Why don't you wait in the front room?" said Alex. "The dog is in the bedroom, and the door is closed."

Stefan walked into the living room and sat down in his usual place on the big couch. A musky odor lingered in the room. Corinne, and a scent she sprayed on her hair.

Alex went down the long hallway to the bedroom and opened the door. "Come out, girl. Someone is here," he said.

Stefan waited a few seconds, and then called out, "Neenee, come see me darlin'. I'm back!"

"Whoa," said Alex, and there was the skittering, scratching sound of sharp toenails on flooring and Neenee rushed out of the doorway and skidded to a stop, legs splayed. She took one look at him and leaped across the room and into his lap, whining piteously. Stefan held her and stroked her as she writhed in his arms. She finally began to calm down and rested her chin on his shoulder and up against his neck, still whimpering.

Stefan pressed her to him and rocked her gently. She licked all over his face and hands and looked at him with large, liquid eyes as he spoke softly to her, making comforting sounds, and finally she calmed and curled up in his lap and stayed there.

Alex came into the room and smiled at them. "She loves you," he said.

"And I loved her mistress," said Stefan. "What will happen to Neenee?"

"I imagine Mister Ariska will decide that along with what will happen to Red Castle. He might take her back to Gan. We hope to hear from him within a few cycles."

"If he'll agree to it, I'd like to have Neenee live the rest of her life with me. I can provide a good place for her on Alpha, not as luxurious as this place, but nice enough, and a few other people have dogs there," said Stefan, stroking Neenee's head in his lap.

"Ask him. When he sees you like this, I think I know what his answer will be," said Alex.

"Have you met him?"

"Only by voice," said Alex, and looked away from Stefan. "He is a serious man, and quite influential on Gan. I found him somewhat cold, but we expect him to keep our casino open and retain our staff. He knows we have a good business here. And I'm sure he'll contact you when he arrives. Corinne made him aware of her relationship with you."

"He didn't call her directly, though," said Stefan. "A colleague of his visited here from Gan and I met him briefly. Corinne must have told him about us, and he passed it on."

"Ah, yes," said Alex, not looking at him. "I remember the man. He was also quite cold, I thought. Would you like something to eat or drink? Alas, it's all synth for now, but we're expecting fresh food deliveries before we open again."

"No thanks, Alex, I just had something downstairs, but I do have a big favor to ask of you, if you don't mind."

"Oh? What is it, Chief Fechter?"

"You know that I was staying overnight with Corinne when I came here."

Alex smiled. "It was a poorly kept secret, sir."

"I would like to sleep here again tonight, one last time in the big bed, and Neenee was usually with us. One last time."

"I understand," said Alex. "I'll prepare a dinner for you and breakfast in the morning, as was my habit when you and Corinne were together." His eyes glistened.

"You don't have to do that," said Stefan.

"I do, chief. I, too, have fond memories of those times. I'll return at 1700 to prepare an imaginative dinner, and then at 0700 next cycle. I think I remember seeing some eggs in the cooler. In the meantime, I do have a casino to run. I'll be in the office downstairs. You can press 2 on the console to reach me. It's nice to have you here, Chief, though I'm feeling sadness about it, but life does go on. Enjoy your stay and be careful getting up. I think Neenee has gone to sleep in your lap."

The dog was sound asleep. Alex left the suite, and Stefan sat with the dog for over an hour, dozing until Neenee woke up, squirmed in his lap and found a hand to lick. He got up and wandered around the suite, the dog following him everywhere. He explored kitchen, bath, and the little room Corinne had used for entertainment and the mysterious scanning device which she used for meditation. The device was no longer there. He played music cubes until Alex arrived to prepare dinner and watched while the man turned a collection of synthetic powders and mush into something not only edible, but quite tasty.

Alex left again, and Stefan retired to the bedroom he had shared with Corinne, and again felt an ache in his chest. Her scent was still there: the air in the room, the sheets, the pillow beneath his head. His eyes began to burn, and he closed them when the room was darkened.

In twilight sleep, he dreamed that Corinne was there with him, her back warmly pressed up against his, but when he awoke later it was Neenee there, snoring softly.

CHAPTER THIRTY-ONE

Nathan Czapia spent two painful hours in a busy clinic at the edge of Pleasure City proper. The diagnosis was a fracture of the jaw, and he was wired accordingly and told he'd be eating with a drinking straw for one week and perhaps two. This he found little different than the krack porridge he'd been eating since his arrival at Port Nexus.

His surviving cell members had disappeared, taken away to somewhere in a van, but there were two other Black Hats in the clinic with him, both being treated for gunshot wounds during the attack on the downtown police precinct station.

"We were set up," said one of them. "They had snipers in every window on both sides of the street. We didn't even make it out of the truck."

"This whole mission was a fugging mess," said the other. "I don't think our intelligence guys even knew what was here."

"Yeah, well someone knew *we* were here." He pointed a finger at Nathan. "That guy's cell got taken before the fight even started."

Nathan nodded, his jaw frozen. The Bishops didn't give a krack. They expected us to die, he thought.

A med tech came in to see them. A trooper was with him, rifle unslung.

"Well, how are y'all doing? I'd welcome you to Pleasure City, but you've already seen it and overstayed any welcome we want to give you. Only a few of you are left alive, and that's just fine with me. Now you can enjoy some quality time in the jail you tried to blow up. Doc has okayed your releases. Your escort here will show you to the van, so good-bye and good riddance."

The tech spit at them at a distance, and it fell short. He shook his head and stalked out of the room.

The trooper gestured with his rifle, gave them a steely-eyed glare and marched them out of the clinic to a waiting van that took them six blocks down the street to a precinct building swarming with workers. Already, the old facade of the building was beginning to reappear.

They were marched into the back of the building where there was a substantial cell block with a dozen large cells, half of which were already jammed full of haggard looking men.

An officer pointed to a corner of the block. "Wounded go there," he said. There were already two men in that cell, both with heavily bandaged heads and hands. They stood back when the officer opened the cell door. There were four bunks and five men in the cell, a basin, toilet and bench. Nathan quickly sat down on a bunk, another man crowding in next to him. The door clanged shut, was locked, and the trooper went away without a word.

They sat in silence for a while, each of them wondering what might come next. Nathan wondered about his brothers. Had they really gone AWOL? Were they even alive? He'd heard nothing about the fight above the city, but it was probably lost too. The locals were saying nothing about it.

And quite suddenly, news arrived.

A police officer and the trooper came back into the cell block.

"Attention, all of you!" yelled the block officer, then he stepped forward and spoke in a loud voice.

"Gentlemen, you are now officially prisoners of war under the jurisdiction of Gan, and subject to the rules governing such prisoners. You will not be subject to torture or execution, will receive proper medical care and physical necessities during your incarceration. The war between Gan and Kratola has come to an end; efforts to take Port Nexus have failed, and all invading ships have been destroyed.

"Gan has retaliated by invading Kratola with the bulk of its space force and ten thousand troops. The Bishops of Kratola have been killed, and their palace and tabernacle eliminated from this universe. The occupation of Kratola began at 0500 this morning Gan time. The Kratolan army has surrendered without a shot, and their space force is destroyed. According to Gan officials, an armistice will be declared, and repatriation of prisoners is expected. Each of you will be interviewed and mustered out of an army and special forces that will no longer exist. This process will begin soon. We'll give each of you a number to be called by, but in the interview, you'll need to provide your true name to be mustered out and become eligible for release and return to Kratola."

The policeman paused and closed the power pad he'd read from.

"You might be feeling guilt or shame right now. I can understand that, but I have an opinion about this war, and it is not a favorable one. You have been gun fodder for a dishonorable war begun by dishonorable, cruel people who cared only about power. Now Kratola has another chance, and so do you. Choose your new government wisely."

He turned and left the room.

The Bishops are dead, thought Nathan, but what about my brothers?

The block officer was going from cell to cell with a box full of little slips of paper with numbers on them. Nathan pulled out 17, highest number in his cell. Numbers were called randomly, and men left their cells for interviews in another room, and did not return. It was a slow process, with two to three men being called each hour. When interviews ended for the day at 1900, Nathan was left with one cellmate and the population of the other cells was noticeably diminished.

Dinner was a slab of mystery synth, a tasty bowl of potato and vegetable mix and a large slice of buttered bread. The coffee tasted thin. He was in his lower bunk nearing sleep when the lights went out at 2300.

The lights went on again at 0700 for a breakfast of grainy gruel and toast. Interviews began at 0800 and Nathan's number was called at 0920, He followed a trooper out the door and down a short hallway to a small office with a desk and two chairs, one occupied.

The man sitting behind the desk was Zeke.

Nathan sat down across from him and was silent.

Zeke shuffled some papers, and then looked at him.

"How's the jaw?" he asked.

Nathan's mumbled reply was slurred. "It's broken. You broke it."

"Yeah, well, sorry about that. Had to make it look good, but got a bit carried away. You *are* alive."

"Doc says two weeks before I can eat regular," mumbled Nathan. "Have you heard anything about my brothers?"

"I have, in fact," said Zeke. "They did go AWOL, and everyone was looking for them. One of the Bishops was killed by a long-distance rifle shot, and whoever did it almost got the first bishop as well. All the AWOL people were suspects."

Nathan tried to smile but couldn't. "They said they'd do it. Both of them had sniper training."

"We must find them to muster them out. If they're the villains, they did us a favor. Now what are we going to do about you?"

"Send me home, I guess."

"Do you want to go home?"

"My brothers are there. That's where I should be. We have the farm."

"Okay," said Zeke, and looked at some papers. "I don't have to ask you about any remaining loyalty to the Bishops."

"I'm glad they're dead. They murdered my parents. I hope it's my brothers who killed one of them."

"Well," said Zeke, "we can check that one off. How do you feel about Gan occupying your planet?"

"Don't know. Depends on what they do."

"Gan will try to establish a democratic government on Kratola."

Nathan snorted. "If the rich guys will let 'em do it. The Bishops got all their support from them. The rest of us had nothing to say about anything. And my fugging jaw is hurting."

"Sorry. I have what I need. I'm sending you home, but you'll be in a holding camp for a couple of weeks before you get your release papers, and then you're free. Hold on to this ticket. Waiting room is down the hall, with some other guys. You'll be taken to your ship at 2000 prompt."

"That's it?" said Nathan.

"That's it, kid. I'm sorry about your folks, hope you find your brothers okay, and we do appreciate your help. Here's something else for you. Keep it in your shoe."

Zeke handed him a small coin, blank on both sides.

"What's this?"

"A credit chit. It's worth ten thousand Gan credits. Anyone with a bank account will take it. Don't be too quick to spend it. You might need something big someday."

"Wow. Thanks, Zeke."

"You're welcome" Zeke reached across the desk and handed a little card to Nathan, who looked at it and nodded.

"Gan Intelligence, and a Colonel, yet."

"That's me," said Zeke. "You can reach me at that number if you ever get to Gan. You never know. Good luck, kid. Now get out of here."

As per instructions, Nathan put the coin in his shoe with an extra piece of fabric under his heal, and shook Zeke's hand.

Zeke smiled as Nathan left the room, and then looked down at his papers again. *Okay, who's next?* He thought, and then, *Hope the kid does good.*

* * * *

During the attack at Kratola City, Jule and Jon Czapia had been a hundred and fifty miles to the south, but they had seen the fireworks in the sky, and then the sun blotted out during the descent of mountain-sized Guppies clear down to the horizon.

"We're finished," said Jule when the Guppies had moved out of sight to the north. "They're heading to the city. They'll destroy everything"

"Good," said Jon.

"But our unit is there, and all the guys we went through training with," said Jule. "We have friends there."

"Maybe they'll have sense enough to give up. Their choice. I just want the Bishops all dead, not just one of them. Any new government has to be better than what we've had, and it's time for us to go home, Jule. Nobody's going to be looking for us anymore. Even without a ride, we can walk it in four days."

"And then what? The house is burned to the ground. We don't even know if the village is still there. Our old neighbors know we went AWOL, a war has been lost, and now we'll be occupied. If we're seen again, someone will turn us in for sure. We could be shot, Jon."

"So we change our names, abandon our property, and hoe onions for the rest of our lives. Is that what you want?"

"No, I don't mean that, but let's wait until things have cooled down and we know what's going on. I'm worried about Nathan, too," said Jule.

"He's probably dead," said Jon. "That whole thing at Port Nexus must have failed, or we wouldn't be getting invaded now."

"But what if he's alive and comes back here and we're still missing. Mom and pop are gone. All he'll come back to is a burned down house and a farm he can't make a living with."

"Nathan can take care of himself," said Jon. "I don't worry about that, but I'd like to see him again and know he's alive."

"Fred would hide us. He did it before."

"What?"

"Fred Engel. He hid us in his basement when we first disappeared. He didn't turn us in, Jon. We could be safe with him, just for a while, you know, to check things out, set up a contact in case Nathan shows up."

"It's risky," said Jon, thinking.

"Our lives have been worse than risky for a long time, Jon. I'm fed up with this. I'm going home, with or without you."

"Okay, okay, give me a minute," said Jon. "We'd have to stay away from roads. If we stick to valley streams between hills, it's a four or five day walk. We'd be living on fish and bread."

"Let's do it," said Jule.

"Nothing out there," said Jon. "If we get hurt or sick we could die."

"Okay. Let's get going," said Jule.

Jon shook his head, smiled, and put a hand on his brother's shoulder. "You have the money. Get us two big loaves of bread at the bakery and a small brick of orange cheese. I'll make up some hooks, and we'll head out this evening at dusk."

"Got it," said Jule, and he rushed away.

So I gave in, thought Jon. Guess I really want to go home, too. I just want to get this whole mess over with and settled one way or another, as long as we don't get our asses shot off doing it.

* * * *

They traveled for four nights and five days without seeing another human being. The weather was good to them, and the evenings were warm. They saw no game, and it was no matter, for they had abandoned their service pistols by burying them weeks ago. Sheathed knives were their only weapons. Using cheese chunks and bent pin hooks they caught six-inch fish in the creeks and valley streams and ate them raw on bread that became drier each day, but the water was cold and fresh. They lit no fires and slept hidden under piles of branches and brush each night, and on the morning of the fifth day they reached the top of a hill and saw a familiar village nestled in a broad valley below them. Plowed fields surrounded a cluster of small houses and buildings, and the fields were showing a faint green from recent plantings.

They walked down the hill towards a small house on the edge of the village. A few people were on the street, but didn't seem to notice them, and they kept them out of sight most of the time as they approached the house.

Fred Engel was chopping wood behind his house when he saw them coming. He shielded his eyes and started towards them, waving.

Jon waved, put a finger to his lips, cautioning. Fred stopped, and they walked to him. The hugs were warm and welcome. "You made it alive," said Fred. "The war's over. Have you heard about it?"

"We saw the Guppies come down after the fighting above us," said Jule.

"We don't want to be seen," said Jon.

Fred led them to his house and shop, where he lived alone and crafted shoes and boots, purses and belts and the occasional harness or saddle for the surrounding region. His large basement with its many compartments for supplies had previously been a perfect safe haven for them, and Fred had been a best friend of their father's.

They went inside the house, Fred cooked up fresh eggs for them to go with the last of their bread and told them about everything that had happened: the deaths of the Bishops, the destruction of the palace, the surrender of the army without casualties.

"There are broadcasts every day on audio and video," said Fred. "They say the occupation will be short, that Gan is here to establish a new government that will be a friendly and responsible neighbor. An armistice is coming, and there will be total amnesty for all non-commissioned and most officers in the armed forces. They're mustering everyone out. We'll only be allowed a police force, now."

"You believe all that?" asked Jon.

"Why not? They're saying their war was with the government of Kratola, not the people. Yeah, I believe it. They blew up the Bishops, but there hasn't been a single civilian casualty. You guys get amnesty. You're safe, now."

"We were AWOL, in case you don't remember, Fred," growled Jon. "Everyone was looking for us."

"Still are," said Fred.

"What?" said Jon and Jule together.

"Car came by two days ago. Gan Expeditionary Force, the guy said. They have a list of missing soldiers, and you're both on it. You must be interviewed to be mustered out. They said that's all there is to it. You're not in any trouble."

"Not likely," said Jon. "We've had a rough few days of marching, Fred. Can we have your basement a couple of nights for rest, and then we'll move on?"

"You don't want to be mustered out?" asked Fred.

"We don't want to be arrested, and I don't believe what any government official has to say," said Jon.

"Well, it's your choice, but I think you're wrong. They're just trying to get everything back to normal again. Stay as long as you like, Jon, but I don't feel obligated to cover for you anymore. There's just no reason for me to be a liar for you."

"Understood. We'll be here a night or two, and then we're gone. And we won't be back again."

"I'm sorry, Jon," said Fred.

"Yeah, me, too. We won't hold it against you. You've been a good friend, and you think you're doing the right thing."

"I am," said Fred. "You know where the basement is. Let me know when you want something more to eat. I'll be in the shop."

They parted ways, Jon and Jule returning to a hidden compartment they had used before in the basement.

"If there's amnesty, and we're mustered out we'll be free men, Jon," said Jule.

"If you can believe the propaganda," said Jon.

"I don't want to be running away the rest of my life," said Jule.

"Just for a while," said Jon, "until we can be certain that everything we've heard is true."

Upstairs, Fed Engel had not waited. The Gan representative had left a card with him. Fred picked up his handheld in the shop, called the number on the card and told that representative that the two men he'd been looking for were now hiding in his basement, and would only be there for a night or two.

The next morning the Gan representative arrived in a military car and was accompanied by two troopers.

CHAPTER THIRTY-TWO

Things were nearly back to normal for Stefan Fechter. Condolence letters had been sent, and in a private ceremony he had pinned Gold Orb medals on five young ace pilots in the fighter squadron that had suffered such terrible losses in the fighting. His biggest pleasure had been presenting a Distinguished Service medal to Aaron Silver, a very embarrassed Tech 4 who had saved the day at Moon G with a hasty repair that had reopened the Gate to Gan.

Cleanup in the city was proceeding swiftly. Stefan had gone to meet with Pavel and inspect the progress at the military installation there. He found it to be far ahead of progress in city center, so complete that one would think nothing had ever happened.

Being in the city made him think of Corinne again. Pavel could sense it from his mood, sad and detached as they sat in Pavel's office.

"Carra says the casino will be open again in a few cycles," said Pavel. "Corinne's father is coming here, might be here already, and he's promised a special announcement. He did say it'll be business as usual, and all the staff jobs are safe. Have you heard anything from him?"

"Not a word about anything. No word about Corinne, or what happened to her. How cold can a person be? I know they didn't get along very well. There was some problem with Corinne's mother."

"Yeah, but my bet is you'll be meeting him soon. He must know how important you were to his daughter."

"She was more than important to me," said Stefan, and felt an ache in his chest again. "I don't know if I can talk to him about it."

But it was only a few minutes later that Stefan's world began to change again when Pavel's handheld buzzed.

"Hi Carra. What's up?" Pavel listened, then, "Yeah, he's here with me. I'm sure he'll want to come. We'll leave now."

Pavel raised an eyebrow. "Justin Ariska came in late last cycle, and he has an important announcement to make. The staff is assembling by the elevator, and you and I should be there. Let's go."

Stefan hesitated, and Pavel scowled at him.

"Up and on. Here's your chance to talk to the guy, Chief. You haven't started to heal yet. You've got to do this. Come on."

Stefan reluctantly followed him. They walked the two short blocks to Red Castle Casino. Inside, all was neat and orderly, the machines flashing colorful lights, some pleasant food odors in the air. People were gathering at the back of the casino near the elevator to upstairs, and the sight of it brought a new pressure to Stefan' chest. He suddenly wanted to leave, but the elevator door opened, and Alex was standing there, saw him immediately, and beckoned to him.

Stefan stepped forward as Carra rushed up to Pavel and hugged him. When he looked back, she waved, and there were tears in her eyes.

"Mister Ariska wants to talk to you upstairs before the announcement," said Alex. "I don't know what it's about. He is not an easy person to talk to and is terribly secretive. I haven't even seen him in person yet. But he says there will be no announcement before he talks to you, so it sounds important to him. I'll take you up to the residence."

Stefan stepped into the elevator. Pavel and Carra were staring at him, and he shrugged at them with some confusion. The doors closed, then opened again at the residence foyer.

"Good luck, chief," said Alex. Stefan stepped into an empty front room as the elevator door closed behind him. He waited a moment, and then sat down on the big couch there.

A moment later, the big sliding door leading to the dining room opened, and a man was standing there, a man around fifty dressed in a white business suit.

The man was Justin Renick.

Stefan stared, hesitated, and then said, "I'm here to see Justin Ariska. I'm Stefan Fechter, Chief of Security."

The man smiled, did not offer a hand. "And of course we've already met, Mister Fechter. Sorry for the little deception. I was persuaded it was necessary at the time. I am Justin Ariska."

"Corinne's father? I was told he's in his eighties."

"So it was. A little cloning and some digital magic with persona and memories, and here I am. Fifties is much better than eighties. The process is simple, but the technology is not. Perhaps you'll make use of it yourself someday."

"I don't understand," said Stefan.

"Of course not," said Justin. "You're not one of us, yet. It's all mythology to you. But let me get to the point. I understand you've been very upset by the death of my daughter."

"Really? Her heart stopped and she died, and I loved that woman to the core of my soul. Yes, I've been upset about it. It's called grieving, and I haven't been told anything about what happened to her after she got on that Guppy. That's pretty lousy."

"I suppose that appears to be correct. An oversight. Things had to be done quickly. But my people see death differently than yours. Sorry about that. Anyway, that's not what I want to talk to you about. I want to apologize for misjudging you, for holding you responsible for something you had no personal responsibility for many years ago. You were a soldier doing work for a tyrant, you rebelled and paid a price for it. One of the dangers of getting old is the casting of old memories in concrete and not seeing the entire picture. And now you have cast a blow for freedom. I was wrong about you, Mister Fechter. I hope you will accept my apology for it."

Stefaan's anger still roiled inside him, anger at a man who seemed not to care about his daughter's death.

"I accept your apology, Mister Ariska, but it won't bring my Corinne back to life. I just wish she'd been here to witness that apology." Stefan put his face in his hands to hide the sudden tears.

Justin sighed. "Oh, Mister Fechter, I never said that my daughter was still dead. I've had my say, dear. Your turn. I'm going to make myself a drink before we go downstairs."

What? Thought Stefan, and then he heard her voice, coming from his right, and his heart leapt.

"Stefan? It's me, darling. I'm here. I'm okay."

He took his hands away from his face, opened his eyes and turned to his right.

Corinne was standing in the doorway to the hall leading back to the bedroom. She was dressed in her form fitting flaming red business suit, and her long, dark hair was done up in a bun at the back of her head.

She stepped towards him: a dream, an illusion, an impossibility of his imagination, and her eyes were filled with tears. "I've missed you," she said.

Stefan stared as Corinne knelt in front of him, took his hands in hers, leaned forward and kissed him softly on cheeks and mouth. His vision was blurred by the tears and his throat was constricted, making his voice a ragged whisper.

"I thought I'd lost you," he said.

"They brought me back on Gan, darling. Our medicine is not a myth. I'm new, I'm healed, and it's me, and we're together again. There is nothing to be sad about, if you still want me."

"Want you? I want to spend the rest of my life with you," said Stefan, and then he grasped her arms and pulled her to him, and the kiss was long and firm.

"I want to marry you, Corinne," he said.

"That sounds like a good plan to me," she said, then put her arms around his neck and crawled into his lap, nestling there.

There was a shout from the bedroom. "Blast! I opened the door, and she was right there! Dog is loose!"

Neenee shot out of the hallway door and skidded in making her turn. Two leaps, and she was on them, burrowing into them from her side of the couch, whining and licking until they had her tightly cuddled and she was sniffing every part of Corinne she could reach as she calmed.

"When I first arrived, she actually shied away from me until I talked to her," said Corinne. "all the hospital odors confused her at first."

"Well, she's not confused now," said Stefan, and got a lick on his cheek when he spoke.

Justin came out of the dining room with a tall glass filled with something blue in his hand. "Well, that looks cozy, and the mood in this room has certainly improved. Don't forget our big announcement."

"Does anyone else know you're alive?" asked Stefan. "Everyone downstairs has been told you died."

"Father brought me in late all bundled up. I don't think anyone saw me, and Alex was working in the office."

"Ah, then you are the big announcement. Your father has some feeling for drama."

"I have my moments," said Justin, and downed half of his drink in two gulps. "We should get to it, if you can help me get Neenee back into the bedroom."

"No," said Corinne. "I'll get her leash. I want everyone to see us all together."

Corinne struggled up to get the leash. Neenee remained cuddled by Stefan but wagged her tail furiously when she saw the leash.

They called up the elevator, which arrived unattended. Justin had called the office to make sure Alex was downstairs with the others. He and Stefan stood behind Corinne and her dog, and the elevator descended for only a few seconds.

The doors opened, and Corinne stepped out in her red business suit to smile at a hundred shocked faces there, quickly followed by bedlam.

People screamed and shouted her name. Tears gushed from many faces, and then applause came with clapping and foot stomping on a hard floor. Alex was standing nearby, his hands covering half of his face, eyes wide. Pavel smiled but lowered his head to hide an emotion. Carra did not hesitate and rushed to Corinne to encircle her in a crushing embrace.

"Neenee, no," said Stefan, when the dog growled.

The hysteria went on for several minutes before calming, and Corinne was shaking everyone's hand and looking happy and beautiful, and tears were disappearing around the room and a person could hear the machine sounds again.

Justin found a traveling microphone at a kiosk and handed it to his daughter.

"Hi everyone," said Corinne. "I'm glad to see all of you here for our big announcement, which I guess is me."

There was polite, nervous laughter in the room.

"I wish we could have told you I was okay sooner, but the Guppies were busy and there was no rapid communication coming from Gan. My wound was very bad, and they had to bring me back on Gan, but they made me good as new, and I'm ready to work again. I'm ready to work with my friends and colleagues at the Red Castle Casino to open up again in just five cycles, and I can already smell the food cooking."

Cheers from the crowd nearly drowned out her words until she was shouting, "All staff will receive chits for dinner, drinks and a show. It's time to party again!"

Corinne held up her hands for quiet, and it came. "You know my dog Neenee, who is now behaving herself, but there are two very important men in my life you might not know."

She beckoned to Justin, and he stepped up beside her, looking serious as she put her arm around him.

"This is my father, Justin Ariska, who has been my inspiration and teacher and business partner, bringing me to where I am today. I love you, Daddy."

Corinne hugged him as the audience applauded. Justin looked closely at his daughter, and for one brief instant there was a hint of a smile.

Corinne held out her hand to Stefan, and he took hold of Neenee's leash as he stepped forward. Corinne leaned close and put her arm snugly around his waist.

"Some of you know this man as Chief Stefan Fechter, head of security at Port Nexus and the man who has just successfully led us through a war."

Applause and some cheering interrupted her.

"To me he is Stefan, my man who I love and adore," she said, and looked up at him with a look that made his face flush.

"So I have another announcement to make. You see, Stefan has asked me to be his wife, and he's waiting for my answer."

There were soft gasps in the crowd, and then silence.

"My answer is yes, darling, forever yes."

Stefan leaned down and kissed Corinne with controlled passion while the crowd of onlookers screamed and cheered their approval. Carra was jumping up and down, while Pavel smiled and clapped his hands together.

"Thank you for coming. I'll see you all again soon," said Corinne, and handed the microphone back to Justin. She went to Alex, who still seemed in shock, and embraced him. Tears came to his eyes, and he struggled for control.

"Welcome back, Ma'am. We were quite worried about you. I'll gladly resume my normal duties now."

"My right hand," said Corinne, hugging him. "How did you like operating a casino?"

"I found it interesting, Ma'am, and challenging in new ways."

"Good," said Corinne, and Stefan saw her wink at her father.

Pavel and Carra came up to them, excited. Pavel shook Stefan's hand. "Congratulations," he said.

"Oh, it's so wonderful," gushed Carra. "The steakhouse is open. Have dinner with us tonight. Real meat has arrived again."

"Father?" asked Corinne.

"I've had enough of crowds," he said.

"Father, five people are not a crowd," said Corinne.

"Okay, then, just tonight," he said.

And that night they enjoyed a steak dinner together at the one table occupied in the steakhouse. Justin had three drinks and seemed to be enjoying himself by the end of the meal. There was little talk about the war, and more about the future. Justin had his eye on black Diamond Casino, which was going up for sale. Pavel and Carra were planning their own wedding soon. Stefan and Corinne were in constant physical contact the entire time and mostly listened, their thoughts and dreams private for the moment.

Pavel and Carra retired to her apartment for sleep, and breakfast the next cycle.

They went upstairs to Corinne's suite. Justin had put his things in the second bedroom and happily went to bed a few minutes later. In the master bedroom nothing seemed changed. They undressed in sight of each other and crawled into bed. There, they cuddled. Stefan whispered into Corinne's ear, "I have a million questions, you know."

"I'll bet you do," she said, and nibbled his ear.

"I love your perfume, and whatever you put in your hair. I could smell it in the bed while you were gone."

"Oh, sweetie, I'm here. I'm me, and I do love you."

"Me, too," said Stefan, nearly asleep as they cuddled together.

If there were thoughts of sex, nothing came of it. They were both exhausted by events of the cycle past, and they fell deeply asleep in each other's arms. A few minutes later the room lights turned off automatically. Neenee jumped up on the foot of the bed and went to sleep there, snoring peacefully.

CHAPTER THIRTY-THREE

Thirty days in a holding camp were more than enough for Nathan Czapia, but he was still surprised when his name came up on the list for mustering out and exit interviews. There were seven thousand men in his camp, and the interviews had only begun the previous week.

He had been shipped on a freighter from Port Nexus with thirty other survivors of a futile escapade and returned to a planet without a government. The palace and tabernacle were gone, and a ten-foot fence surrounded an intact military base he had trained in before the war. Barracks and mess hall were intact, the food simple but sufficient for a military stomach. There was no exercise except walking around a fenced in field filled with thousands of bored men with nothing to worry about except their futures. All of them had been professional military, and now the word was that Kratola would no longer have a military force, at least for the immediate future. Only limited police personal would be allowed after occupation.

Nathan, too, wondered about his future. His brothers were missing, his family home burned to the ground and there was only a small plot of untilled land that was worth anything at all. All his worth was in his right shoe. He could buy some land, or a business, but what? His whole life had been the military. Now he only knew one thing he had to do. He had to find his brothers. They were all he really had left of importance to him. And to start a search for them, he'd have to go home.

So, when the time for the interview came, Nathan was eager to do it. He was called to an office in what had once been the officers' mess. The man who interviewed him was named Ben Ellis, and he had a file about Nathan of substantial thickness. He gave Nathan a serious look as he opened the file. Immediately, Nathan was nervous.

"I want you to know that the information in this file will be kept secret by the Gan Intelligence Service," said Ben.

"Sir?"

"It concerns both you and your brothers, and your activities during the war. That includes the help you gave us at Port Nexus. I assume you'd not like to have that exposed."

"I did it because I hated the Bishops, sir. They killed my parents. That was my only reason. I hope you don't intend to use it against me."

"Certainly not," said Ben. "Eventually, you might agree that we're not the bad guys. The bad guys are dead, Nathan, and we're pretty sure your brothers were involved in the death of one of them."

"I heard guys talking about an assassination before the war," said Nathan. "My brothers went AWOL. They hated the Bishops as much as I did, and for the same reason."

"We know that," said Ben. "The Black Hats were looking for them with orders to shoot on sight. Your brother Jon was a trained sniper. One Bishop died, another missed death by inches, both shots from nearly a mile. They'll probably deny it, but we have little doubt about who did a favor for us."

"My brothers are still missing?" asked Nathan.

"They've been found in a little village called Ester about seventy miles south of here. A van left this morning to interview them."

"Ester is my home," said Nathan. "If they did you a favor, then leave them alone. Don't arrest them."

"I said interview, not arrest," said Ben. "We're mustering everyone out, and you have to have papers. You're all getting amnesty, but you need papers to travel. You people haven't known real freedom for a long time. You must trust us, Nathan. Do you want to go home?"

"Yes!"

"Then let's get this interview over with, fill out your papers and get you transportation south. If your brothers don't shoot someone again, you should have a nice reunion."

The rest was a blur. The questions were familiar: name, origin, rank, serial number, political affiliations, skills, interests, etc., etc. Nathan signed a paper. Ben countersigned and stamped it and handed it over.

"You're a civilian," said Ben, "and a veteran. We'll be setting up offices in a few weeks to match people with available jobs if you need it. Amnesty will be formal in a month or so, but with the clearance of a formal discharge you can travel now. Good luck, Nathan. Be here at 0800 tomorrow morning, and a van will be here to take you and some other guy's home."

Nathan hesitated to stand up and seemed confused.

"It's a new day, Nathan. You can thank me some other time. Now get out of here," said Ben, smiling.

Nathan left without saying a word, and the reality of his situation really didn't hit him until he was packing a small bag back in the barracks, and he saw the lost expressions on some of the other former soldiers there.

* * * *

A scraping sound woke Jon and Jule nestled in their little hideaway behind some boxes in Fred Engel's basement.

Jon peeked out. Two men were moving chairs around a small table, and one of them was a trooper with a sidearm. Jon pulled back with a jerk, and a box rattled.

"Ah, you're awake. If you are indeed Jon and Jule Czapic, come on out of there and we'll get these mustering out papers done for you. Your war is officially over."

"Come and get us," growled Jon, and saw the trooper's hand move towards his handgun.

"Oh, don't give me krack," said the other man. "We're not here to arrest you. We have your files, and we're here to muster you out before your brother gets here in about an hour and a half."

"Nathan!" said Jule. "He's alive."

"That's right, and he'd like to see you stay that way. We know you're not armed, so get out here so we can get this done. We have four more guys like you to see today." The man sat down behind the table and opened a file in front of him. The trooper still looked alert for trouble.

Jon came out first, then Jule, both with hands up at shoulder level.

"Put your hands down. I said this is *not* an arrest. Sit down, please. Let's see; Jon and Jule Czapic. Jon is the sniper. Thank you for getting rid of a Bishop for us. It would have been better if your second shot was two inches to the left, but close does count."

"I don't know what you're talking about," said Jon.

"Of course not. We'll just forget it, and this file will never be seen by anyone outside of Gan Intelligence. Same is true for your brothers' files. I have everything filled in for you. All you have to do is sign it, and we'll be out of here."

"How did you find us?" asked Jule.

"We have eyes in the sky," said the man who remained anonymous the whole time they were with him. "Sign here."

They were discharge papers for both of them. Jon looked them over. "What's the catch?" he asked. "This is all too fast and easy."

"It is for you and your brother. You're all special cases, courtesy of Gan Intelligence. Makes my job easier. Just sign here, and here, both of you. Corporal, start the van. We have to get out of here. Two hundred miles of driving today."

The trooper left.

Jon looked at Jule and shrugged. "Okay?" he said.

"I'm tired of running," said Jule.

They both signed the papers.

"Keep those safe and make copies. You can't travel off planet without them before amnesty is declared," said the man. He closed the file, stood up and extended a hand to Jon.

"Good luck, shooter, and thanks," he said, shook Jon's hand, then Jule's, and climbed the stairs out of the basement.

Jon and Jule stood quietly for a moment, discharge papers in their hands. "Do you believe this?" asked Jon.

"Only because I want to," said Jule.

They went upstairs and found Fred Engel at the front door, watching a military van drive away. He looked at them anxiously.

"They were just outside when I got up this morning. Are you okay?"

"We're discharged from military service. They said Nathan will be here today."

"What? Oh, that's great. You're all still alive. See, I told you things were looking better. Did they say how they found you?"

"Eyes in the sky," said Jon. "Nathan should be here in an hour or so."

"He'll be hungry, too. I'll fix us a big breakfast," said Fred, and he hurried away to the kitchen.

In an hour the odors of food cooking filled the house. There were corn cakes and eggs and slabs of smoked meat, and bread slathered with sour butter laced with honey, and coffee strong enough to make a heart flutter. It was all nearing completion when a covered military truck pulled up outside the house. The driver got out, went around to the back and yelled something to the occupants inside. A young man appeared from inside and jumped to the ground with a light pack on his back. Tall and thin, he rubbed his eyes as if he'd been sleeping on the truck.

Chairs scattered as Jon and Jule rushed to the door and outside, yelling, "Nathan, Nathan!" and they came together in a tangled embrace. Men inside the truck hooted at them until the driver got back inside and drove the truck away for his next delivery.

Fred Engel joined them and shook Nathan's hand. "Good to see you alive, boy. It has been a long time," he said.

"Fred hid us when we went AWOL," said Jule, "so we came back to his place after the takeover."

"Thanks, Fred," said Nathan.

"Breakfast just came off the stove," said Fred. "Let's eat and talk."

They went inside and sat down, and Fred covered the table with platters of food, half of which was eaten before they really began to talk.

"We're all lucky to be alive," Nathan finally said. "And things we've done are making it easier for us now. I heard the black Caps were after you for killing a bishop. The orders were to shoot on sight."

"I told you they hadn't quit looking," Jule said to Jon.

"We said we'd do it, and we did it," said Jon. "If you forgot why, I can show you where mom and dad are buried right behind what's left of our house."

"I'm not faulting you, I turned myself in to Gan Intelligence for the same reason at Port Nexus and spied for them. That makes me a traitor, Jon, but I'm glad I did it. What we did helped to get rid of the Bishops and allow Kratola a new start."

"Better keep that to yourselves," said Fred. "Some people won't see it that way. Some are ashamed that our soldiers threw down their guns and ran when the Guppies came. They're ashamed about losing a war. They see a Gan truck, they hide. There was no big reception for you here today. Don't expect any welcomes home. There are hard feelings here, at least for a while."

"Then we should leave," said Jon.

"Not so fast," said Nathan. "We just got home. We must figure out what we're going to do."

"What can we do?" said Jule. "I'm not a farmer, and how much could we make out of a five-acre plot of land?"

"Not enough," said Fred, "except maybe fruit or nut trees, and that would take several years to production. George Reny has done it. He asked me weeks ago what was going to happen to the land if y'all were dead. Soil's good, hasn't been farmed, it's gotta be worth five to ten thousand credits. Sell it to him."

"And then what?" said Jon.

"Learn a new trade, maybe drive a truck. I did enough vegetable picking when we were on the run. No more farm work," said Jule.

"I know guns and killing," said Jon.

"I know everything I was taught in Black Hats," said Nathan, "and that includes motivational and organizational skills, and quick thinking on my feet. There should be lots of things we can do in civilian life, but the opportunities have to be there, and I don't see it happening here for a long time."

"You want to leave? That takes money, lots of it," said Jon.

"Where could we go to?" asked Jule.

"Gan or Galena," said Nathan, "but the mega-city on Gan is probably the best. Everything is there. Galena is more agricultural and small towns."

"Doesn't sound possible to me," said Jule. "We need money, contacts, a job offer from a company paying living wages a place to live, lots of stuff like that. Our chances are better here at home, even if the neighbors won't like us anymore."

They sat silently for a moment, the mood somber, a sense of defeat hanging in the room. Fred cleared the table and served coffee.

"Wow," said Nathan, "that is good."

"My heart is thumping," said Jule.

"If you boys want to sell that land, I can talk to George for you. He has the money for it," said Fred.

Jon and Jule were silent, and then Nathan suddenly said, "With or without you, I'm going to Gan. I have a chit in my shoe worth ten thousand credits anywhere. A Gan Intelligence guy saved my life at Port Nexus, and I was working for him. He also gave me his telephone number and said I should contact him if I made it to Gan and needed something. That sounds like an opportunity to me, and I'm taking it. Come with me or not, your choice."

Nathan took a long swig of coffee and thumped the cup on the table to emphasize his statement, "Well?" he said.

Jule and Jon looked at each other.

"It's pretty quick, brother. We'll have to think about it some," said Jule.

"I can't wait long," said Nathan. "Amnesty is coming up, and we should travel before that to avoid the rush."

"We'll figure it out before then," said Jon. "In the meantime, maybe Fred can talk to George and see how serious he is about buying our land."

"I'll talk to him tomorrow," said Fred.

CHAPTER THIRTY-FOUR

Seven months after the Gan occupation of Kratola, John Haight made the first of three trips by Guppy to evaluate the progress in governmental and constitutional reconstruction underway there. He was pleased by what he saw.

Two committees had been formed by selected leaders in industry and education as well as locally elected union members and people from individual tax districts on the planet. A new, detailed constitution was being written to replace the one-page statement of religious authority that had been used by the Bishops. Various governmental models had been considered and one quite similar to the new model used on Gan was receiving most of the support because of its emphasis on equal representation and distribution of power.

There had been little change in rural life before, during, and after the war. Only changes in tax structures would affect the people living there. The main issues to solve were for the vast industrial capital of the planet, and the several industrial-centered cities near it. Unions were to enjoy new freedoms after dangerous persecution by the Bishops.

Nicholas Zahn led the committee on governmental reform and had impressed everyone by his insights and his ability to reach a consensus with such a diverse group of representatives. There was talk of Zahn serving as Prime Minister in a future government, an idea supported even by union representatives who had had dealings with him. Haight talked to Zahn at length privately and came away impressed by the man.

The Kratolan army of some ten thousand men had been mustered out and dispersed, and efforts to place them in civilian jobs were underway. The problem was complex, since retraining would be necessary in many cases and new educational programs would depend on the skills and interests of the trainees.

The Kratolan space force had been decimated, with no survivors except for a few men who had remained on the ground during the war.

Arrests had been made, mostly senior officers responsible for an earlier slaughter by the palace gates and more than a few lethal incidents at small villages. Acting on orders from the Bishops, they were nonetheless held responsible by occupation forces, tried, sentenced and imprisoned far away from civilization.

Otherwise, complete amnesty had been declared for everyone, and all travel restrictions were lifted, including travel to Port Nexus, Gan and Galena.

Haight made several public statements of support for what was going on and reiterated the desire for friendship between the Kratolan people and those of Gan and Galena, all of whom shared a common ancestry. "We are all one people," he declared. "We must never again allow political ambitions or differences to get in the way of our friendship."

John felt good about his four-day visit, was energized and optimistic as he took a shuttle up to Kratola Station and the entrance to the great wormhole to Port Nexus. The station was busy, and his appearance was an event there. There was polite applause as he was escorted by two aids and three troopers to his gate where he would board a tourist ship bound for Nexus and then transfer to another tourist vessel bound for Gan. He would not stay at Nexus for a visit since Petyr was already there and acting in his behalf.

He had mixed feelings about the people standing in line to board the ship. Many were obviously tourists, dressed nicely and ready to have a good time at Port Nexus. There were a few businesspeople and government workers classically dressed and headed for Gan. All established, knowing where they were going and why.

The people he noticed most were the ones who were quiet among themselves, looking apprehensive, perhaps a bit frightened, not dressed well and with small bags they could carry aboard the ship. These were the first emigrants from Kratola to Gan, traveling at discount prices on one-way tickets to an unfamiliar planet to begin a new life.

John's appearance had been announced and there was more applause as he approached his gate, where he would be the first to board the ship. He noticed three young men who looked like brothers, sitting close together on a bench by the gate. They were thin and hard looking, with close cut hair, and were probably ex-military. Now they were likely in search of a new life on Gan. John looked directly at them as they studied him, and he gave them an encouraging gesture by slightly shaking a closed fist in their direction.

Good luck, boys. Hope you find what you're looking for, he thought.

The tallest and probably the oldest of the three gave him a tired version of a military salute, and smiled at him.

Somehow, that salute made John feel a little better as he boarded the ship.

CHAPTER THIRTY-FIVE

Corinne Jean Ariska married Stefan Carl Fechter in the Grand Ballroom of the Red Castle Casino. Seven hundred staff, friends and invited well-wishers attended the event. The bride wore red lace, and the groom was in formal dress blues. Pavel and Carra Fiala served as witnesses, and the civil service was conducted by the Honorable Gerald Newton, a friend of the bride's family from Central city on Gan. The bride's father, Gan industrialist Justin Ariska escorted his daughter to the stage, and Red Castle was closed to the public for one cycle for the wedding and following reception. Bride and groom looked forward to a delayed honeymoon at the family-owned estate at Lake Ariel Fish and Game Preserve on Gan.

By the beginning of red light, it was all a wonderful blur to both of them. The service had been simple, short and quick and they had said their lines with reasonable intensity. The nuptial kiss had been soft and long and produced much loud cheering from the guests. Corinne had to keep her eyes off of Carra, who blubbered silently through the entire ceremony.

Corinne would remember looking up at her father as they walked towards the stage and seeing the tears in his eyes.

Stefan would remember his first sight of his bride in a flowing red dress and veil, and how for just a moment his knees felt weak and shaky.

Now they sat at the head table with Pavel, Carra and Justin, trying to hear each other over the background noise in the crowded steakhouse. Staff serving the dinner had watched the wedding on private cable and would be treated to their own dinner and reception the following week.

Toasts were numerous, before and after a delicious meal, but Stefan and Corinne were careful to take small sips with each, and by the end of the celebration several guests wished they had done so as well.

No gifts had been requested, but there were more than a few anyway, to be opened later. The one large gift was announced by Justin Ariska, who stood and presented Bride and Groom with the ownership papers of Black Diamond Casino across the street, bought and paid for by himself. Corinne accepted the gift with mixed feelings, acquiring a business owned by a man who had murdered her, but expanding a business she loved dearly. Stefan was stunned and saw the gift as a kind of justice meted out by a father.

The party was still in full swing at 2300, but it was the traditional time for the bride and groom to make their escape for their wedding night. Stefan and Corinne made the rounds of the tables, thanking guests for coming. There had been two notable exceptions. Kira Madelia and Petyr Vlasok had earlier called to apologize for not attending the nuptials. Both had been with John Haight on Gan at the time.

The bridal couple slipped quietly out of the steakhouse, but many guests slyly watched them leave. Alex followed them to the elevator and opened the door for them. "Would you like breakfast after sleeping tonight?" he asked with a faint smile.

"It might be very late," said Corinne, looking at Stefan. "I think I'll do some cooking for my new husband. Thank you, Alex."

"Ma'am? I need to mention this. Your father asked me if I had any interest in managing Black Diamond Casino. I told him I'd think about it. Is this a problem for you?"

"I'd hate to lose you as a close aide, Alex, but I think you're qualified, and it's a good opportunity for advancement. We'd still be in the same family. I think you should do it. Just tell me when."

"Thank you, Ma'am," said Alex, as they arrived at the residence. Stefan shook the man's hand as they got out of the elevator and whispered into his ear. "Do it," he said, and smiled.

Alex looked pleased as the elevator door closed.

They were alone in the residence as a married couple for the first time. Stefan picked her up in a hug and twirled her around.

"My beautiful wife," he said. "I've had dreams, but this is better than all of them."

He kissed her softly, melted under the loving gaze of her dark eyes, and finally allowed her feet to touch the floor again.

Neenee met them at the bedroom and relished their attention. When they began undressing, the dog curled up in the corner of the room. She was a polite animal and understood when their privacy in bed was to be respected, even for preliminaries.

They slipped into bed and cuddled.

Stefan ran his hands softly all over her and buried his nose in her hair.

"Everything is the same, even that little cinder on your wrist. I'm still struggling with this clone thing," he said.

"New shell, same old me," said Corinne, and she kissed his ear.

"I feel weird, like I want to laugh, but what's funny?" said Stefan.

"Maybe you're happy, dear. I don't think you've had a lot of that in your life."

"Because you weren't there. And for a while, I thought you were gone for good. I couldn't see how your father could be so matter-of-fact about it."

"Death means change to my people., Stefan, but we always have a choice. My mother chose to end it because of a mental imbalance. She didn't commit suicide; she just deliberately destroyed her only clone. It hurt my father terribly. I keep hoping he'll find a new woman to love. Now that he's younger again he might try it."

"I must be in love with a much older woman," whispered Stefan.

"I am thirty-eight years old," whispered Corinne back.

"Once you said you were 250 years old," said Stefan, chuckling.

"But you didn't believe me, right?"

"Right."

"So, let's stick with thirty-eight for now."

"I really thought you were in your forties," said Stefan, still kidding her.

"New shell, new age. You're physically older than me by a few years, but you have my permission to take advantage of me." Her lips brushed his.

"I love you, wife," he said, and kissed her firmly, passion growing.

"Me, too," she said. "I want us to be together for a long time."

"A lifetime," he said.

"More," said Corinne. "We'll be going to Gan. An initial scan takes four hours in a hospital setting, and some skin or hair samples for DNA analysis is all they need. You have a choice, darling. We can be together a very long time if you want it."

"Wow," said Stefan. "But what about kids? Can we have them?"

Corinne smiled. "Do you want children?"

"I do with you, boy or girl, I don't care which. I never even thought about having a family until I met you."

Corinne pressed her cheek against his and murmured, "In all my years, you are my only husband, but I will have your babies for you if you really want them."

Stefan smiled. "Yes? Can you have them? I mean—"

"—I am a fully operational woman, dear, but I'm thirty-eight, and I'm not getting any younger right now. If we're going to have children, we'd better get started on it pretty soon."

"How about right now?" growled Stefan.

"It might not be the right time," said Corinne, "but if it isn't, we'll just have to keep working on it until it happens."

Corinne put her arms around his neck and pressed herself tightly against him, feeling satisfied with what she felt there.

They were in love, and living in the moment, with little thought about the future. But that moment was the beginning of a great house, a dynasty spreading to Gan and beyond to Galena over the centuries, an empire built by Stefan and Corinne Fechter and their many descendants. And they would all be together to see it happen.

"Shall we?" she said.

Neenee watched their joyful activities out of one eye from her corner of the room. And when they were finally finished, exhausted and falling to sleep in each other's arms, the dog leapt up onto the foot of the bed, curled up as close to them as she could without touching them, and went to sleep with her new family.

ABOUT THE AUTHOR

James C. Glass won the Golden Pen Award of Writers of the Future in 1991. Since then, he has published eleven novels, four story collections, and over seventy stories in anthologies and magazines such as *Analog*, *Pulphouse*, *Digital SF*, *Talebones*, and *Aboriginal SF*. His website is author-jamesglass.com, and he is often seen at conventions. He divides his time with wife Gail between Spokane, Washington and Desert Hot Springs, California. James was a physics professor and dean in his professional life, and retired in 1999 to write and paint.